IN REMOTE WOODLAND SANCTUARIES, ELVES AND WITCHES WORSHIP AN ANCIENT SPIRIT.
From the strife of the Middle Ages to the conflicts of our own era, these six novellas from the celebrated author of the *Strands* books will transport you to a world of starlit wonder.

"Charity" introduces the kind carpenter Andrew—and his epic struggle, with the help of Varden the Elf, to undo the hatred of the village's most estranged citizen.

In "Lady of Light," the shadow of the Inquisition creeps into the village of Saint Brigid—as a tormented woodcarver toils between the power of the crucifix and his love of the forest.

Roxanne is a witch with a great deal to learn about the Goddess and herself—and in "A Touch of Distant Hands" her journey of self-discovery may cost another's life.

In "Elvenhome," a hardworking professional named Joan must cope with the dizzying power rising within her—and discovers its incredible meaning from an unexpected source.

In "Please Come to Denver," Lauri flees Los Angeles for Colorado—and lands a job with an employer who teaches her a great deal more about herself than she was ever willing to believe.

"Shadow of the Starlight" finds Lauri a changed woman—and confronted by a deadly danger that her Elven talents might not be able to stop.

Spires of Spirit

Early Stories in the World of
Strands of Starlight

Gael Baudino

A ROC BOOK

ROC
Published by the Penguin Group
Penguin Books USA Inc., 375 Hudson Street,
New York, New York 10014, U.S.A.
Penguin Books Ltd, 27 Wrights Lane,
London W8 5TZ, England
Penguin Books Australia Ltd, Ringwood,
Victoria, Australia
Penguin Books Canada Ltd, 10 Alcorn Avenue,
Toronto, Ontario, Canada M4V 3B2
Penguin Books (N.Z.) Ltd, 182–190 Wairau Road,
Auckland 10, New Zealand

Penguin Books Ltd, Registered Offices:
Harmondsworth, Middlesex, England

First published by Roc, an imprint of Dutton Signet,
a division of Penguin Books USA Inc.

First Printing, February, 1997
10 9 8 7 6 5 4 3 2 1

The original version of "The Shadow of the Starlight" was published
in The Magazine of Fantasy and Science Fiction, April 1985.

Cover art by Tom Canty

Map of Adria by Jan Bender

Printed in the United States of America

To my readers, the strangers

Contents

"It's all been so lovely."
  —Bessie Grahame

Introduction

This book gathers together the six novelettes that form the foundation and background of the four *Strands of Starlight* novels. All six were written between 1981 and 1984, most of them taking shape between the first and second drafts of *Strands of Starlight* itself.

Their history, though—and, therefore, the history of the novels, too—goes back much farther. As much as a decade before the first of the novelettes, when I was making my first attempts at putting words on paper in a coherent form, I was already dealing with the village of Saint Brigid and some of its inhabitants in stories with names like "The Witchmark," "The West Wind," and "Edrich Frühr."

Pounded out, first on an old Royal manual typewriter, then on an IBM Selectric II, and then, finally, on an Apple IIe, these novelettes and their predecessors not only formulated situation, geography, and character, but they also firmly established the themes that would illuminate the books: compassion, redemption, faith, spiritual search, and the paradoxical bitterness of joy. Nor did this influence work solely in one direction: there was, in fact, much cross-fertilization between the novelettes and the novels, and, in the course of the preparation of this manuscript—the last revision of these stories (on a Pentium-driven Windows platform!)—the fully fleshed world of the novels was always available to add clearness, sometimes providing detail not previously present, sometimes demanding that certain phrases or descriptions be altered so as to bring consistency to the saga as a whole.

I do hope you enjoy these novelettes, for they occupy a special place in my regard. It was when I wrote them that I first felt the magic of creating an alternate world to which I could give some semblance of independent existence, in which I could express belief and optimism.

The belief and optimism are, alas, gone, but the stories remain, an embodiment and a fading echo of a happier time. Once the foundation of a long, long tale, they now find themselves in a loftier place: final flourishes, distant spires stretching up into the light, rising from the ruins of a very small, very personal cathedral.

Some acknowledgments are in order. Some are, I fear, terribly overdue.

Edward L. Ferman liked "The Shadow of the Starlight" enough to buy it and to publish it in the April 1985 issue of *The Magazine of Fantasy and Science Fiction*. It was my first meaningful publication. My deepest thanks to him.

Two years later, Cherry Weiner, my agent, read

the second draft of *Strands of Starlight*, loved it, and sold it. Christopher Schelling, who was then my editor at NAL/Roc, persuaded me to cut the novel by 37,000 words (and, yes, the cuts made it a much better book) and subsequently shepherded the entire series through the editorial and publishing process. As I am greatly indebted to Ed Ferman, so am I also indebted—immensely, eternally—to Cherry and Christopher for their belief in and care of the *Strands* books.

Amy Stout, my subsequent editor at Roc, was gracious enough to be open to the idea of this collection. Moreover, throughout our association, she maintained her equanimity and good humor ... even when confronted with the haphazard ridiculousness of the *WATER!* trilogy. I do believe she is in line for canonization.

To Tom Canty, who created the breathtaking cover for the original Signet edition of *Strands of Starlight*, who later sent me a signed and remarked print of same, and whose lovely work graces the covers of the other books—and of the present volume—my sincerest appreciation.

My beloved Mirya Rule has kept me going through the last eleven years. She has encouraged me, held me through my sleepless nights, and comforted me through my black depressions. Those of you who have read my other books know that I always mention Mirya in my acknowledgments. Those of you who know Mirya understand why.

I also need to thank you. Yes, you. You have perhaps been patient with my novels. You have perhaps

liked them enough to be interested in these stories.
Some of you have written to me. Some of you have
sent e-mail to me or have posted on my topic in the
Science Fiction Round Table of GEnie. Some of you
have made me optimistic. Some of you have disturbed me. Some of you have scared me to death.
Regardless, without you, I would not be writing
this . . . perhaps I would not be writing at all. Therefore this book bears the dedication that it does.

Englewood, Colorado
November 1995

Then . . .

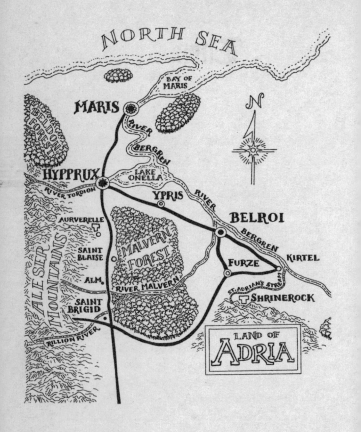

Charity

There was a black shadow lay on the village street that morning. Andrew, the carpenter, had seen it before, many times in his life, but still he half turned away from it as he worked, turned his shoulder to the old woman who hobbled down the street, her back bent, her stick making small taps as she went.

"Leather," she called, her voice rasping like a saw on hard wood. "Give me your leather!"

Andrew lifted his head. His tool belt lay on the bench, its straps torn. He had done without it for a week now, and the cry of the old woman made him think of every instance in which he had reached for something at his hip and found it not there.

He looked up through the open shutters of his shop and found that she was already watching him. She knew that he had business for her. She was that way.

The village hated her for it.

Picking up the belt, he swung open the half door and stepped out into the dusty street. The old woman was waiting, and, without a word, he handed it to her and watched while she ran her cold, lake blue eyes over it. Without another glance at him, she

17

put it in her sack. "Day after tomorrow," she said, and she turned away slowly, as if in pain, her black shadow a pit of darkness on the ground.

Andrew looked after her as she dragged herself up the dusty street. He had never before thought of her as being in pain.

They all called her the Leather-woman. They called her worse things too, though not to her face, for that would have been folly. Folly, too, it would have been to have driven her away from the village, for she knew the ways of revenge well. Svengard the herder had felt her anger most recently, for he had lost the better part of his flock after imitating her crippled walk in the village square one afternoon. He had held a stick to his leg in imitation of the iron brace she wore, and those nearby had laughed . . . until her cold shadow had appeared. She had looked at him— only looked—and a month later the shepherd was all but penniless.

And there were others who had felt her touch. Some of their stories had been told many times over before Andrew had married Elizabeth and had started a family, and some had been told many times over even before Andrew had been born. But the years had passed, and the Leather-woman still lived in her miserable hut at the edge of the village, still hobbled down the street, still supported herself by mending small items of harness and tackle. Her work was good, and she made a meager living. And fear let her remain as she was.

When she returned Andrew's belt two days later, the hide had been patched and mended perfectly and near invisibly, and the material seemed to have a suppleness that it had not possessed before. Andrew paid her well, and she nodded curtly to him before turning back up the street that led to the edge of town.

In the bright, harsh light of the midsummer sun, she looked frail and thin. Too thin, he thought. Her shadow seemed to have more substance than her body, in fact, and the black shawl she wore was tattered and sere, like a dry leaf barely clinging to a stripped branch. Again, the thought struck Andrew that she was in pain, and for a moment, he forgot about Svengard and the others, forgot about the shadow that clung to her house, forgot about her cold, blue eyes.

"Is there anything I can do for you, Mother?" he blurted out suddenly.

The Leather-woman stopped in her tracks. As she turned around slowly, leaning heavily on her stick, Andrew found himself staring at the iron brace that stiffened her right leg. "You say . . . what?" Her voice was desiccated, but it had an edge to it, like black ink on dusty parchment. "You call me *mother*?" There was no humor in her words. "I've never been anybody's mother."

"Can I . . ." Andrew found himself regretting his words even as he spoke them. "Can I get anything for you? Do you need help?"

She tottered back to him, her eyes fixed on his face, but then she bent and spat on the ground at his feet. "Help?" she rasped. "I needed help eighty years ago, when I was born, when I killed my mother. They gave me this for help." She tapped her brace with her finger, and the sound was as of bone on metal. "That was all I deserved then, and that's all I deserve now. Don't I frighten you, scrapling?"

Andrew said nothing.

Svengard visited his family that night for dinner. Since he had been paupered by the loss of his flock, the villagers had, as a community, adopted him, making sure he had what he needed. No questions were asked, there was no talk of repayment. Svengard needed help, and he got it.

In the firelight, the old shepherd looked worn. Elizabeth led the blessing on the food, and Andrew found his gaze resting on the ham on the table. What was on the table of the Leather-woman this night? She looked so thin . . .

He felt Elizabeth looking at him, and he met her eyes. "Are you not well, husband?" she said. Her voice was as soft and sweet as it had been when he had married her twelve years ago, and it brought out the shy boy in him. He smiled sheepishly and shrugged.

"I'm thoughtful tonight."

"Thoughtful!" Svengard snorted as he broke off a piece of bread. "Thoughtful! Leave that to the priests, carpenter. Why, I'm sure that Jaques Alban thinks fully enough for ten men!"

The children laughed and giggled, and Elizabeth shushed them.

The shepherd continued. "It's no good for you and me to be thoughtful. I was thoughtful that day I played the clown in the village square, and you see where it got me! Nearly starved out!"

"Now, Svengard," said Elizabeth, "it did teach you

a few things . . . for instance how not to be a stranger in the village. You did not visit us often before."

Svengard buttered his bread with short, stabbing motions. "It taught me to stay away from witches," he said. "And the same should be true for everyone. I noticed your belt, Andrew."

The table fell silent. Elizabeth, her gray eyes calm, simply looked at Andrew as if to say, *I trust you.* The children, though, were frightened.

Andrew cleared his throat. "It's true," he said. "I had her do some work on it."

"Unwise, unwise," said the shepherd. "Stay away from her."

"Don't you think," said Andrew suddenly, "that the more we shun her, the worse she becomes? I got to thinking today—"

"Thinking again!"

"Peace, Sven. I got to thinking about what her life must be like. Can you imagine living in a hut like that? And during the winter? Why, it's said that even the Elves hide in deep caves to stay warm during the cold season, and her house is more full of holes than a beggar's pouch. And she can't eat very well—"

"She's a witch, Father," said James, the eldest. "She can eat stones."

"Hush, child," said Elizabeth. "She is flesh and blood like us all, and must needs eat."

The shepherd laid down his bread. "Stay away from her, Andrew," he said, pointing at the carpenter with a knobby finger. "Let her live out her life and then let her go. Her kind's best left alone."

Andrew was silent.

"Take it from me," said Svengard. "I'm old, and I know what I'm talking about."

Elizabeth spoke up. "Sven, you must remember how the Leather-woman came to be. How did it happen?"

Andrew looked across to her, saw the half smile in her eyes. She knew what he was thinking. Bless her, he thought. Bless her as often as there have been moments we have been married.

Svengard had his mouth full of ham. He squinted at Elizabeth and shook his head, but when he swallowed, he spoke. " 'Twas about fourscore years ago she was born. Ugly thing. Still is. Always had that bad leg, and always had that hoarse voice. People made fun of her, especially the little ones. She used to laugh about it herself, until she understood what it all meant. Father died. Mother passed on giving her life.

"She got by, though she had to beg a lot. Couldn't even make a good whore: too ugly . . . and that brace got in the way. Francis' father used to make them for her out of charity . . . until he got too old and young Francis took over the forge. Now it's the youngster does it."

Svengard fell silent. Andrew wondered if he was thinking about charity. "You said she had to beg."

"Until she learned leatherwork, aye. Then she made her own way. People didn't like to deal with her much, but they did. And there was some that still laughed. She just sort of holed up in that house of hers and got real strange."

Elizabeth was wiping her youngest's face. "It sounds as though she has much to be bitter about."

"Well," said Svengard, "she used to laugh. She

could have stayed that way. But, no, she just got bitter and nasty. Then she went and killed my sheep."

James looked at Svengard. His young eyes were troubled. "It doesn't sound fair . . ."

"God takes care of everything," said the shepherd through another mouthful.

"Sometimes I wonder . . ." said Andrew, lapsing into thought.

"First thinking, and now wondering! Watch it, Andrew: next thing you'll be out dancing in the forest with the Elves! God help you, you'll have a change-ling in your cradle!"

"I'll be all right," said Andrew softly.

The Leather-woman was much on Andrew's mind over the next weeks. The tool belt, to be sure, was a constant reminder, but it was more than that: the memory of the thin, crippled old woman tottering down the road, alone, with no family and no friends and only a stick to lean on . . . The image haunted him.

She used to laugh, Svengard had said. But had she not been given sufficient cause to stop laughing? Andrew, pausing in the middle of planing a tabletop, considered. What might her life have been if no one had laughed at her? What if everything could have been turned around? For a moment, Andrew saw her, crippled still, and hoarse still, but seated under the oak tree in the square, playing with the children, telling them stories, bringing out herbs to heal a cut or scrape or illness. Loved . . .

He laid his work aside and sat down on his bench, for his sight had turned blurry. Jaques Alban, the village priest, had condemned her (though he would not move against her, even with the Inquisition firmly in control in the cities to the north), but Alban, most everyone agreed, was a fool, and so, though Andrew had no doubt that the Leather-woman had destroyed Svengard's flock, he discovered, in the other pan of the balance, many years of loneliness and pain, and he was not at all sure that the latter was not the heavier.

Why had it happened that way? Why not another way?

Near noon, Elizabeth found him with his head in his hands. Concerned when he could not answer her questions, she could only hug him and make him eat what she had brought him.

"I'm just dizzy, my love," he murmured between tasteless mouthfuls. "I'm thinking too much. Maybe Sven's right."

"There's nothing wrong with thinking," said Elizabeth.

"I wonder."

Uncharacteristically, he gave up on his work that day and wandered out to the forest, away from the tilled fields. The trunks were shadowy, indistinct, but all the same, they were familiar things. Trees. Good, solid trees. Wood, living and growing.

The sight of them calmed him. Here were earth and water and wind, and sunlight dappling the mossy forest floor. He breathed the air and sighed. Hermits, he was sure, had the right idea: to leave the random and quarreling houses of men and dwell in the woods, finding peace among the trees. Perhaps they spoke

with the Elves, and why should they not? Jaques
Alban had assured the villagers that, like the Leather-
woman, the Elves were beings to be avoided, soulless
creatures who led godless lives . . . but everyone knew
about Alban; and in any case Andrew knew that the
priest had no more knowledge of the Fair Folk than he
did himself. Far more likely there were mistaken ideas
in currency, even among the priests, for anyone who
knew the woods as well as the Elves knew it could not
but be, like the hermits, and in accordance with their
own ways, gentle and godly folk.

He rested, leaning against a thick oak, and as his
thoughts calmed, he resolved to help the Leather-
woman, regardless of her spitting and her evil deeds.
Maybe he could undo something of what had been
done. And would it not be a godly task to win a soul
back from evil?

Something flashed among the shadows of the trees,
and Andrew started when he realized that it was a pair
of eyes . . . then started again as the figure to whom
they belonged came forward: a young man dressed
simply in green and gray, with a gray cloak fastened
at his throat. His face was almost womanly, with dark
hair that fell to his shoulders and deep blue eyes that
mirrored more light than Andrew expected.

"Be at peace," said the stranger. "Forgive me if I
frightened you."

Andrew pulled off his cap, felt absurd, put it back
on again. "What can I do for you, messire?"

The young man smiled. "Is that the village of Saint
Brigid?" he said, pointing. His voice was quiet:
pitched just loud enough to carry, no more.

"Indeed it is, messire."

"There is no need to call me *messire*. My name is Varden."

"God bless you, Varden. I'm Andrew."

"Blessings upon you this day, Andrew. There is a woman in the village who works leather, is there not?"

"Aye, messire . . . er, Varden. She lives in a hut on the other side of town. I fear I must warn you: she is a witch."

"A witch? Indeed?"

"She has done evil."

A smile. "I thought you said that she is a witch."

"I did . . . uh . . . I thought I did . . ."

"Peace to you, Master Carpenter." Varden laid a light hand on his shoulder.

"Uh . . . thank you." Andrew peered at Varden through the dappling of leaf shadows. The brooch that fastened the stranger's cloak had the fashion of an interlaced moon and star, and, indeed, the light in his eyes seemed like that of the stars on a clear night. Andrew found that his hands were shaking. "May I ask . . . what brings you to Saint Brigid?"

"I want to look in on the woman. I am . . . concerned about her." Varden looked Andrew full in the face. "Do you know her name?"

Andrew realized that he did not. She had always been the Leather-woman. He admitted as much to Varden.

"Perhaps that will be remedied someday," said Varden. "I must go now. Farewell."

He bowed and then he was gone, his gray cloak blending into the trees, his footfalls silent. Andrew suddenly wondered how Varden had known to call him *Master Carpenter.*

When Andrew returned home, he was still shaking. Elizabeth noticed, and her eyes were thoughtful as he told his story. "I imagine he was some kind of traveler," said Andrew. "Maybe a relative."

"Maybe. I wonder . . ." Elizabeth looked at the unshuttered window where the last of the afternoon sunlight was glowing.

Dinner was quiet that evening, and, afterward, Andrew stayed up into the night. Long after Elizabeth and the children had retired upstairs, he sat watching the fire as it burned low, the dying embers flickering redly, and if thinking was bad, then he was most assuredly becoming addicted to the pernicious habit, for he mused alternately on the Leather-woman and on Varden. He was suspecting something about the latter, but he was afraid to admit it to himself. Then, too, Varden's question about the Leather-woman's lack of a name kept coming back to him. She did not even have a name anymore. Had it come to that? Names were . . . names were important. They could not just be forgotten.

Eventually, he could stand it no longer, and he rose, threw on his cloak, and went out. Unseen, he made his way through the village, his boots crunching on the stones of the street. Finally, the last house but one was behind him, and the Aleser Mountains bulked against the horizon, visible only because they blacked out the stars. Closer was the small hut—

thatched unevenly, full of holes—where the Leather-woman lived.

Cautiously, he crept forward, stepping with care, wishing he could move as silently as the young man in the forest. His mouth was dry and tasted of fear, but he forced himself to press on: around the rocks, through the heather, up to the wall of the hut.

There was a fair-sized crack at about eye level, and yellow light glimmered uneasily from it. With a prayer that he might not be blasted, Andrew peered through it.

Across the shabby room was a table, and there the Leather-woman sat on a flimsy stool, her back to Andrew. She was chanting tonelessly, and from her movements, he judged that she was mending. Aside from a dying fire, a small candle was the only light, and he wondered that she was not blind. He wondered, too, how and what she ate: he did not see much resembling food in the house. She was thin, too thin, and he suddenly became afraid that she would die . . . and she had no name. And who would bury her?

The Leather-woman moved, dropping her work and covering her face with her hands. A low sob drifted through the dark air. It had no more resonance than a gong of lead, but Andrew heard it, and he heard also her hoarse murmur: "Let me go."

His vision was blurring again, and he stepped back and wiped his eyes. When he looked again, the Leather-woman had turned around and was glaring at the chink as if she had sensed his presence. Hastily, he retreated.

As he reentered the village, his thoughts were

whirling again. *Let me go.* The murmured plea and the moan that went with it were, in his opinion, enough to rive the gates of hell itself.

And she could die. And without even a *name*.

He was so lost in thought that he did not at first notice that he was no longer alone in the street. Someone had appeared from between the buildings and had fallen in step beside him.

"Good evening, Master Carpenter. Are you going my way?"

Andrew cried out in fear, but he recognized Varden's smile and shining eyes even in the darkness. Indeed, a soft light, like a shimmer, appeared to hover about the young man.

His cry, though, had been heard, and a shutter opened above his head. "Andrew? Is tha' you?" came the gruff voice of the smith.

"Uh ... it is, Francis," said the carpenter. He noticed that Varden had faded quietly back into the shadows.

"Wha' in God's holy name are you doing out in the middle o' the night, man?"

"Uh ... taking a walk."

"Ach! Yer brain is addled with wood chips and sawdust! D'ye need help?"

"No thank you, Francis. I'm on my way home."

"Good night to you then. May God sit on yer pillow!"

The shutter banged to, and Varden reappeared. "It seems," he said, "that you are indeed going my way."

"Where?"

"To your house. I want to talk with you."

"To me? But . . . but why?" The carpenter was both baffled and frightened.

Varden took him gently by the arm and guided him away from the smith's window. "It appears that we share a concern." With light, soundless steps, he accompanied Andrew to his house and entered quietly behind him.

The carpenter hung up their cloaks on the wooden pegs by the door and turned to face his guest. Even among the commonplace furnishings of the house, Varden kept his shimmer and his mystery. It was as though some wild thing had entered to pay a visit to its domestic kindred, bringing with it an ambiance of forest and river, mountain and lake.

Varden smiled. "Be at peace, Andrew."

"What is it you want, Varden?"

"May we sit?" Varden gestured to the chairs by the fire. Andrew nodded and guided his guest to one of the seats, then sat down facing him, watching him in silence for some time.

Varden at last spoke. "You are worried about the Leather-woman."

"I am."

"I watched you at her house this night."

"I shouldn't have done that."

"Should not have done what? Shown compassion for a fellow creature? Exhibited concern for her welfare? I believe you are a Christian, Andrew. Are these things not good for one of your faith to do?"

Andrew passed a hand over his face. "She'll more than likely curse me for a meddler . . . like she did Svengard."

"The shepherd?" Varden shifted as though sitting in a chair was not something to which he was accustomed. "Perhaps. But have you ever seen a starving dog? Frightened creatures—creatures in pain—will snap even at a hand extended in compassion and friendship. And the Leather-woman has been starving for a long time by your reckoning of years."

Andrew watched the flames of the fire. The pine crackled and spat. "Did you find out what her name is?"

"I did not. That information appears to have been lost."

Andrew looked up. Exposed by the open collar of Varden's tunic was a pendant in the form of a moon and rayed star. It caught the light and sent a flash across the fireplace stones. "Who are you, Varden? Are you an Elf?"

Varden's voice was soft. "I am."

Andrew was silent. He had said the word. He should have been terrified, but instead he felt only relief: there seemed to be nothing even remotely frightening about Varden. He laughed quietly, releasing the last of the tension. "I've never talked to an Elf before."

"I have never guested with a human before."

"Why did you decide to start?"

Varden grew serious. "For this reason: the Leather-woman has lived for eighty years. She is old, and bitter, and she has done evil, and she will continue to do it. Her life could have been otherwise, but it was confounded."

"How do you know that for certain?"

Varden leaned toward Andrew. "I will tell you this, Andrew: each life lived is many lives. There are patterns of chance and circumstance that form and change with each breath we take. It is so even with Elves, and those of your race are even more affected because in many ways you walk your lives in blindness. There was another life open to the Leatherwoman. You saw it in your daydream: she could have been loved, and she could have loved in return. But she was denied that life and that love. Perhaps it could be set down to fate, destiny, happenstance, caprice." He shrugged. "Regardless, her sorrow is great, and my people are troubled. Other creatures we would heal, or release from their burden of life, but we cannot so deal with the Leather-woman. Her help must come from human hands."

"And so you come to me?"

"In eighty years, you are the first to look upon her with compassion."

The Elf's statement fell on Andrew like an oaken beam. "Varden . . . the first? Surely you're mistaken . . ."

The light flickered in Varden's eyes. "I am not. My memory goes back far beyond yours, dear mortal."

Andrew spread his hands helplessly. "But what can I do? You said yourself that she's like a starving dog."

"Are you unwilling to try?"

"You're asking a lot. I have my family to worry about, too."

Varden nodded. "That is so."

"So what right do you have to ask me such a thing?" Agitated, Andrew jumped up and went to the unshuttered window. The night was warm, and the song of the crickets was loud and clear.

"None whatsoever."

"Good. Because ... because ..." Andrew was looking off into the night, but in his mind he was looking once more through a chink in the wall of a shabby hut. "I've got to do something."

"And will you?" said Varden behind him.

"Probably." Andrew smeared the dampness from his eyes and turned around. "And I'll probably get hurt, and my family—"

The Elf held up a hand. "Peace, friend. Do you think I would ask and give nothing in return? You have the protection of my people. We will shield you as we can. Do not be mistaken. Your action will still be dangerous, but generosity and compassion shall not go unrewarded."

He reached into a pouch at his side and extracted a green stone. It was about the size of an egg, faceted, and shining with a soft light as of a forest meadow. "This is a beryl. Keep it with you, Andrew. It will shield you from all but the greatest powers."

The carpenter took it. The stone felt warm. "And if it fails?"

Varden only looked at him. "There is danger in your task."

"Why can't you and your people do something, Varden? You have ... have ... powers. I've heard the tales."

"And what would that teach her?" said Varden. "That love and concern are not to be found among those of her own race? That only the terrible Elves

of the forest can find it in their hearts to love her?
That she can expect sympathy only from those whom
the Church condemns? Were her situation other than
what it is, were its origins different, we might consider such an action. But it is not so. It is a mortal
hand that must help her, that must itself be redeemed
by her."

"Redeemed? What could she possibly—?"

There was an edge in Varden's voice, like a sword
blade sheathed in velvet. "Your people rejected her.
The fault lies with them, with their choices, with their
actions. Through your actions, however, they will
have the opportunity to show that they are of a different stuff than the Elves believe. As I said, I have
never guested with a human before, and for good
reason. Now I find that a spark of love exists in a
race that hunts down and burns my sisters and
brothers. Do not protest, carpenter: Inquisition rages
in the north."

Andrew had indeed lifted a hand, but at the mention of the Inquisition, he let it fall to his side. "I'm
surprised you even speak to me."

"Forgive my words. They are indeed overharsh
considering your actions." The Elf rose gracefully
from his chair. "I will come again, Andrew. My people are fading, but maybe before we depart altogether we can find some friendship among our
younger cousins."

"I never thought I'd be helping the Elves ... or a
witch, for that matter."

"Ah," said Varden, "but the Leather-woman is not
a witch. Those who do harm never are. Those who

practice the Old Ways have many things in common with my people." The light in his eyes turned troubled. "Including being hunted by the Church. This age is an unfortunate one, in which ancient wisdom is held cheap ... and hated."

There was a rustle on the steps leading to the loft. Elizabeth's voice carried down to them. "Andrew?"

"We have a guest, Elizabeth."

She descended, a robe clutched about her, and as she came forward, her eyes were on Varden. "Good evening to you, my lord. If my husband had awakened me, I would have shown you greater hospitality."

"Elizabeth," said Andrew, "this is Varden. I ... met him in the forest this afternoon."

Varden bowed, touching his hands to his forehead. "Fear not, Elizabeth. Your husband has seen to my comfort."

Elizabeth's eyes suddenly grew wide. "Fair One! You are welcome here! You do us great honor!" And she curtsied deeply.

For a moment, Varden stood, looking from Andrew to Elizabeth. Finally, and with reverence, he took the woman's hand and pressed it to his lips. "And you do me honor also, madam. I find that there are indeed jewels among the shards."

He donned his cloak. "I will say farewell now. I will be near. Be at peace."

Andrew let him out, and the Elf vanished silently into the darkness. The beryl felt warm and strangely heavy as he turned to Elizabeth, but she was looking at her hand, at the place where the strange, immortal lips had touched.

Summer passed, and the year drew toward harvest. The fields ripened in the warm sun, and the days turned hot and dusty. Nonetheless, those in Saint Brigid who were weather-wise read the signs of a coming harsh winter, and so, even in the heat, Andrew was busy mending shutters for the village folk, preparing for the cold season.

Andrew kept the beryl with him always, carrying it nestled in a leather pouch he wore next to his skin. In the warm weather, he had not worried about the Leather-woman's comfort at night, though over the weeks since he had talked with Varden he had done his best to see to it that she had gotten a fair price for her work and a fair weight for her money. He had tried to be innocuous, but his efforts had been noticed . . . and not only by elvish eyes.

He was sharing a skin of wine with the smith one afternoon while they negotiated the price and number of some pole pins. The business was pretty much done when Francis leaned back on his stool and fixed the carpenter with his black eyes.

"So now, Andrew. What are you up to?"

"Up to?" Andrew took the skin and drank.

"Aye, man. Up to. Yer acting dard pretty about the Leather-woman, and so I'm asking. You know I a'ways pay her a fair price for her doings, though I'm not sure about others. And now yer looking into it?"

"It's true," Andrew admitted. "I think she should

be looked after. She's old, and the winter will be hard. I wouldn't like to see her starve . . . or freeze."

"There's many folk in Saint Brigid wouldn't regret tha'."

"Yes . . . that's true."

The smith watched him silently for some time, a rivulet of sweat running down through the soot on his face and into his black beard. "Let me know if you need help, man."

Andrew was startled. "Why . . . why do you say that?"

"I mak' her braces for her. Done so all my life. My first time at the forge, my father was making her a brace—did you know that? 'Tis true. The first iron I ever beat went onto her leg, and though she's done sa' bad, sure enough, I canna but feel that there's sa'thing in her worth guarding. In spite o' what she's done."

Andrew stared at the leather wineskin in his hands. She had taught herself how to work leather. "Someone told me once that her life could have been better . . . if things had been different."

"Aye, Andrew. But life takes its turns."

"I'm wondering if we can't . . . well . . . turn it back."

The smith chuckled and wiped at his sweat. "Turn it back? Andrew, that's wha' miracles are for, and He that di' them is gone from us until the Last Day. More's the pity for us, poor devils."

"I wish there were some way . . ."

"Maybe a wizard, Andrew, if you can find one."

"Or ... Elves?" Andrew was suddenly acutely conscious of the stone at his side.

The smith's eyebrows went up. "Elves? D'ye talk from tales ... or experience?"

Andrew colored, and stood up. "Just thinking, Francis. If we can get her through the winter, it'll be well."

But there was a tapping from the street, and Andrew recognized the sound of the Leather-woman's stick. In a moment, she had entered the smithy and they were face to face.

"Good day," said Andrew.

"No *mother* today, scrapling?"

He shrugged and shook his head.

"Do you need leather, Francis?" she rasped past the carpenter.

"Aye, madam," said the smith. "Come in an' be comfortable. Does your brace fit well enough?"

"Tolerable, thankee." The Leather-woman had not moved. She was talking to the smith, but she was looking at Andrew ... or rather, she was looking at the place in his shirt where he kept the stone. When he tried to leave, she stepped directly into his path, bringing him up short. Their gazes met, and he shuddered at the chill in her lake blue eyes.

"Magic can get you in trouble, scrapling," she whispered. "Look at me, and beware."

He pressed his lips together and swallowed. "Let me know," he said evenly, "if you need anything. Now, or this winter."

"So the old black hen has some friends, eh?"

"More friends than she thinks."

"Go to hell." She brushed past him, but he felt her grab for the stone. He stepped back involuntarily, but she had already drawn back her hand as though she had been burned. She looked at him for a long moment. "Mind yourself, scrapling," she said at last. "The Folk of the Wood have no power over me."

"Nor do they want any," Andrew returned without thinking.

She spat and turned away. Andrew bid Francis good day and went out into the light. He was already a good distance up the street when he heard her shout behind him: "And the next time you come peeking at me you'll get an eyeful of something!"

The first winter winds were cold, sweeping down from the mountains to the west, smelling of frost. There was little snow as of yet, but the air was frigid, and heavy cloaks and quilted jackets came out of storage chests early. Andrew could not wear mittens when he worked, and he was glad when Elizabeth brought him something hot to drink, for he could warm his hands on the earthenware mug.

He saw the Leather-woman only from a distance now, but he did not cease thinking about her. The frosty winds had made him consider once again her miserable hut, so full of holes that it might as well have possessed no walls at all, and a plan was forming in his mind. To be sure, it was a foolhardy one, but the beryl by his side was a constant reminder of Varden's words: *Her help must come from human hands.*

And so he spoke to Francis and gained his cooperation. All he needed was some time, and since the

Leather-woman stopped regularly at the smithy to see about necessary bits of harness, Francis had only to find some plausible excuse to delay her for an hour or so.

And when he did that, the Thursday after the feast of the patroness of the village, Andrew went to the Leather-woman's hut with a trowel and a bucket of plaster, and, working quickly, filled in the worst of the holes before the wind half froze him. Shivering, he returned to his house, and Elizabeth wrapped him in a blanket and sat him close by the fire. He was shaking, but only partly because of the cold.

At least, he thought, she will be a little warmer. At least I've given her that.

"Do you think I'm wrong, Elizabeth?" he said aloud. "Do you think I'm being foolish?"

She sighed. "I've been afraid of her too," she said. "I've kept the children indoors when she's gone by, lest she . . . do something to one of them. Now . . . I'm not sure. I'm finally seeing her as . . . as someone like us. Someone who just went wrong. Maybe . . ." Her voice drifted off, then: "Maybe she's someone who needs a second chance. Maybe she's someone who can actually do something with a second chance."

Andrew saw the Leather-woman neither the next day, nor the day after that, but on Sunday, as he walked alone in the forest, he came around a turn to find her waiting for him.

The light was weak, the sun shining through a thin overcast, and her shawl looked more like an autumn leaf than ever. She looked thinner, too, but her eyes burned at him. "Why?"

Andrew was silent.

"I said: *Why?*"

"I ..." His tongue was nearly frozen with fright, but he forced the words out. "I didn't want you to be cold."

"Stay away from me, damn you. I don't want your help. Far better it would be if I were dead."

"No, it wouldn't. Don't say things like that."

"And why not, scrapling? The village wouldn't have to pay for a sexton. Just light my house, and let me burn. It'll be cooler for my corpse than for my soul, I assure you."

"*Don't say that!*" His fists were clenched at his sides. Fear? Passion? He did not know. "You've got to *try*. There are some who care."

"Like the Elves? Don't start, Carpenter. I've known that they've been spying on me. They'll fare no better against me than you ... or your friends. Now, stay away from me!"

She lifted her stick, and a blast of wind whirled leaves and dust into Andrew's eyes. When he could see again, she was gone.

The next day, in the late afternoon, he heard about the accident at the forge.

He was there within minutes, and Francis' wife met him at the door, her face white with worry.

"What happened, Hester?" he panted.

"A crucible exploded," she said vaguely, still in shock. "Metal went everywhere. The men put out the fire, but Fran's ... he's ... his hands ..."

She put her own hands to her face, sobbing. Andrew held her and said what words of comfort he knew until her eldest daughter came and took her away.

"He's been bespelled, Carpenter." It was Jaques Alban, the priest. His face was plump and pallid, and in his voice Andrew heard a note of fear.

"And what have you done for him?" said Andrew.

Alban was looking toward the door as though wanting to escape. "I did what I could. Fever is setting in now. It will probably take him in a few days."

Andrew exploded. "You're damned hopeful, aren't you?" He pushed past the fat man and into the chamber beyond. He heard the smith's labored breathing.

A woman was kneeling beside the bed, wrapping a white cloth about Francis' hands. She lifted her head. "Andrew?"

"Blessings, Roxanne. How is he?"

Roxanne sighed and tucked the comforter up around the smith's chin. Francis was pale under his coating of soot, and his teeth were clenched even though he was unconscious. On the other side of the bed, a slight blond boy was on his knees, praying. Andrew recognized him as Kay, the smith's oldest son.

Roxanne stood and drew Andrew out into the hall. Though she was a weaver, she was skilled in herbs and healing, and the villagers often turned to her for help. But her expression today was bleak. "Most of the flesh is burned from his hands," she whispered. "Some of his fingers are just stumps. He'll never hold a hammer again, even if he lives. And there's a fever coming."

"Alban said as much."

"That priest . . . He should stay away." Her dark eyes flashed.

"What chances are there?" Alban was right about at least one thing, though: magic had a hand in the accident. The beryl burned at his side, and Andrew recalled the words of the Leather-woman.

Roxanne looked up at him. He read the answer in her face.

"We'll have to take care of the family," he said.

"Unless Kay can work the forge."

"Kay?" The boy was young and thin: undeniably better suited for a tonsure than a smithy. Francis had been amused that he had sired a monk, but had always shrugged it off. "Mak's up for me own youth," he had chuckled.

"Please, sir." It was Kay, standing in the door of the bedroom. "I heard you. I can handle the forge. I'll have to."

"Kay, you want to be a priest."

"I have to do it. If Father can't."

Andrew looked at the boy, then at Roxanne. Even a breath could alter a lifetime. How much more so a pair of fleshless hands?

"I'm going for help. Roxanne, please tend to Francis and try to keep him comfortable. Kay . . . please pray."

He turned and left the house. By the time he reached the street, he was running, and he headed out of the village and into the forest. The air was cold, and it burned his lungs and his throat, but he did not stop until he stood deep among the trees.

He was gasping by then, and he had to lean

against a leafless oak. When he had caught his breath, he scanned the trees around him for a moment, then cupped his hands about his mouth and shouted: "Varden!"

His voice echoed among the bare trunks and ended in a cold sigh. The forest was silent and still. A trace of snow clung to the matted branches. He was about to shout again when he felt a touch.

"You need not shout, Andrew. I am here." The Elf was wrapped in a gray cloak, nearly invisible amid the colors of winter.

"Varden, we need your help. Francis, the smith, is hurt. He tried to help me with the Leather-woman, and she struck at him. His hands . . ."

The light in Varden's eyes flickered uneasily. His face was without expression save a kind of sadness.

"I've been trying to help her, Varden. I'm not sure that it's possible. She'll kill anything that shows her love."

The Elf was gazing beyond him as though searching among the trees. Or perhaps his sight was turned inward, turned toward some vision that only the Elves could know. "Anything is possible," he murmured as though to himself. "Anything. There are only different degrees of probability."

Andrew stood facing him, hoping. "Please, Varden. You said that compassion shouldn't go unrewarded. Maybe you don't believe it, but my race has tenderness too. Francis is in pain, and I doubt that he or his family is going to care if help comes to him from a human or an elven hand."

The Elf nodded slowly. "Take me to him."

With the Elf at his side, Andrew returned to the village. There was a small cluster of friends and neighbors at the smith's door now, and they turned to look at Andrew and his companion. Varden had pulled up his hood so that his face was half hidden, and, amid puzzled stares, they entered the house and approached the room where Francis lay.

Alban was standing near the door. "And who is this? Do we bring spectators to a man's deathbed?"

"One might almost think you wanted him dead," said Andrew. The priest snorted. Varden doffed his cloak and went toward the bed. The light in his eyes flashed as he turned to face Alban.

"It might be well for you to leave, reverend sir," he said quietly. "I have work to do that you will find distressing."

Alban had shrunk back a step. Andrew knew that he sensed something terrible about the stranger.

"Is this not the time for the prayers your people call vespers?" said the Elf.

"It is." The priest's voice was almost inaudible.

"Then go and say them. And add two requests. One for the health of our friend and brother Francis, and the other for yourself, that you might not always decide upon death as the only outcome of misfortune."

Alban was frozen for a moment, then, with a rush, he departed, his shoes clattering on the flagstone floor.

Kay, small and thin, was still in the room. He was staring at Varden. "My lord ... can you help my father?"

Varden met his eyes. "I will do what I can, young one. You wish to become a priest, do you not?"

"Aye, my lord. I would like to come back and be priest here in Saint Brigid."

Varden rested his hand gently on Kay's head. "And what kind of priest will you be? What do you learn from studying under such as Alban?"

"Everything, sir."

"Indeed?"

"Everything not to be."

Varden sighed softly and removed his hand. "Blessings upon you, Kay. Be a good priest."

He turned toward the smith, who was still unconscious. The shimmer about him brightened as he knelt by the bed.

"*Hyrealle a me.*" The Elf's voice was a faint murmur.

Andrew felt the beryl turn warm. Without thinking, he covered it with his hand.

For a moment, Varden stared into the smith's face, then he took the bandaged hands in his own and bent his head. The ephemeral light grew brighter, and Andrew found that he was seeing, as though just at the edge of sight, a skyful of stars. Faint strands lay among them, shimmering like threads of light, weaving in and out and through one another, forming a complex web; and the carpenter realized that Varden was changing the pattern. He watched as warp and weft were altered, saw several strands fused while others were separated.

There was a sudden change in the air, and then the stars and the web faded. Andrew blinked at the commonplace room, wondering, but Varden straightened, took a deep breath, and stood up. He looked at Andrew. "Be at peace."

Taking up his cloak, he fastened it at his throat and put up his hood. His light was shadowed, but Andrew could see his eyes. "Later, Carpenter," said the Elf, "we will talk again. Let our brother sleep, and feed him well tomorrow." A pause. A trace of a smile. "And you might as well unwrap his hands."

He passed to the door. Roxanne, who had been standing there, was inadvertently blocking his exit. She came to herself at the last moment and stood aside, but as he passed she reached out to him, and he stopped and watched with curiosity as she lifted the hem of his cloak and kissed it.

"Master," she said. "Thank you. I was powerless."

"You did well," he returned. "Be at peace, my lady." He bowed deeply to her and, with silent steps, moved off down the hall. The folk at the door made way for him.

Roxanne went to Francis and removed the bandages. The smith's hands were whole and sound, without even a singed hair or a discolored knuckle.

Kay was on his knees again. Andrew was gripping the beryl still, his hand clenched tightly, the muscles stiff with the strain.

Francis slept through the night, rose, ate breakfast . . . and was back in the smithy the next day. At first, his time was taken up with repairing the damage done by the fire, but soon he was hammering metal as lustily as ever, and Andrew was present when, about a week later, the Leather-woman came into town and halted in shock before the door of the forge. Francis eyed her for a moment, and then he laid aside his hammer and thrust a piece of glowing metal back into the fire. "Good morning," he said. "I ha' need o' leather."

She had noticed Andrew sitting in one corner. Her eyes turned venomous. "You should be dead," she said to Francis.

"But I'm not." The smith rubbed his beard. "By rights I should be angry, but I'll tell you again: I ha' need o' leather."

"Then you'll have to get it somewhere else," she snapped. She looked at Andrew. " 'Twas your friends helped you," she cried. "I'll have my say to you later on, Carpenter."

Andrew stood up wearily and spread his hands. "I'm trying to—"

"I don't need help. But you will. Believe me. And you won't find it in elvish hands." Dragging her crippled leg behind her, she turned around and slowly made her way up the street.

Francis watched her. "How well d'ye know that Elf o' yours, Andrew?"

Andrew shrugged. "How well can you know an Elf?"

"Well, I hope y' have confidence in him, as you'll be wanting his help afore this is through."

Andrew's hand went to the stone. "I don't doubt him."

Heavy snows came the next month, burying the village deep. Andrew stayed indoors for the most part, as did the other villagers. No one saw the

Leather-woman. Andrew reassured himself that she was still alive by periodically checking to see that there was smoke rising from the hole in the roof of her hut, but he was unwilling to risk further contact with her.

But as the snowy days continued, and as the cold increased, he found himself thinking and wondering again. She could not have much food in her house, and the snow more than likely made it impossible for her to get more. The certainty grew in him along with the worry, and by the first Sunday in Advent he was brooding about it. The village was approaching the winter feast days of joy and plenty, and he did not like to think of an old woman starving while others danced.

So, one evening, he asked Elizabeth if she would gather together some bread, and preserves, and smoked meat, and other good things that would keep. Elizabeth did not ask why, but Andrew knew that she guessed, and her quick hands soon had a large basket packed and covered with a cloth. Andrew was wrapped in his cloak and his furs by the time she was finished, and she put it into his mittened hands as he stood before the door. He looked at her, and she nodded. "We have to try," she said.

"I trust Varden," he whispered.

"So do I."

She kissed him, and he went out into the night.

He checked the following day. There was no basket by the Leather-woman's door, and so he assumed that she had taken it in. But as the days passed, and as a sense of oppression grew about him, he thought of the smith and prayed that his family would be spared.

Then Varden came one evening, cloaked in blue and white, his eyes flashing as brilliantly as the moon and star at his throat. Elizabeth was just sending the children to bed, but when the Elf stepped into the firelit room, the youngsters stopped at the foot of the stairs to look. Varden met Andrew's eyes, then bowed to Elizabeth and the children. "Blessings upon you this day."

James, twelve years old and fearless, strode directly up to him. "Are you an Elf?"

"James!" Andrew was aghast.

"Peace, friend." Varden smiled and turned to the boy. "And what do you think, young one?"

James looked him up and down, scrutinizing carefully. "You don't look like what they say in the tales."

"And what do they say in the tales?"

"That Elves are tall and strong, and have cows' feet, and breathe fire if they want."

"I have never breathed fire in my life," said Varden, still smiling. "Although I confess there have been times that I wished that I could. So, what say you?"

"I think you are."

"In spite of the tales?"

"I don't care about the tales," said James stoutly. "You . . . just feel like an Elf. I don't think the Elves in the tales would feel that way at all."

"Well said," replied Varden. "And quite correct."

Regardless of James' stated conviction, Varden's confirmation made the boy's eyes open wide. Elizabeth came and took him by the shoulders. "To bed with you," she said, and marched him up the stairs. The other children followed, whispering and looking back until they disappeared into the loft.

"And may the Lady send you sweet dreams," the Elf called softly after them.

Andrew was standing to one side, his arms folded.

"And how are your dreams, Andrew?"

"Troubled. Last night I saw my family slaughtered before my eyes. Elizabeth woke me. She said I was crying out. My children were frightened."

The Elf sighed. "So perhaps it is too late for love." He spoke softly, almost to himself.

"She's bitter. Very bitter. And now I fear all her hate is directed at me."

Varden moved to the hearth and sat down cross-legged, his back to the flames. Elizabeth came down the stairs. "If I would not be intruding," she said, "I would like to hear what passes."

"It is well," said Varden. "Please join us, my lady." He spoke to her as though she were nobility, and she blushed; but she sat by the fire with her needlework, her hands moving of their own as she listened.

Too agitated to sit, Andrew paced. "It's not working, Varden. It's just not working. If anything, she's worse. She hadn't done anything against anyone in the village for months, and now ..."

Varden's voice was soft, grieving. "I had hoped that this would turn out otherwise. Though a tree in the forest may be struck by lightning, or broken by the wind, it can be propped up and tended to, and can grow straight again. But sometimes . . ."

Elizabeth spoke. "She was broken many years ago, and her wounds were never tended."

"I'm afraid she can't be mended," said Andrew. "She's like . . . like a starving dog."

Varden nodded. "I believe I described her as such, when we spoke of the danger involved in the task."

Andrew was not sure if he was being reprimanded, and the Elf's face gave no clue. "At that time," he said, "we both thought that there was some hope."

"You do not believe so now?"

"I'm not sure." Andrew stopped pacing, rubbed at his cheek. "It seemed like a good thing to do. To help her, I mean. But at that time, she hadn't tried to kill Francis, and she hadn't threatened me. And now, more than ever, what about Elizabeth? What about the children?"

"Her anger," said Varden, "is directed at you alone. There is nothing to cause her to attack your family."

"Except revenge."

"Elizabeth and your children have the protection of my people. They are beyond the reach and power of the Leather-woman. What, then, is your will, Andrew? Do you wish to end this matter now, and leave the Leather-woman to her fate? Or do you wish to continue?"

In the back of his mind, Andrew felt the beginnings of a headache—a sharp pain, then a dull throbbing—that rose and fell quickly, then departed.

He sensed that it was not natural, that it came from somewhere outside of himself. "It's . . . it's too late now. I plastered her hut, I've spoken kindly to her, I've given her food. Even if I turned back, she'd still hate me, and she'd still work against me."

Varden did not speak.

"So I'm going to have to go and meet her, one way or another, sooner or later. I can feel her around me, testing me. And look at this." He pulled out the leather pouch, displayed the beryl. It was palpably shining, filled with a radiance as of sunlight. "It's been getting brighter," he explained.

"It counters her working," said Varden.

"For how long?"

Varden stood up slowly, went to Andrew. Extending his hands, he clasped them around Andrew's, around the beryl. For an instant, the carpenter stared into the Elf's starlit eyes, and then his vision blurred. He saw the stars, shining brightly, remote and yet close. He was floating in a night sky.

He saw a web again, as he had at the smith's house, but it was a different web now, and as he examined the strands, he felt certain that it had to do with the Leather-woman. He heard Varden's voice in his mind.

"Each life is many lifetimes," came the words, softly, almost wearily. "I told you that before, and now this is what you see before you. Each weaving of the lattice you see is a choice in the Leather-woman's life: past, present, and future. The web is herself, all of her. Look back at the past, and see the tangled interactions that forced her along the paths she now travels. Look to the future, and see the possibilities she once had. There is a strand there that represents you, Andrew. See how it changes the pattern."

"I can't interpret the change."

"Nor can I. There are many possibilities that branch from that intersection."

As Andrew looked, the stars brightened, and their light flowed into the strands. The pattern shifted subtly, and he saw that, although the Leather-woman's futures remained hazy, his own thread traced its way through the intersection and on into another maze of possibilities.

"There is nothing she can do to harm you," said the Elf. "As she exerts her powers, so the stone alters the futures so that you are shielded."

The room flashed back into existence around him, and he shook his head to clear it. Elizabeth's brow was furrowed, and she seemed half of a mind to rise and draw him away from their strange visitor, but he smiled thinly at her. "I'm all right."

He turned back to Varden. "You're very sad. And very tired," he said simply.

Varden released his hands and stood back, nodding. "You see clearly, Andrew. It is so. For a minute, though, you have seen with our eyes, and so you should understand our feelings. We see what is, and we also see what might have been. There were many futures that led to peaceful coexistence between my people and yours, and instead we have the present situation. The Leather-woman might have been loved, and yet she was not. Missed opportunities. Wrong choices. We see them all. We delight in the good that has happened, and we grieve for that which has been missed, ignored, lost."

"But I saw the strands change, Varden. Why can't you—"

The Elf shook his head. "Our power is limited. Terribly limited. Still, though, we try as we can. That is why I made the stone you hold."

"You . . . you *made* this?" Andrew stared at it.

"I did. I have watched the Leather-woman grow old, and I have watched her bitterness rage. To reach out among the patterns of her life and alter them without her consent is a course of action that is denied me. But if I could in some way aid one of her own kind who wished to help her, if I could protect him and guide him, then I would be acting within my constraints. My hand can set a seal on whatever you do, Andrew, but it is you who must do it."

"Do . . . do what?"

"I do not know."

The Elf stood in the firelight, his hands at his sides. The shimmer gleamed about him, the starlight shone in his eyes, but, for a moment, he seemed no more than a creature of the world, someone who was trying in his own, groping fashion to do good, who was baffled by the often vague and indefinite turns of events. Even the Elves could be unsure.

Andrew hefted the stone, slid it back into its pouch. "I'll do what I can. I can't promise anything."

Varden bowed. "Nor are you asked to."

Christmas drew nigh, and the Leather-woman kept to her miserable hut. Late at night—despite the cold, despite her hate—Andrew would sometimes go to the edge of town and drop a bundle of firewood at her door. The bundle would be gone come morning. Still, he imagined that he could hear her voice carried along by the wind from the mountains, an old, dry voice, rasping as it had from infancy: *I don't want your help. Far better it would be if I were dead.*

No, he thought as he turned away one night, far better it would be had you not suffered as you have. Far better it would be had you not been born in a body that made you an object of laughter. Far better it would be if those about you had remembered compassion and common charity.

He trudged up the street, head bent, hood pulled well forward against the cold. It was but four days before the Nativity, and already, in defiance of the self-denial of Advent, the villagers were setting out their decorations: bunches of elder, mistletoe, and birch adorned the doors of many of the shops and houses.

He felt again the shade of a headache that touched and departed, felt the beryl inside his shirt flicker and glow as it altered chance and destiny to protect him. The Leather-woman was still seeking vengeance for the good he had done her, and yet he found himself casting about in his mind for something more he could do to bridge the abyss of fear and bitterness with which she had surrounded herself. It seemed impossible. No matter what he did, he stood condemned in her eyes.

The headache touched him again, and again the beryl glowed and turned it aside.

How foolish! How wonderfully useless!

Again, the headache.

She had food, and she had warmth. Maybe that was enough for now. Maybe, in the spring, when the weather was better and the land was smiling with green leaves and early flowers, maybe then he could reach out to her and have his hand accepted. An improbable occurrence, but then had Varden not said that anything was possible?

The headache strayed into him again, lingered for a moment . . .

He stopped, shook his head slightly. The beryl flared . . .

. . . and then his brain itself seemed to detonate, throwing him to his knees as a knife of pain buried itself in his skull. Hands to either side of his head, he gasped, for so great was the agony that he did not even have the strength to cry out. At his side, the beryl turned into a small star, shining even through cloth and leather . . .

. . . and suddenly the pain was gone.

Weak and shaking, he stood up, feeling sick, his vision blurry. But he gathered his strength and faced about, turning back in the direction of the mountains. It was going to be tonight. It had to be tonight.

He returned the way he had come, pushing through the dry heather and bracken at the edge of the village, scuffing through the crusty snow that covered the rude path to the Leather-woman's hut. When he reached the door, he did not hesitate, but pounded loudly. "All right, Mother, I'm here!" he shouted.

But there was no answer. The door swung inward. Though the fire burned on the hearth and the air was thick with the smoke of herbs, the hut was unoccupied.

Andrew stepped back, puzzled. She had wanted him: of that he was sure. Where—?

He turned. Out toward the mountains, where the foothills began amid bare rock and tumbled boulders, he saw a dim red light. It flickered, grew brighter. Nodding inwardly, he turned his steps toward it and followed a trail in the snow that led into the rocks.

The slope was steep, the stones beneath his feet jagged and uneven, the boulders so thickly strewn that at times there was barely enough room for him to squeeze through, and he found himself wondering how she had dragged herself along this path. Still, he continued, and as he did, the wind rose, shrieking through the rocks, howling among the tumbled boulders.

He had thought that the night would be clear, but he saw now that it was clouding up. Already, the growing overcast was overtaking the full moon, but Andrew continued in the direction of the red light, now brighter still, and at last he rounded a turning to find a flat expanse of packed earth and bare rock surrounded by a ring of tall boulders. The wind had swept it clear of snow, and at the center burned a low fire.

Behind the fire stood the Leather-woman.

The flickering light set her shadow rising hugely behind her, dancing back and forth on the rocks. Her stick writhed in her hand, and her tattered shawl blew in the wind. For a moment, Andrew stayed within the cover of the stones, but the beryl glowed as he grasped it for reassurance, and he left his shelter, approached, and stood across the fire from the Leather-woman.

She did not speak at first, only eyed him up and down as though astonished at this common laboring man who had dared oppose her. "I warned you," she said at last.

"I know. It didn't do any good. I still care."

"You're a fool."

"Maybe." He searched for words, hoping to find something that would make a difference to her. He came up with dust.

"Fools suffer for their foolishness." She lifted her stick, but the beryl glowed in response. Andrew fingered the stone through its covering of cloth and leather and laughed nervously.

"Why don't you just accept the fact that someone wants to do you a good turn?" he said. "It doesn't cost you anything. I fixed your house, and I've given you food and wood. I've left you alone other than that. So, other than that, you can live as you want."

She lowered her stick, grounding it. "Live as I want? What do you know about my living? You don't know how many nights I've huddled in my straw and prayed for death. I don't want life. Not like this. Keep your life." Her voice cut through the wind like a file.

"But you ate my food, and you didn't tear out the plaster."

"Yes ... damn you. That's true. All of it. I pray for death, but I don't have the will to destroy myself. I thought for a while that I could ... and then you came along with your damned gifts."

"It could be different."

"Could it? Can you take away the fear? Can you undo eighty years of hate, can you make me young again and take away my crippled leg and my harsh voice? Can you? Get to work then, Master Carpenter, you with your elven magic and your stone of protection." Her eyes were cold even in the red light of the fire. There was no hope in them. Hope had fled long ago. "It'd go hard with you if you didn't have that beryl, I'll tell you."

Slowly, Andrew removed the pouch from his shirt and slid the stone into his palm. It shimmered with the light of a thousand stars, patterns of life forming and reforming within it as though it were alive.

He looked at her suddenly. "Would it? When I saw you in the street months ago, I saw you for the first time. All my life you'd been the Leather-woman with her evil and her spells, and then, all of a sudden, you turned into a person, someone who ate and slept just like me, someone who felt cold and hunger and pain ... just like me. I've been lonely, too. Maybe not as lonely as you, but I know what it's like. Now you're looking at me, and maybe now you're seeing *me* for the first time. And maybe I'm not just an interfering young ... scrapling. Maybe I'm Andrew, the carpenter. Maybe I'm someone who has some love to offer. Maybe I'm someone who wants to help. Maybe ... maybe I'm even someone who feels sorry for what happened to you and wants to try to make up for it."

The beryl gleamed, starlight dancing through it. Andrew looked the Leather-woman in the face, saw, just for an instant, a flash of uncertainty. Maybe . . . maybe . . .

Before her thoughts could harden again, he spoke. "So I don't believe you when you say you'd strike me down if it weren't for this stone. I think you're willing to try once more."

He could not tell for sure, but he wondered if her eyes were, perhaps, glistening. "I . . . I don't want anything," she choked. "I just want to be left alone. I just want to die . . . and get it over with."

"I won't leave you alone. I won't let you die. I'm not asking you anymore. I'm telling you. It's going to change. It must change."

The beryl was suddenly ablaze with light. Gritting his teeth, shaking, he stretched his hand across the fire, offered the stone to her. "Here. Take it. It's yours . . . and it's you. Maybe you need it. Maybe it can give you something that I can't. But I don't believe that you'll hurt me if I don't have it. Take it."

She reached out, hesitated.

"I trust you."

The words galvanized her, and she snatched the stone and whirled half around, pressing it to her chest. It did not burn her, and, after a minute, she straightened as much as her bent frame would allow. She gazed down at the gleaming beryl, then lifted her eyes to Andrew.

Her mouth worked for a moment. "Why?" she

managed. It was not a demand. It was, rather, sheer bewilderment.

"I told you. I trust you. I'm going home now, but if you need anything, come to me. Let's try to—" He choked and forced his jaw to stop trembling. "Let's try to be friends."

He turned around and walked toward the trail. He did not look back. He kept himself from looking back. When he reached the edge of the clearing, he continued on down through the boulders and the scattered rocks. Afraid. Waiting.

Hoping . . .

A bend in the trail brought him around to face the clearing again, and only then did he look, climbing up on top of a boulder in order to see. The Leather-woman still stood by the fire, the beryl shining in her hand, and as she suddenly lifted it over her head, Andrew could not but wonder whether, in the next moment, his head would suddenly split. But when the Leather-woman brought her hand down again, it was not to hurl a curse, but rather to fling the stone onto the hard ground.

It shattered on the rocks.

A blast of incandescence, as though a star had come to dwell in the stone circle. Mounting blindingly, mounting hugely, it expanded, widened, reached out as though it would encompass the world. Leather-woman, stones, fire—all and everything vanished within the searing light.

Andrew had but a moment to stare before it reached him, lifting him up and throwing him back off the rock. For a moment, he hung suspended, arms outstretched, feet dangling uselessly, and then, the blast passing by, he fell heavily onto the ground. He had a brief glimpse of lattices of shimmering lines weaving themselves into new patterns, and then blackness overwhelmed him.

When he awoke, it was morning, the winter sun just rising over the plains to the southeast. He was cold and stiff, and he was infinitely grateful for his thick cloak. More than likely it had saved his life that night.

Still groggy, he pulled himself back up to the top of the boulder and looked around. There was the clearing, and there was the circle of stones ... but there was no trace of the Leather-woman; and when he made his way back up the trail, he found nothing more than what he had seen from a distance. Even the ashes of the fire were gone.

The world suddenly looked very bleak, and he felt empty and sad. But he turned away, turned toward the village, for he knew that Elizabeth and the children would be frantic about his absence.

Slowly, he descended through the boulders and into the bracken and the heather, and when he came to the Leather-woman's hut, he found that its fire had died. The dwelling now looked untenanted, even more forlorn than before. The wind stirred the dead heather, and snow was blowing in through the open door.

Andrew stood for several minutes, grieving over his failure, for the hut was almost accusatory in its desolation. She was gone. There would be no more chances.

But then he heard weeping. A soft, quiet voice.

He wiped his eyes and followed the sound, and in a clump of heather he found huddled a young girl, not more than seven summers old. She was dressed in rags that looked woefully inadequate to the cold, and Andrew tore off his cloak and cast it about her shoulders while she looked at him, wide-eyed.

"Don't be afraid," he said.

She had great self-control for one so young, and she blinked back some of her tears and managed to whisper, "Thank you, sir."

"Who are you?" said Andrew. "Where are you from?"

"I . . ." Her hair was long and dark, and as she stared at him out of eyes as blue as mountain lakes, her lip trembled. "I don't know. I don't—" She suddenly winced and looked down at her legs.

Andrew was puzzled, and when he pulled the cloak aside, he had to stifle a cry. Her right leg was perfectly straight, sound, and healthy, but it was imprisoned in a harsh, iron brace that bent it unnaturally.

"I couldn't get it off by myself," she said.

Andrew stared for a moment, then pulled out his knife and cut away the old leather fastenings. He eased the brace from her leg and rubbed warmth and blood back into the flesh. "Who . . . who did this to you?"

He looked into her face as he spoke, and then he knew, for she was staring at the iron brace with a dim flicker of pain and recognition, and her eyes were growing troubled. But Andrew stood, picked up the brace, and threw it as far away as he could; and then her pain and recognition faded . . . and her memory, he supposed, faded too. Her eyes cleared and shone. They were lake blue, tranquil.

Andrew knelt before her. "What's your name, maiden?"

"I don't know. I don't remember. I don't think I have one."

"Nor home, neither?" But he knew the answer already . . .

"No, sir."

. . . just as he knew his own reply, for: "You have one now," he said. "You'll come and live with me and my wife, Elizabeth, and our children. My name is Andrew."

"You're a . . . a carpenter," she said suddenly, then looked uncertainly at him, smiled, and shook her head as the last trace of remembrance fled.

He picked her up and carried her home. The villagers marveled at the pretty young waif from the bracken, and they marveled more at how she had been abandoned by all, to be rescued only by chance. But Elizabeth met him at their door, and she kissed the child and bade her be welcome, and she gave her warm clothes and a hot breakfast. She met Andrew's eyes, and he knew that she had guessed.

They named her Charity.

Lady of Light

The west doors of the church were open, and the reddening light of sunset spilled in, setting the length of the nave aglow and illuminating the bare wooden cross above the altar. David's hands were in his tunic pockets, and he kept them there while he examined the cross, lips pressed together, uncomfortably aware of the priest who stood beside him.

"I want it finished by next Easter," said Jaques Alban, lacing and unlacing his fingers inside the sleeves of his soutane. "With your talent, David my son, it will be a fitting masterpiece to crown my church. People will come from miles around to see it."

David shifted uneasily. Outside of town, the forest was full of autumn color—red and russet, yellow and gold—its final celebration before the death of the year. He had received the summons from Alban an hour before, and he had scuffed through piles of those glowing, fallen leaves as he had taken the road into the village. He had known even then why he had been called, had known, too, that he could not avoid this meeting ... or the demand that would be made of him.

Still, he sought to evade the inevitable. "I hope you realize," he said, "that I have other commissions to attend to. Members of the baronial houses desire panels and statues for the churches and cathedrals they're building in the cities to the north." He kept his voice polite.

"Pah!" said Alban. "Rivalries. Blood feuds, too, I imagine: stabbing each other in the back amid the reek of taverns. Fine people to set up carvings before God!" He laid a fatherly hand on David's shoulder and did not notice that the carver winced. "This village is your home, David. Your birthplace. You grew up here, went to school, received the sacraments. If I'm not mistaken, you thought about a vocation for a while, eh?" He patted David's shoulder . . . and did not notice that the carver winced again.

David did not reply for some time. The bare cross, he thought, was sufficient for the church: a stark counterbalance to a lavish interior in which stained glass windows soared up on all sides, stone carvings peered out from corners of the elaborate vaulting, and an inlaid floor gleamed in the light of candles in gold (gold!) holders. Alban had wanted a fine church, and he had built one; but though David could see that it was attractive enough in its own way, all its opulence and ornament, in his opinion, found a resolution only in the simplicity of the cross—a vertical and a horizontal beam, the wood smoothed and planed and polished, no more—as if that simplicity were a reminder not only of the poverty of the One who had suffered there but also of the point of that suffering: that the cross should eventually be bare, the tomb empty.

He found himself thinking of the autumn leaves through which he had walked on the way to this meeting. The harvest: yellow fields, dying leaves. Soon, the grain would be gathered in, and the fields would be left stripped and forsaken ... like this cross. Autumn was a hard season for David. There was too much death in autumn, too much of a sense of futility as the life of summer guttered into cold and dark. Only the distant spring made the bleakness at all bearable.

If only Alban had asked for some other carving! Doors, maybe, or maybe a screen. David could see either project easily: trees, forests, animals peering through carved trunks and bunches of flowers, intricate filigrees. There could be life there, and love, and the touch of a Hand that had brought healing and comfort.

"David?"

Death.

"David?"

Death. Death. Death.

He dropped his eyes, unable to think of anything to say.

"I want that crucifix."

"Are you ordering me, master?" said the carver. "I'm a free craftsman." A thought came into his head. "How much are you willing to pay for such a carving?"

Alban looked shocked. "Pay? Your whole life you have benefited from the Church, and now you talk of payment? Look at this fine church, David! All the love that I could muster I lavished upon it. The men who worked here were compensated for their labor, true, but they were from the north, from Hypprux and Maris and Belroi, and they did not care about a church in Saint Brigid. You, though, David ... you grew up here. Surely you would be willing to donate a carving to—"

David's patience finally broke. This priest had come to the village hardly five years ago, a complete stranger sent down from the north. By what right did he go on about birthplaces? "To God?" he said. "Or to Jaques Alban? Tell me, master: would you have to give up a fat capon on Saturday nights in order to provide me with a decent wage?"

"I am simply reminding you about obligations." Now they were facing one another over ten feet of stone flooring: priest with fists at sides, carver with fists in tunic pockets.

"I am simply reminding *you* about food, tithes, and rents."

Alban remained standing for a moment, then wandered over to a prie-dieu and knelt, propping his head on his folded hands. "You have a sister in the convent, do you not?"

Sunbeams poured in through the western door. The day was dying in sunset, its death as vibrant as that of the forest.

David watched the priest warily. "Yes. What of it?"

"The convent of Saint Barnabas. Near Hypprux, I believe. Cloistered."

"Yes."

"There have been witch burnings in that region, have there not?" The priest's voice was bland, matter-of-fact. "Elves and other demons consorting with humans and such. There have been outbreaks of ... possession ... in a number of the cloistered orders."

David's mouth worked for a minute or two. His hands were still clenched, but he could feel the blood go from his face.

The priest did not look at him. "You are overproud, David. Perhaps your not-insignificant talent is the cause. It would perhaps be good for you to undertake some work in the service of the Church. A crucifix, for example."

David felt ill, dizzy. His sister ... possession ... the Inquisition ...

"Consider."

He found his voice. "Yes indeed, master. I will." His words were hoarse, almost inaudible, and he felt as though he must immediately collapse in fear or explode in anger. But he did neither: instead, he made his way down the nave as if blind, groping through the glory of the sunset. Behind him, Alban regarded the bare wooden cross appraisingly, as if visualizing the wonder that would replace it.

David carved wood, and he carved alone. His house lay well outside the village, within the growth of trunks and leaves at the edge of Malvern, the great forest that grew to the northeast. He had built it himself, raising the walls years before when he had left the Carvers' Guild in Maris and returned to the place of his birth. At the time, life in even a small village like Saint Brigid had not appealed to him, for it had reminded him too much of the city, and therefore he had made his house in the forest, and in its facade he had duplicated weathered bark, incursions of lichen, and boughs of randomly scattered leaves with a skill so great that it was impossible to say where the wood of the forest left off and that of the house began.

There, hidden and alone, he worked. In solitude he wrought the carvings that had made him famous throughout the land, carvings that seemed to live, breathe, and grow as his skilled fingers freed from the wood the designs and the figures that sprang from his imagination. His leaves curled and fluttered in wooden breezes, his animals romped in ligneous fields, his kings, queens, barons, and bishops looked out of their vegetable matrix with eyes that mirrored faith and inner strength.

But he had never carved a crypt, or a tomb, or a crucifix. He had, in fact, gone to great lengths to avoid any work that smacked at all of death or mortality. His flowers were always in bloom, the faces of his men and women healthy, alive. And though this pointed omission was occasionally noticed and commented upon, he was forgiven. Because of his talent. Perhaps because of his solitude.

But this evening, solitude was no refuge for him, and when he reached his house, he slammed the door behind him and sat down heavily on a low stool by the unshuttered window of his workshop, his face in his hands as though he would hide both from the priest and from the bright dying outside.

A crucifix. To be sure, it was a common enough thing to carve, and he supposed that the Church needed its crucifixes ... but he hated them. And if Alban had his way, the face on the suffering Figure would be as contorted as the body, racked with pain and sorrow, something the children would be frightened of, something to trouble the dreams of the townsfolk.

"A fine thing to hang in the house of God," he muttered bitterly. "The image of a dead body for a fat priest in exchange for peace of mind and my sister's life."

Alban was capable of anything. Anything. David had not liked him from the beginning, when the priest had arrived in Saint Brigid on a fine horse with a harness set with gems. Ignoring the villagers, he had ridden directly to the small chapel that had been built two centuries before, and, after examining it, had been overheard to mutter with some distaste: "This will not do."

And that *will not do* had clung to the village like a leech for seven years, with the priest exhorting the villagers to give more and more in labor and money for the building of what he considered to be a fitting church. During that time, too, Alban had deserted his cure for trips to the coastal cities to plead for funds, sold (some suspected) fake relics to the nobility, used what influence he had among the churchmen and the barons to fatten the building fund, and, upon occasion, done ... even more.

Two years before, Alban had attempted to extort money from Andrew, the carpenter. Andrew was

well liked—cherished, in fact—by the folk of Saint
Brigid, and if he had some dealings with the Elves
of Malvern Forest, no one was inclined to fault him
for it, for the dealings (if, indeed, there were dealings) had certainly done nothing to make him an
undesirable neighbor. Quite the contrary, in fact.

But Alban had found out about Andrew's dealings
and had, after mass one Sunday, threatened him. The
carpenter himself, smiling and kind, would neither
confirm nor deny the accusation, but Francis, the
smith, who stood well over six feet in height and
who, it was said, did not fear the Devil himself,
pounded, that evening, on the priest's door. With his
largest hammer. Another threat was made, this time
to Alban, and the matter of the Elves was dropped.

But David's sister was miles away in the convent
of Saint Barnabas, and who knew what influence
Alban had with Church dignitaries, or with the pros-
ecutors of the Inquisition? Upon whose door would
Francis have to hammer in order to keep Catherine
safe? Upon whose door *could* he hammer?

Rising suddenly, David went to the window and
shouted out into the forest: "Damn you, Alban!
Damn you!"

The trees seemed to trip up the words, which fell
flat among the leaves and branches. He worked his
mouth for a moment, then turned back to the room.
Leaning against his workbench was the first of the
panels he was creating for the cathedral in Hypprux.
It was partly finished, and the face of Baron Roger
of Aurverelle stared out from a network of vines,
flowers, and scurrying squirrels.

He ran his hands over its surface. It was life. Like the forest, like the crops, like the rising and setting of the sun and moon. And from this he would have to turn away ... for a crucifix.

Reluctantly, he took his hands from it and left his house, taking, once more, the road for the village.

It was becoming dark by the time David reached the home of Andrew and Elizabeth. In response to his knock, Elizabeth peered out from a window, then quickly opened the heavy door. "David! What brings you out so late?"

"Is Andrew here?"

"He left some minutes ago ... for the forest. He often takes evening walks." Elizabeth looked at him, a half smile on her face, as though her words held more meaning than was obvious.

David, agitated, concerned about the crucifix, panicky about Catherine, did not notice her expression. "I have to talk to him, Elizabeth. Tonight. Which way did he go?"

"Take the East Road, David." Elizabeth met his eyes, and David could see that, in her opinion, what he needed right now was something hot to drink, a chair by the fire to sit in, and a sympathetic listener. But he could not stay. He could not even allow himself to think about comfortable and pleasant things right now.

"Thank you, Elizabeth. Good night." He turned and started to run off.

Her voice followed him. "God be with you, David."

Above the nearby rooftops, the spire of the church was visible against the darkening sky, and the carver felt that it was watching him as he left the village and trotted off down the East Road. The image of Alban, fat and smug and kneeling at the prie-dieu, stayed in his mind and quickened his steps, but the sky was covered with stars and the full moon was well above the horizon by the time he made out the smudge on the road ahead that he guessed was the carpenter.

David started explaining when he was still some distance away. "Andrew," he called. "I need some wood. Some good wood. Oak if you have it. Big." He gestured with his hands to indicate an indefinite, but very large, size, but it was only when he reached Andrew that he realized that the carpenter was not alone.

Andrew's companion was wearing a gray cloak that blended with the darkness, and, unseen, he had stood to one side, calmly watching David's approach and gesticulations. His face was smooth, gentle, almost womanly, and there seemed to be a faint light hovering about it.

"You are the woodcarver, are you not?" he said. His voice was quiet: pitched just loud enough to carry clearly, no more.

David stared at him, his mouth open.

Andrew put his hand on David's arm. "Varden," he said to his companion, "this is David, a friend of mine. David, Varden."

Unnerved, David found himself groping for words. "God be with you," he blurted out.

Varden smiled. "Hello, David."

Fair skin, David noticed. Dark hair. A clasp in the form of an interlaced moon and star holding his cloak closed at his throat. Eyes that reflected more light—starlight—than they should have. And that face . . .

Yes, Andrew often took evening walks.

David found that his heart was pounding. "Maybe . . . maybe . . . maybe I'd best talk to you . . . ah . . . tomorrow."

"No need," said Andrew. "You're here tonight."

"And you are upset," Varden put it. "There is no reason for you to return to your house in such a state."

The starlight was holding David's gaze. Abruptly, he half turned away and rubbed his face, trying to clear his thoughts. First Alban . . . and now this . . .

"What do you need the wood for, David?" said the carpenter.

The thought of the task ahead of him brought the carver's thoughts up short. "Alban," he said. "He wants a crucifix from me. I don't want to do it, but he's forcing me." He told them of the priest's words in the church.

Varden's eyes flicked down to the ground. "A grave mistake," he murmured.

"I can't put Catherine in danger," David went on. "I didn't want her to enter the convent in the first place, but after the plague took Mother and Father, she seemed to think it was her duty. I imagine Alban has friends up there. He could . . . he could . . ."

He shut his eyes, trying to keep away the possibilities that, like the dying leaves of autumn, seemed bent on pressing close around him. He could smell death in the air.

He felt a hand on his shoulder.

"Peace," said Varden.

"That's an easy thing to say."

Varden dropped his hand. "That is true."

"You usually find your own wood, David," said Andrew. "Why are you coming to me now?"

"I don't want to cut a living tree," David said, opening his eyes. "Not for this. It's . . . it's not worth it. Alban's not worth it. It would be like . . . like sacrilege."

Andrew looked at the moon thoughtfully. "David . . . I'll tell you, I don't think I have a piece of wood big enough for what you need."

"I don't want to cut a living tree," David repeated. "I have to carve a dead thing. I hate death."

Varden suddenly looked up, looked him in the face. "Death is very popular in the cities," he said. "And in the country, too. Many people think of death a great deal. Much has been written of it, and painted . . . and carved."

"Yes, yes. That's one of the reasons I left the capital." David's voice was sharp with annoyance. Why was this stranger belaboring the obvious?

Varden continued to look him in the face. "But there is death, nonetheless," he said simply, even though the light in his eyes appeared to deny that.

David noticed that his hands were shaking. "The Savior died to bring life," he said, trying to ignore them. "I want to glorify that life. But people like Alban, like the ones in the cities . . . they're only seeing death. What's more, they seem to be worshiping it, reveling in it. It's like a . . . a horrible mistake. And I have to become a part of it now." He struggled with words for a moment, then suddenly burst out: "And he'll probably want every single little scourge mark lovingly tricked out in the very best red paint. That . . . that—"

"You hardly sound like a man with a sister in the convent," said Varden.

Still those starlight eyes. David felt for a moment as if they were searching his face for something.

But: "A mile from here," Varden said suddenly, "there is a dead tree. It is quite large and well seasoned. I believe it will do for your purposes."

Andrew was nodding slowly. "That one, Varden? Yes. And it would certainly save time. A new-cut piece of wood takes a while to season. And I assume, David, that you want to take care of this quickly."

The carver groaned. "It will take time, regardless. It will be a huge carving. Massive."

"Shall we go look at the tree?" said Varden. He beckoned them to follow, then led them along a nearby forest path.

The tree was in a clearing near the top of a hill, brightly illuminated by the rising moon. It was as Varden had intimated: the thickest part of the main trunk soared up gracefully about six feet, and, near its top, a large branch separated from it, curving out and up.

When he saw it, David stopped, staring, for the tree gave him an odd feeling about his heart. There was something strangely haunting about the stark whiteness of the trunk in the moonlight, and, even in death, the branch seemed to be uplifted in blessing.

Andrew was examining it closely, running a hand over it with a carpenter's touch. "It looks like a very good piece of wood."

"I'm . . ." David tried to speak, but he could not get the words out. "I'm . . ."

A little distance away, Varden was watching him, his eyes mirroring the starlight, his face as calm as that of the pale moon floating over his head.

David stood before the dead tree. "It's beautiful," he managed at last.

The next morning, David, Andrew, and two men from the village went into the forest, carefully cut the dead tree off at ground level, and hoisted it into a wagon. Before they left the clearing, though, Andrew planted a small sapling next to the stump.

David watched. "Interesting sapling."

"It's a beech. Varden gave it to me."

"Who is Varden?"

Andrew looked up as he wiped the earth from his hands. David was rather afraid of the answer to his question, was, in fact, rather astonished at his temerity in asking it; but Andrew only gave him one of those impish half smiles that one might well exhibit when extending two closed hands to a child and asking: *Which has the sweet?* Of course, in Andrew's case, there was more than likely a sweet in *both* hands. "A friend of mine," he said.

"What is Varden?" David felt he had to ask.

Andrew's smile broadened. "A friend of mine."

And as the wagon jounced and rumbled down the road to his secluded house, David was half wondering if he were seeing that same peculiar starlight in Andrew's eyes. The carpenter had his elbow propped on the side of the wagon, and he was whistling a jaunty tune as he watched the forest go by.

Idly, the carver let his hand rest on the trunk beside him. The wood was surprisingly smooth to the touch, hardly weathered at all considering that the tree was seasoned well enough to have been drying for at least two years.

Andrew's genial little tune danced through his head. The carpenter was a very good whistler, and now he was adding ornaments to the melody, little turns and graces that could not but lift David's spirits in spite of the task he was facing.

Blue sky, yellow sun. David settled down comfortably beside the tree, his hand still on the warm, smooth wood, and as his thoughts drifted away from the wagon and into the forest, dancing with Andrew's tune among the leaves and squirrels, leaping and jigging down by hidden brooks and ponds, he suddenly felt as though, in the wood beneath his hand, something stirred.

He jerked his hand away as though he had put it on a hot stove, and, frightened, looked at the tree; but there was nothing overtly unusual about it. It was only good, solid, warm wood. Yet he was now seeing shapes in it, shapes that he, a carver, could release. The tree itself was telling him what should be carved from it. In fact, it was telling him what *must* be carved from it, and the vision that leaped into David's head was so overpowering that it made him giddy.

The problem was that it had nothing whatsoever to do with a crucifix.

The wagon reached David's house by noon, and the carver's companions set the tree up in his workshop, said farewell, and left. For several hours, David busied himself cleaning the wood and preparing it for carving, and then he backed off a few feet and looked at it.

And, two weeks later, angry, frustrated, and almost afraid, he was still only looking at it. In the fields surrounding the village, grain was reaped and gathered in, melons ripened, and apples reddened; but David's mallet and chisel lay untouched on his workbench. He had spent the days nervously pacing back and forth in the shadow of the tree, picking things up and putting them down, staring out his window for long minutes: despite his efforts to banish the vision that had come to him on the wagon, the vision that dictated imperiously the final form of the tree, it would not be banished. In fact, while what tentative ideas he had forcibly fostered within his imagination for the design of the crucifix had grown hazy in his mind and threatened to disappear altogether, the vision had not only persisted, but actually intensified. He had only to look at the weathered surface of the trunk and he would see the face, the uplifted arm, the calm eyes. The tree itself was only an overlay, a veil that dimly hid what was already present in the wood, what he, a carver, had to release.

After nearly a month of impotent staring, he was reduced to sitting on a stool with his face buried in his hands. Through his tightly shut eyes, he could still see what he had to carve, and he was roused from his turmoil only by a knock on his door.

He shook himself out of his frustrated trance and rose, but Alban had already entered. The priest's eyes lit up when he saw the tree.

"Ah, David! A fine piece of wood! Some of the men in the village were saying that you had found material for the crucifix, and now I see that it's true. Excellent, my son!"

David watched him, hollow-eyed.

Alban folded his hands inside his sleeves and wandered around the trunk, examining it from every angle. "Just the right size, too. I assume you'll be adding the outstretched arms later?"

David's anger was building. "Have you ever thought about asking permission before entering a household?" he said as evenly as he could.

Alban paid very little attention. "And this upper section," he continued, "you can see the face right here. See how this line runs down and forms a grimace? Why, the mouth is almost ready-made. You can feel His pain, the terrible throbbing in His hands where the pagans drove the nails through." He looked at David. "Can't you, my son?" The silence grew, ominous, and Alban turned quickly back to the tree. "Such a fine piece of wood. A suitable crucifix it will be to crown my church."

But then he suddenly turned to face the carver.

"Why have you not started work?"

David merely looked at him, feeling something welling up that he knew would be disastrous to let out. Grimaces and pagan nails . . . He glanced at the tree, and the calm face of a woman regarded him almost appraisingly in return. He did not know who she was, but her still-imaginary eyes held his.

"Are you going to answer my question or not?"

David tore himself from the vision and confronted the priest. "You wanted a crucifix," he said. "I will carve it in my own good time." He tried to keep his voice calm. He succeeded. Partially.

"Your own good time?" Alban was incredulous. "What about God's time?"

"Theoretically," said David, glaring as though he would incinerate the priest with his gaze, "the Deity exists in eternity and is not concerned with human conceptions of duration." Alban opened his mouth, but the carver added: "Or so I was taught in school . . . when I was considering a vocation."

Alban had reddened. "Others," he said, "may not have such time."

"Others," said David, "like a certain Jaques Alban?"

Alban drew close to him and leaned forward. "Others, like your sister, Catherine?"

David was silent.

"I want that crucifix." Alban's voice was cold.

The carver could stand it no longer. Rising up, his fists balled as though he would strike the anthropomorphic pudding before him, he shouted: "You will receive your damned cross when I *decide* you will receive your damned cross! Do you understand, priest?"

Alban blinked for several moments, then recovered. "So, you . . . you set yourself up as an equal before God. I see. There have been precedents. Very interesting, my son. Very interesting."

"Get out."

Alban started for the door. "Very interesting indeed."

"Get out of my house!"

Pausing at the door, Alban looked at him for a long moment, then turned and left.

David stood, shaking, until the sound of the priest's shoes crunching through the dead and dry leaves outside had faded away. He knew the meaning in Alban's eyes as plainly as if the priest had spoken aloud: *You have no choice.*

Fists still clenched, the carver lifted his eyes to the tree, seeing only what was inside it, what he had to release. The woman's face was turned toward him, her gray eyes calm and clear, her dark hair falling softly about her shoulders in waves that only he could carve, her slender arm uplifted in benediction upon him.

He pressed his fists to his temples. "Why are you doing this to me?" he screamed at her. "Why? Have you no pity whatsoever? My sister is in danger and you . . . you . . ."

Turning, he flung himself out the back door of his house and ran down the forest path that led into the shadows of the trees, his hands holding his head as though it would burst.

The path's twists and turns were familiar to him, for he had followed them many times before in calmer moods. But now, heedless of anything save his fears for Catherine and his inability to save her, he plunged wildly along the trail, half falling over roots, almost braining himself on overhanging branches, seeing very little of anything, in fact, including the large oak that suddenly loomed before him . . . into which he ran full tilt.

When he regained consciousness, it was quite dark, though a little starlight and moonlight managed to filter down through the forest canopy—just enough to let him see the trunk that had felled him. The earth was cool against his cheek as he lay at full length, breathing harshly, the days of built-up rage and fear and frustration hammering inside his skull.

"Damn you, Alban. *Damn you.*" The words were hoarse, whispered, inadequate to the burden of hate that he wanted them to carry.

Everyone knew of the burnings in the north, and David had, in fact, seen one of them during his time in Maris: the frail, abused figures tied to the stake, the kindling fired, the rising smoke. But, even so, it had never seemed quite real to him, not even when he had fled from that long-ago square, his hands over his ears to shut out the last, faint screams from the condemned, his eyes frantic to look anywhere but at the sight of that tongue of flame lapping against exposed and bruised flesh.

And he had, in much the same way, fled from the sight of crypts, too, and from the mystery plays that depicted death and dying. It was all terrible, to be sure, but it had always remained little more than a spectacle. Theater. Unreal. Until now.

Catherine . . .

Was it not in this very forest, near the river, that she had seized his hand, once upon a time, and, laughing, pulled him into the water? "Come on, silly," she had cried. "You can swim. I've watched you!" Then, their mother and father had been alive and well, and though they had not been wealthy, they had not been hungry, and the love they had shared had made up for any lack of money.

Catherine especially had looked forward to the trip to Maris and had talked excitedly about it for months before they had set out, going on and on while she helped their mother with the housework. But the plague had struck Maris at the height of the festival, and it had taken their mother and father, and David and Catherine had been left alone.

It was strange to think of her now in that convent, cloistered, she who had chattered about Maris now vowed to silence. David had not seen her in years. But Alban knew of her.

He sat up suddenly, the cool forest air and the multitude of autumn scents making his thoughts far clearer than he wanted them to be. There was no way he could carve the crucifix for Alban. His hands would refuse to obey his commands even if he could bring himself to try. He could not carve death in any case, but most assuredly he could not carve it in the

face of what he saw in that tree. His spirit revolted
at the idea, rebelled, filled his imagination with white
blankness when he contemplated the action.

And, as a result, Catherine's silence would be broken by her screams.

Sitting up, he leaned against the oak, tilted his
head back until it rested on the rough bark, and
wept. Above him, a few stars shone through the tan-
gle of branches and leaves, but their light blurred
into vague swirls as his eyes filled with tears.

Caught. Hopelessly caught between a priest's arro-
gance and his sister's life. It seemed obscene that the
former should outweigh the latter. It would be easy
for Alban: a word here, an accusation there. Such
things had been done before, and there was no reason at all to doubt that they could be done again.
And Catherine . . .

His cheeks were dripping, his hair damp and matted when he noticed that the bleary swirls above him
had become more numerous. They had also brightened considerably, and the oddity finally forced its
way through his grief far enough that he wiped at
his eyes with the sleeve of his tunic.

There were no leaves above him: the forest was
gone. He was in the open, leaning against a rock in
the middle of a grassy plain that seemed to extend
for miles on all sides. Above him, a sea of stars glittered powerfully in a black sky, shining with the
strength of diamonds upon jet; and clinging to the
horizon was a crescent moon gleaming as silvery as
the polished ring of a Queen.

But what terrified him more than all of this, terrified him more even than the instinctive and absolute certainty that he was a great distance from his familiar forest, a much greater distance than he could ever imagine or comprehend, was the sight of the woman standing quietly a stone's throw from him, the light of the stars shining bright upon her. Her face was calm, clear-eyed, and her dark hair fell softly about her shoulders. She was infinitely strange, infinitely frightening, and infinitely familiar in that he had been living with her from the day he had first put his hand upon the dead tree and felt the stirring within the dry wood.

She moved, pacing slowly toward him, and the air was so very still that he fancied he could almost hear the blades of grass springing straight in her footprints. Before him now, she went down on one knee and peered into his face, and though the sight of her shining eyes made him avert his gaze, she took his head in her hands and gently made him look at her.

For a moment, he could see nothing but her calm, gray eyes, filled with starlight, filled with the reflection of the moon, then:

"My child," she said, and her words hung quiet in the quiet air. He tried to speak, but he was crying again, and his vision blurred. He felt his hand taken, felt the touch of lips upon his brow, and he buried his face in his knees, sobbing out his grief, his fear, his impotence.

And when he had exhausted his tears, he found that he was back in the familiar forest, that the oak was, once again, behind him, and that someone was calling his name. There was the faintest rustle of leaves a few feet away, and he made out a flash of starlit eyes.

"David?"

"Hello ... Varden ..." His words were mechanical, numb.

"David?" Varden approached, knelt, looked at him carefully. "David? What is wrong?"

The woodcarver opened his mouth, but he knew before he did that speech was useless. He shook his head slightly and stared off at nothing. Stars. The touch of her lips. When Varden pulled him to his feet, his muscles obeyed, but they did so distantly, as though they were not actually connected with his thoughts.

"David, some of my people are gathered nearby. I am going to take you there. Fear not."

The admonition was superfluous: David's emotional capacity had been thoroughly drained. His body submitted to Varden's guidance, but though together they walked paths through the forest, his mind traveled other, oblivious roads.

Then, suddenly, there was firelight about him, and grass under his feet, and the odor of food in the air. The homely smells and sights brought him partly back, and he could see that Varden had led him to a wide clearing beneath the night sky, and that there were others there: men and women dressed simply in gray and green.

"Is that not the carver?" someone called.

"Somebody please get him something hot to drink," returned Varden. "And find some cushions and a blanket for him. He is not well."

David felt a hand pressed to his forehead. "He is like an icicle," came a woman's voice, soft and clear.

"Terrill, where is that cider?"

"Blankets coming."

"Over here, over here. By the fire."

They wrapped him up and sat him down next to a cheerful blaze in the center of the clearing. "I'm all right," David found himself mumbling. "I'm all right."

In the confusion of figures and voices about him, he saw Varden look him over carefully, his nose wrinkled. "That, my friend, you are not. Drink some hot cider. You are thoroughly chilled."

The bowl that was offered him was warm and fragrant, and he took several swallows of the contents in rapid succession.

"That will put him to sleep," came the woman's voice.

"Indeed," said Varden, "I hope so."

The warmth made David realize how cold he had been. Someone took the bowl from his hand ... which was fortunate because he was suddenly on the verge of dropping it. He discovered that there was a pillow under his head, and he muzzily thanked whatever Providence was responsible just before he closed his eyes and let exhaustion take him.

When David awoke, it was still dark, and the fire was still burning. Sleep had distanced him from the events of the early evening, and for a few minutes he did not remember what had happened or where he was. Nor did he particularly care: the fire was warm, the heat of the cider still in his veins. He was content to drift in the twilight of half sleep.

Someone approached and put a few more sticks on the fire. The action was performed quietly, but the motion brought him fully awake, and memory flooded back. He opened his eyes to find Varden sitting beside him. A pendant in the form of an interlaced moon and star hung at his throat, and his face was thoughtful, pondering. He seemed to be looking through the blaze rather than at it, and the starlight and firelight mingled in his eyes.

David stared at him for some time. Varden. His people. The delicate shimmer of starlight. Quiet, silvery voices. And the hint of unimaginable power.

Swallowing, he found his voice. "Elves," he whispered.

Varden heard, turned, helped David to sit up. "How are you feeling?"

Holding the blankets about himself, the carver took a deep breath, stared at the gentle face a few inches from his own. "Elves."

Varden smiled. "It is so, David. You have indeed found us out. Now: how are you feeling?"

"Much better than when you found me."

The Elf looked at him seriously. "What did Alban do?"

David countered with a question of his own. "Why did you direct me to that tree?"

"I do not understand."

David's strength was coming back in force now, and, with it, the full brunt of his fear. "I wanted wood for a crucifix, and you told me about that tree."

"I did," said Varden, obviously puzzled. "It seemed to me to be about the right size for what you wanted. From what little I know about crucifixes, that is."

David clenched the blankets about himself. "I can't carve a crucifix out of that wood. I just can't. It's awful. I . . . I think I'm going mad."

"Peace." Varden signed to someone, and an elven woman brought another bowl. It was wine this time, and as the carver took it from her, he noticed her eyes: shining, like Varden's, with starlight.

"Blessings," she said. "I am Talla. We will have food in a short while." And then she was gone. David took a swallow of the wine, and the whirl of his thoughts slowed.

"Is there something wrong with the wood?" said Varden.

"It's fine wood," said David. "Very fine wood. And I know exactly what to do with it. But I can't carve . . . I can't carve a crucifix . . ."

"Because of Alban?"

David dropped the bowl and shook his hands helplessly. "Because of what I see in the wood!"

But as he had opened his hands fully, something had fallen to the ground between him and Varden, and, looking down, he saw that a head of wheat, bright and golden, now lay on the lush meadow grass.

David stared at it. The stars above the plain. The woman. She had taken his hand.

He finally managed to lift his gaze. Varden was watching him. For a moment, the Elf examined the wheat, and then he met the carver's eyes once more. "What is in the wood, David?"

"The face and figure of a woman. It's too strong. I can't fight it." He looked fearfully at the wheat. "I must be mad."

"You are not mad," said Varden. "You are simply upset and afraid." He considered for a moment. "I hope you are not afraid of us."

"Right now, Elves are the least of my fears."

"I am glad to hear that."

The wheat lay on the ground, palpably real. There had been no wheat in his hand when he had left his house, and its presence now meant that he could not discount the woman he had seen as a mere hallucination brought on by his encounter with the oak tree. But that meant . . .

"What does the woman in the tree look like?" said Varden.

David did not even have to close his eyes to regain the vision. "Tall. Slender. Dark hair . . . gray eyes . . ."

David saw Varden start, saw his gaze flash back down at the head of wheat. He followed the Elf's eyes, noticed that the wheat was oddly intact and whole, even after having been crushed in his hand for several hours.

Varden spoke at last. "Have you . . . have you ever heard the name *Elthia*?"

David searched his memory. "I've . . . I've heard Andrew say it once or twice."

"Just so. Andrew has learned a few things from us."

David hesitated. It was difficult to ask the question

because he was, again, afraid of the answer. "You say it's a name. Who is she?"

Varden smiled. "Everything," he said. "You. Me. Talla and the others over there. The grass we sit on, the trees about us, the air we breathe. This fire, and this ..." He reached out to the wheat, held it up. "... this head of wheat."

David stared.

"She made us," said Varden. "She *is* us. And upon occasion, She wears an outward form for our convenience." The Elf looked past the wheat at David.

The carver hesitated again. He did not want to hear the answers to his questions, did not, in fact, want to ask them in the first place. "What ... what does She look like?"

Varden was silent for a moment, then: "Tall. Slender. Dark hair ... and gray eyes. She is robed in—"

"Blue and silver," said David, shutting his eyes. The words continued as though of their own accord: "Her girdle is of amethysts and emeralds." He felt the Elf put a hand on his shoulder, but he continued to speak. "Her hair ..." he faltered, "is ... is caught back on one side ... with a ... a ... a ... golden clasp ..." His throat was constricting. "A-and the stars ... they go on ..."

"How do you know this?"

"... forever ..."

"David?"

"I ..." David put his hands to his face, covered his eyes.

"David, how? You saw all this in the tree?"

"I saw *Her*, Varden. In the forest. Just before you

found me." David's voice was tight, strained. He had seen ... had met ... "I wasn't in the forest anymore, and She was there. She made me look at Her, and She called me Her child. Then She kissed me and put ... and ... and ... She must have put that wheat into my hand ..." He wept. "Why is She doing this? Why is She tormenting me so?"

"Is She tormenting you?"

David dropped his hands. Varden was still holding the wheat.

"My sister," said the carver, "is in danger. I can only save her if I carve a crucifix for Alban. I can't carve the crucifix because I see Her in the wood. You ask me if She's tormenting me. What say you, Varden?"

"As I recall, David, you could not carve a crucifix because you hated death. Why now do you blame my Lady?"

The wheat in Varden's hand glowed golden, embodying the harvest, the gathering in. David recalled the ripe fields, the hues of red and russet in the autumn leaves. It was death. Death given form and color. But then again ...

"I don't blame Her," he said, realizing that, given Varden's explanations, as much as the wheat embodied death, it also embodied *Elthia*, and that meant ... "I only want to save Catherine."

... that meant that ...

"And deny death." The Elf's statement was stark.

David pressed his lips together. "What do you know of death, Varden?" he said after a time. "As I recall, you and your people are immortal."

"Immortal?" Varden smiled sadly. "Maybe. But we can be killed. And we have indeed been killed, as you well know. In any case, we are fading. Another century, perhaps two, and the Elves will be no more. Mortals cannot comprehend our ending." He turned his gaze on David. "We face death in our own way, friend. And you?"

He shrugged. "I'm mortal. I'll die eventually."

"You run from death," Varden pressed. "You will not even carve a crypt to hold the bones of one who might have passed honorably from life."

"You should see what they're doing with death these days, Varden."

"I have seen." The Elf held the wheat reverently. "They have turned death into a god. And they worship it. And you, David, have turned life into a god. And you worship it."

"Life seems to me to be a better god than death."

"Really?"

"Yes." David was astonished that the Elf would respond in such a way. "Death is suffering. Death is pain." And suddenly it came back to him, and the words tumbled out. "Death is your mother and father covered with boils and blotches in a strange city . . . and no one caring because the streets are already so choked with the dead that two more bodies don't make any difference. Death is a boy and girl wondering what happened to mama and papa, wondering what they're going to do now. Death is your sister entombing herself in a convent, because she thinks that's all she can do. Death . . . death . . . death is . . ." Suddenly, he was wandering once again through the plague-ravaged streets of Maris, and his eyes filled with tears and his voice fled.

Varden held him as he wept. And when at last David came to himself and to his present enough to raise his head, he saw in Varden's face a touch, an echo, of the face of Elthia, as though, through the being of this Elf, She was watching him.

"I know, David," Varden said gently. "I know. But is that death . . . or merely the prelude to death? Your mother and father died, and their bodies rotted. But what about your parents themselves?"

"Yes . . . yes, that's true." But his agreement was of the mind only. It held no savor of belief. "They're in Heaven, I suppose. But that doesn't change what I saw, and it doesn't change what Catherine and I went through."

"True. It does not," said Varden. He considered a moment. "I want to tell you something, David. You have loved life, and have honored it, and have re-created it in your art. I have seen your carvings. They are beautiful. An elven hand could not have done better. But though you love life, you have missed something important. Tell me, Carver," he said, lifting the wheat and holding it before David's eyes. "Is this stalk of wheat alive or dead?"

David stared at it. The head was ripe, golden, but its color came only from its dryness, and its stalk had been severed. It was dead, and he was about to say so when he remembered that the seeds held within it were themselves alive, and would sprout into next year's crop, green and growing under the warm sun.

"Answer me, Carver."

"It's . . ." In his mind's eye David saw the plowed fields, cleared and barren and with the first snows sifting down to cloak them in white. But they were full of seed. And the cold ground contained the dens of animals who would give birth during the winter. And if there were only an endless summer, what would happen? There would be no planting, and no harvest, no ripe melons, no golden wheat . . .

"Alive or dead, Carver?"

"It's . . . I don't know. It looks dead. Dry. But it's alive . . . I guess. Or else it has to die in order to make the seeds for the next crop." He looked at Varden.

Varden looked right back at him. "Can you contemplate this," he said, "and insist that death is evil?"

The Elf held the wheat out to him. Trembling, David took it in his own hand. The wheat seemed to shimmer with a light that hovered just at the edge of seeing. "I can't love death," he said.

"Death does not ask to be loved," said Varden. "It asks only that you do not run from it or deny it. Death comes in sorrowful ways, true, but there is sorrow in life also. I called the Lady *Elthia*. Her full name is *Elthia Calasiuove:* Bright Lady Shining with Clear Radiance. But She has another name, one that is yet longer, and in your tongue it would be Star of Light, Abyss of Darkness. Without light, darkness could not be seen, and in the absence of darkness, light would be unrecognizable. And so She is both. Totality. Completion. Wholeness."

"Why . . . why did She come to me?"

"Have you not realized it yet? You have loved Her passionately in your own way, and you have given Her honor in your craft. You could not bring yourself to deny Her. You share much in common with our folk."

"And Catherine?" David demanded. "All this is going to do her no good at all if Alban has his way. I want her safe. I don't care about fat priests, or wheat, or ... or ... or *anything* if Catherine is in danger."

Varden held up a hand. "No harm will come to Catherine."

"How can you say that?"

"I said—"

"I heard what you said!"

Varden simply looked at him, and David sensed the power that dwelt behind those starlit eyes. The thought of who and what he was talking to forced itself through his fear and anger.

"I'm ... not afraid of you," he said.

"That is well," said the Elf quietly. "You have nothing to be afraid of. Alban, however ..." He shook his head. "It is not our nature to fight. Perhaps it was once, but no longer. Now, when the Albans of the world threaten us, we withdraw. In that withdrawal, we lose brothers, sisters. And then, sometimes, something happens that makes a particular withdrawal too costly, the thing threatened too precious." For a moment, he looked terribly haunted, and David wondered what friend—or, perhaps, lover—Varden had lost. "So it is now. I said that Catherine will be safe. She will be. The Lady's favor

to you will not come to nothing. It cannot. I will not
let it. Carve the tree as you see fit, David."

"But if I do, then . . ."

Varden held his gaze again, and again David
sensed the power in him, sensed a deep loss that
years, numberless years, had not diminished in the
slightest.

"Do what you must do," said the Elf.

The next morning, Varden guided David back to
his house. The paths they took contorted themselves
in odd ways, ways that the carver had never seen
before, and he was not overly surprised to find that
the oak he had run into the night before had
vanished.

Varden looked at the place where the tree had
been, but said nothing about it. He was strangely
quiet this morning, and when they reached the door
of David's house, he broke his silence only long
enough to wish the carver good morning and good
luck before he disappeared back into the trees, his
gray cloak fading into the autumn hues of the forest.

Some inward premonition made the carver nervous as he fumbled at the latch, and when he swung
the door wide, he nearly cried out: for a moment he
thought the Lady Herself was waiting for him in the
middle of his workshop. But it was only the tree, the
dead tree, his vision now possessing it utterly and
telling him what it should be, what it *had* to be.

Silently, he went to his workbench and picked up
his tools. No preliminary sketches, no chalkmarks,

nothing but his inner eye and the compelling presence of the dead—yet living—wood before him.

He was dimly aware that his arms were raising the mallet and chisel . . .

The tree was alive beneath his hands. It had stood in the forest, spreading leafy branches in the sun for countless years, and then it had died, and summer heat and winter ice had dried it and frozen it . . . and yet now it lived again. Now it seized some inner part of him, pulled him into itself, folded itself about him, welcoming as it did so the strokes of his mallet and the cuts of his chisel as if its former death in the forest had been only a prelude to this infinitely more glorious rebirth.

David felt it. At once, he was carver and carved, artisan and art, releaser and released. He, too, felt the blows of the mallet, felt the fetters of dross imprisonment falling from his limbs. Life poured into his wooden arms, and starlight and sunlight mingled in his soul, blasting through layers of dry paralysis, twining through and revitalizing him. Before his eyes, he watched the wood change, watched himself change, and as he carved, he felt himself standing in a sea of stars, their light shining brilliant in the darkness, while about him the sun whirled, the earth turned, and the moon waxed.

He did not stop. He could not stop. Dragged by the vision, but dragged willingly, he worked without pause. The face grew. His face grew. He no longer knew who he was, did not care. She was looking at him, he was looking at himself. Clear-eyed, bright-browed, arm upraised as if calling the essence of life to Her side, She took shape even as She gave him his own form. Carving Her belt, he was carving amethyst and emerald, he was carving gems, but it did not seem at all remarkable to him. Nor did it seem at all strange that Her robe—blue and silver just as he had seen it—glowed under his hands as surely as if he were working cloth.

And three days later, when he had finished, he sat on the floor before the statue, hungry, exhausted, and shivering . . . with a flood of peace flowing through him. The vision was reality, the compulsion fulfilled, and the just-risen sun was sending a shaft of golden light in through the east windows of his house, gilding the walls and workbench, wrapping the statue in a hazy glory.

The day passed, and he was still sitting, floating somewhere between one world and another, catching glimpses of a grassy plain and a skyful of stars behind his closed eyes. His strength was returning quickly, as though whatever power had been in the tree was still there, nurturing him, giving him back what it had taken. They were lovers who had been long with one another, who together felt the deep peace of a quiet exhaustion that ebbed away and left only tranquillity behind.

It was a good day, a lovely day, and when he looked out his window at the fields and the harvest, he did not see the bare, stripped land as a termination of the summer's bounty. He saw instead but a step between one season and another, a resting of the world before spring would return once again. It was a cold step, and yes, there was death in it, but death seemed to him now not so much an abyss from which nothing returned as a door, a passage into another land, another life, another season of growth and promise.

It was true. He was sure of it. And in the clear gray eyes that watched him, there was a light that told him that his surety was not misplaced.

And then, when the sun was nearing the western horizon, Alban arrived.

David felt his coming, and though he turned around to face the open door just as the priest stepped across the threshold, the anger that spread over Alban's features had no effect on him, and he watched calmly as the priest circled the statue, examining it from every side as though simultaneously fascinated and repelled.

When he had done looking, Alban turned on David. "Sacrilege."

David did not move. "No," he said. "It's not sacrilege. It's a statue. You can call it what you wish, but that doesn't change what it is."

"I ordered you to carve a crucifix."

"And I did not carve it."

"You refuse to serve your God?"

"Not at all. I serve as I can."

The priest regarded him; then: "Very well, Carver. You have chosen." Shaking his head, he turned to the door.

He stopped short. Varden was standing in the doorway, the starlight in his eyes blazing fiercely, even dangerously. There was a staff of pale wood in his hand.

"You are threatening an innocent life, Jaques Alban." The Elf's tone was surprisingly mild, almost respectful.

Alban found his voice after the better part of a minute. "What is that to . . . to one who has no soul?"

Varden was choosing his words carefully. "It would be best for you to drop this matter."

"It would be best for you not to meddle."

The Elf sighed, but he took a step into the room. "You shall not leave this house until you have promised and sworn by your God that the woman will not be harmed." An edge of steel had crept into his voice. He was stating a simple, inescapable fact.

"I make no promises to the damned."

Varden grounded his staff firmly. Almost imperceptibly, the wood began to glow. Alban saw it and backed away quickly, circling around to put the statue between him and the Elf, but he bumped into David's workbench and could back no further.

"You must promise," said Varden.

But in response, Alban whirled, seized a heavy hammer from the workbench, and hurled it at the Elf.

"Varden!" David cried, but it was too late. There was not even time for Varden to move or dodge, and Alban's aim at such close range was deadly.

Varden simply stood where he was, motionless and, apparently, accepting; but as the hammer passed the statue, it suddenly shone brightly, expanded into a haze of gold . . .

. . . and fell softly to the floor as a shower of new-ripened wheat. The base of the statue was blanketed with the grain.

The Elf bent his head.

Alban stared in shock, first at Varden, then at the wheat, then at the statue. With a small, strangled scream, he turned and fled through the back door.

David's mouth was dry. "Varden . . . he'll kill Catherine. He's a vengeful brute."

"True. And a brute he shall remain," said the Elf quietly. His staff brightened into a rod of fire as he stepped quickly across the room to the door. Ahead of him, the priest was almost lost among the forest trees.

Varden lifted the staff.

A flash . . . and yellow light everywhere. *Everywhere.* Shadows fled. Trees seemed burned into the sky. David's vision reeled as though he were confronted with a sun a hand's breadth away.

Then, as abruptly as it had come, the light was fading, and the world was coming back. Bare trees. Brown earth. A sky blue with afternoon. Rubbing his eyes, David stumbled to Varden's side. The Elf was looking into the wood, and the carver saw a bulking shape that snorted and grunted in the bushes.

"Be off," whispered the Elf, and the shape lifted a tusked head for a moment, stared with bestial eyes, and then bustled away with a crash of underbrush.

David was frightened. "Varden . . . that was . . . I mean . . . you . . ."

Sighing, Varden rubbed his face as though tired. "Catherine is safe. Fear not. The priest will not trouble her."

A distant sound of shaking. A thump of hooves. It

was true, but David, despite his fear, put a hand on Varden's shoulder. "Another will come."

Varden shrugged and grounded his staff. "They are not all like Alban." He looked worn, grief was heavy upon him, and the starlight glimmered uneasily in his downcast eyes.

But a flash pulled the carver's gaze back to the trees, and he caught his breath, for out among the gray trunks and the bare branches, he saw a woman's form. She was standing, tall and slender, among the trunks, and even at a distance, he could see the clear gray eyes, the dark hair, the robe of blue and silver.

His grip on the Elf's shoulder tightened. "Varden . . ."

Varden lifted his head, and David felt the smile break over his friend's face like a sunrise, felt the strength flood into him, felt the sadness and care wash away.

He wanted to say something more, wanted to say something that would, perhaps, give reassurance, or confirmation . . . or perhaps ask for them. But he could not. There were no words to be said. He decided, though, that he was quite content simply to stand in silence and let the vision last as long as it would. And then he decided that it was obvious to him that She had always been there, and always would be; and it seemed a little absurd to him that, living on the edge of forest and field as he did, it had taken him so long to realize it.

A Touch of
Distant Hands

In years to come, Roxanne would remember that morning clearly, as though it were etched in her memory, or wrapped in silk and put away with the wedding clothes that her mother had lovingly made for her ... which lay, unused, in the dark oak chest in her bedroom.

She stood at the edge of the farmlands to the south of the village, naked save for a dark cloak she wore against the pre-dawn chill. It was Midsummer Day, and she was waiting for the sun to rise. She had work to do. She was a witch.

The growing light in the east began to banish the stars from the sky. Venus, a splinter of diamond a hand's breadth from the horizon, was lost in the effulgent flood. Off to her left, Malvern Forest came alive in a chorus of birdsong, and the crops before her were lush and waist high.

And as the sun broke free of the edge of the earth, she let fall the cloak that covered her and lifted her arms. "I am the Mother of all things," she chanted, her voice as clear as the warm light that washed over the fields, "and My love is poured out upon the earth. My life is the life of the world. My promise is eternal, and shall not be broken."

And so she channeled the energies of the longest day, blessing the growing crops, feeling each plant— root and stalk and seed—clearly in her mind. For long minutes she stood thus, an incarnation of the divinity she worshipped, reaffirming Her promise of life and continuance; and then she dropped her hands and walked into the fields, touching the future harvest, wishing it well, loving it as only a Goddess could.

The sun was well into the sky when, her rite finished, she let the energies fade and redonned her cloak. In the old days there would have been others with her, and this would have been only the beginning of much feasting and dancing. But those times were gone, and she was alone. For most of the townsfolk it would be an ordinary work day.

And, for that matter, those who labored in the fields would be arriving soon: best, therefore, that she be on her way, for it would not do to be seen. Kay, the new priest sent to replace Jaques Alban, was from Saint Brigid, and though he had been a kind and tolerant soul as a boy, Roxanne did not know how his seminary training might have changed him. And, indeed, it might have changed him greatly, for he had been trained in the north, in Maris, and the Inquisition was very active there. True, the Inquisition had not stretched as far south as the Free Towns—not yet, at least—but it was certainly better not to give it any excuses, and so she threw on her cloak and headed for the forest, where she had left her clothes.

Why was she out that morning? Why, only to gather fresh herbs, Your Excellency. Their virtue is best at dawn, as I am sure Aquinas says somewhere. The village healer must have her herbs, must she not?

She wrinkled her nose at the imagined conversation. Good, except for the reference to Aquinas. She was a woman, and she was therefore supposed to be ignorant. If she ever had the misfortune to face a bishop across an Inquisitorial desk, her knowledge would undoubtedly trip her up. An intelligent woman, particularly a young and pretty one, was just as bad as a witch. Even if, by some miracle, she managed to deflect her accusers from her religious practices, they would probably burn her anyway just to be rid of her.

She snorted under her breath, reflecting that her jokes were not particularly funny these days.

The path led her close by the house of David, the woodcarver, and the sight of it half hidden among the trees reminded her that there were still some things for which she could be thankful. David's carvings, for example, antic and serious by turns and full of the life of the wood from which they had been carved, graced the village church in profusion, and they comforted Roxanne greatly during her weekly ordeal of mass attendance. His statue of the Virgin was always of particular aid during those interminable hours, and now, as she passed by the carver's house and heard the steady blows of his mallet and chisel, she recalled that slender figure and wondered again if it really was supposed to be a statue of the Virgin at all, for a moon and rayed star, conjoined, gleamed on her breast, and there seemed to be an elven air about her . . .

The Elves. Yes: that was something else she could be glad of, for since Varden had healed the hands of the smith five years before, something gentler and more tolerant had become a part of the daily life of Saint Brigid. She was not sure what to call it. A widening of the heart, maybe, or the touch of an elven hand. Nor could she lay her finger upon any given manifestation of it so as to call it unmistakable evidence of a change. All-pervasive and yet as ephemeral as a soul's bond with its deity, it had seeped into Saint Brigid as though that first healing had opened the smallest of chinks for a slow but steady influx of compassion; and year by year its influence had grown.

Had anyone noticed? Possibly not. Certainly the Fair Ones were no more visible in the village than they had been before, but Andrew and Elizabeth were known to entertain Varden now and again, and their adopted daughter, Charity, had once given Roxanne to understand that that immortal being had been in the habit of giving her pickaback rides through the forest.

She smiled at the image as she reached her bundle and slid out of the cloak, but as she pulled on her clothes, she recalled that she did, in fact, have herbs to gather this morning . . . and it was for Charity that she would gather them. Elizabeth had come to her the evening before to tell her that her daughter had nightmares, and as Roxanne was a healer—well, perhaps something to send the girl sweet dreams?

All-heal, the witch thought as she laced her bodice. And chamomile. And vervain. And ... and maybe just a touch of the white sandalwood her mother had left her. It was rare, and valuable, but Charity was worth it. Charity was worth a great deal.

Fully clothed now, she threw the cloak once more about herself and set off along the path, her ebony-handled knife stuck firmly in her belt. She had a favorite place for herb gathering, but it was some distance away. If she did not dawdle, she could be back home by noon, and Charity would have the mixture that night.

There was a hearty feeling about the forest that day, as though now, at the height of summer, the trees were stretching themselves to their fullest in the sunlight. Roxanne could not help but reach out now and again to touch a trailing bough or a gnarled trunk. How are you today? Wonderful, is it not? And blessings upon you, too.

She was reminded of a morning in early spring, years ago. She had been initiated by her mother the night before, and with the coming of the new day she had taken to the forest in boy's clothes: breeches, shirt, and cloak. The air had been cold, but she had been warm, and she had climbed a hill that, bare at the top, had given her a view of the sunrise. The wave of morning light had rolled across the land, washing her in the dawn, and she had instinctively lifted her arms, feeling, in that moment, the sure and immanent presence of Another in her own being; and thereafter, Roxanne, then thirteen, had sat down on the grassy slope and had cried and laughed the morning away, her heart so full that it hurt.

Now, her boy's clothes put away, she felt it, in a gentler fashion, once again: the Mother of All walking in the world, greeting Her children this Midsummer Day.

The path she traveled took her to a stream, one of the many that wound through the forest, tributaries to the Malvern River. Barefoot, her skirts belted high, she picked her way across a series of half-submerged stones; and it was not until she was sitting on the far bank, tying her shoes, that she noticed that someone was watching her.

He was slender, clad simply in green and gray, and his dark hair fell smoothly to his shoulders. His face was gentle, almost womanly, and something about his eyes made her think of the light of the stars on a clear night. Roxanne recognized him: Varden. She had met him once before, when he had healed the smith's hands. At that time, she had been awed by his power. Now, though, under the spell of the day and her Goddess, she smiled graciously at him, a fellow traveler in this forest on this splendid morning, and she lifted a hand in greeting. "Blessings upon you this day, Master Elf," she called. "The hand of the Lady be on you and your folk."

Varden blinked in surprise, though Roxanne had not thought that particular emotion possible for Elves. But then he smiled in return. "And upon you and yours," he said. He came forward, offering his hand, and helped Roxanne to her feet. "And what brings you this far into Malvern today, Mistress Weaver? I would think that you would have returned home to sleep."

"To sleep?"

"You were awake all night. I had supposed that all humans needed sleep. Or maybe I am mistaken?"

It was her turn to blink. "I see. And was I the evening's entertainment? A naked witch parading about, chanting and waving a knife?" Had they been spying on her? Her methods could only appear crude and primitive compared with those of the Elves, but still, common courtesy . . .

Varden shook his head. "By no means, madam. We had our own . . . commemoration . . . last night, but we saw you enter the forest at sunset, and we felt your worship merge with ours. It was a blessed night."

"I was out in the fields this morning."

"True. And we were among our trees. Our separate kindreds have each their own concerns." He bowed and offered his arm. "Will you walk with me, Lady? I would speak with you this morning."

His use of the old title unnerved her a little. "I . . . have herbs to gather . . ."

"Roxanne, my name is Varden. And my business had somewhat to do with yours. May I go with you to collect herbs?"

She laughed suddenly. "Could there be any question, Varden? I might as well forbid Kay to enter his church as tell an Elf not to walk at will in Malvern."

The starlight in his eyes flickered. "And I might as well show disrespect to my Creatrix as accompany a witch without her leave."

Roxanne stopped her laughter. Varden was an Elf, and she, a mortal, was essentially trespassing in his forest. And yet he treated her with deference and courtesy. She took his arm, wondering at him and at his ways. "Yes . . . yes, of course you have my leave, Varden," she stammered.

The path wound through the forest, branch and leaf pressing in on both sides, and they traveled it in silence. Varden's steps were steady, and Roxanne's were no less sure, though she paused once to loose her skirt from the greenery, wishing as she did that she had not given up her breeches and shirt.

Varden waited patiently for her, watching, and, "It is about Charity," he said quietly as they continued.

"Charity?" said Roxanne. "She is indeed why I'm here today. Her nightmares?"

"It is so. How much can you do for her with herbs and philters?"

Roxanne could not read the tone of his voice. "How much? As much as I can. I can help her to rest at night. If the dreams are very bad, I might have to find out what is troubling her."

Varden seemed suddenly uncomfortable. "And what methods might you use for that?"

The path took them up the side of a low hill, swung out of the trees and into the sunlight, and skirted a meadow that lay like a bright carpet of wildflowers. "Methods?" Roxanne looked at him, but he was gazing at the blossoms. Still that sense of discomfort about him ... something that, like surprise, she had not thought possible for Elves to manifest. "Why do you ask me of methods, Varden? Yours are infinitely more effective than mine, I'm sure."

But Varden stopped, reached down, and plucked a scarlet bloom. It glowed in the sun like a small, petaled flame. "Our meeting, Roxanne, is perhaps overdue," he said. "My people and yours are sundered in many ways, but we hold some things in common, and therefore it may be that we should share others. True, my folk have knowledge. But yours do also, and it should not be overlooked or held cheap. You love Charity. As do I. The girl's nights are troubled. I would ease them, but I cannot touch the life of a mortal without great cause. I ... could assist your efforts, though, were you willing."

He extended the flower to Roxanne and, after a moment, she took it. His gravity and the sense of weight behind his words confused her. "I don't understand," she said. "Charity is just having nightmares."

He made a small, indefinite movement of his head. "I helped Charity once, in the days before Andrew found her orphaned and abandoned. Perhaps it would be better to say that I helped Andrew to help her, for in many ways my hands were tied. I find now that my work is unfinished, and still my hands are tied. You are a witch, Roxanne. Your power is great, though perhaps you doubt it sometimes. May I help you to finish the work that I began years ago?"

The flower glowed in her hand. "Charity doesn't

remember anything of her life before Andrew found her," she said. "Am I to assume that her dreams have something to do with that time?"

"It is so." The Elf started along the path once again, and Roxanne walked at his side.

"She's beautiful, Varden," she said. "She's . . . she's like this flower . . . but she came up in the middle of the village instead of here in the forest. Whatever you did for Charity, Varden, thank you. The whole village owes you its thanks."

"The village owes me nothing. But I fear the flower will be blighted unless we take care to guard it."

"I would do anything to guard it, Varden."

"And so, if the herbs do not help, what then?"

"If they don't help . . . well . . ." Roxanne considered for several minutes, then: "I would question her first. If that achieved nothing, I would, with her permission, look into her mind and try to feel what she feels. Perhaps the view gained by another might give insight. That failing . . . why, I could scry . . . or . . ."

"Or . . . or what, Roxanne?" There was concern in his voice, concern and . . . apprehension.

Inwardly, Roxanne started. Was Varden hiding something?

"I could, if necessary, step between the Worlds," she said, "go back into her past, find out what happened, and help her to deal with it in her waking life." She spoke of it almost casually, but the task she described was both difficult and fatiguing. She stepped between the Worlds each time she stood in Circle, whether worshiping or working magic, but time was an element she did not often invoke. She hoped that lesser means would suffice.

But Varden looked grave. "All right," he said quietly, as though to himself.

They reached a small meadow bordered by a stream and sheltered by tall poplar and oak. Varden helped her to find the best of the herbs that she needed, and as she bent to cut leaf or stalk, murmuring as she did a quiet request for the plant's permission, the Elf stood, watching her, his arms folded and his calm face bespeaking his worry more eloquently than any frown he could possibly wear.

Her pouch was full when she finished, and Varden smiled. "We speak to the plants, too."

"It has always been our way."

"Indeed." His eyes flicked to the pouch. "These are what you intend to use for Charity?"

"Yes," said Roxanne. "With the addition of a little white sandalwood. It doesn't taste very good . . . but then neither does all-heal."

"White sandalwood," said the Elf. "A costly substance in this land. How did you come by it?"

"My mother bought it years ago at the Century Fair in Maris. She passed what was left to me before she died, along with the house, the looms, and her . . . her tools." She suddenly felt awkward. Here she was, standing in a forest clearing with an old leather pouch in hand and a knife stuck in her embroidered belt . . . talking with an immortal. She thought for a moment of her house: the looms set up in what had once been her parents' bedroom, her own tiny room that she kept much as it had been when the Goddess had taken her mother five years ago.

She still slept on a straw pallet next to the oak chest that held her unused wedding clothes.

"I . . . suppose I'll find someone to pass them to when my time comes," she said, realizing suddenly that her silence had grown too long. "I . . . I have no children myself."

A shade of sadness crossed the Elf's face. "Nor husband?" he said. "Nor lover?"

Roxanne forced a smile. "Who wants a village wise-woman for a wife? There's something of the strange and forbidden about us, even if no one thinks of the word *witch*. My mother was fortunate enough to find one of our own people to handfast with. I'm not so lucky. Witches are getting scarce, and who but a witch would understand a witch?" But she looked away quickly.

There was a gentle touch on her shoulder. "The Lady teaches us in many ways," said Varden. "May you find happiness."

Roxanne dragged a sleeve across her forehead, wiping some moisture away . . . blotting her eyes as she did. "Thank you, Varden. It must be nice to have folk of one's own kind about."

"It is comforting, though my people are fading also." The Elf's tone was matter-of-fact, and as such, was heartbreaking. Was so much leaving the world, then? Was it all to go? Closing her eyes, Roxanne bent her head, reaching out in her mind to the land and forest about her, pulling them into herself as though she were gasping air. The land would go on.

Maybe everything of her people, everything of the Elves—everything of magic—might fail, but the land would go on. And that was what mattered.

Varden's hand was still on her shoulder. Maybe, she thought, maybe in these last days of their kindreds, maybe this touch was the important thing. Elf and human meeting, speaking of mutual concerns. Events, Roxanne was sure, were not random things, but were tied up in patterns, intricate dances of cause and effect that depended not only upon past and future lives, but also upon the delicate and distant touch of divine hands.

This is Her work, she thought, reaching up and laying her hand on his, feeling the cool energies of the stars shimmering through his flesh. And then she not only felt the starlight, she saw it too. It was as though she floated in a night sky, gems of bright fire scattered through the darkness, gleaming.

She stayed there for some time, and when she at last came back to the forest clearing, her sorrow was gone. The land would continue. Forever. And there would always be something of magic in it. The Lady taught in many ways, and Her hands lay always upon the life of the world.

Roxanne smiled at Varden, felt sure of the future. This was not faith: though she could not put into words what she had seen, somewhere among the stars was the knowing of the thing, and she did not need definition or utterance to confirm it. "Thank you, Varden," she whispered, her voice barely audible above the rustle of forest leaves.

"Such is the way my people see," said the Elf

softly. "Thus do we face our fading with courage, though with regret. The world changes. We learn." He squeezed her shoulder gently. "Let us go and help Charity."

For a moment, before they turned to the path that led to the village, she looked into his eyes and saw more than she had before.

The herbs did not work. Charity tossed and turned throughout the night, her murmurings vague and confused. The infusion had only drugged the visions: it had not banished them. Worse, Charity's system was delicate, and the girl spent her days foggy and half asleep from the aftereffects, a situation that bothered her intensely ... when she could collect her wits enough to be bothered by anything.

Roxanne tried not to show her worry when she visited the carpenter's house a week after her meeting with Varden. She told Elizabeth to discontinue the infusions and let Charity sleep naturally, but she went home with a furrowed brow. She should have guessed from Varden's involvement that this would be no ordinary case of nightmares, and she began to suspect that whether the Elf had in the past offered his help directly to Charity or indirectly through Andrew, the nature of that help had been more magical than mundane.

Charity was a quiet girl, just approaching the threshold of womanhood. She was indeed much beloved by the entire village, and the fact that her life before the age of seven was a complete unknown had largely been forgotten. But now Roxanne started to wonder what had happened. What could come back to haunt a young woman so? And what ... what had Varden done?

She dropped by the house again the next day. Charity was awake and alert, helping her mother with the baking. Elizabeth sent her to sit and talk with Roxanne.

"I'm sorry the herbs made you feel so bad," said the witch.

Charity smiled, her lake-blue eyes sparkling. "It is well, I'm sure, Mistress Weaver. You tried to help me, and there is no harm done."

Roxanne examined the girl's face. Did she resemble anyone in the village? Some knowledge of her birth might dispel some of the mystery about her. But, no, she seemed to belong only to herself. She was indeed a wildflower that had sprung up among them. "I spoke to Varden last week," she said. "He was concerned about you."

Charity's face lit up. "Varden! How wonderful! Did he take you to dance with the Elves?" She turned to Elizabeth. "Mother, Roxanne has talked with Varden!"

Elizabeth straightened from her kneading, eyed Roxanne with a half smile. "I'm sure it was about time the two of you became acquainted."

"Tell me about it, Mistress Weaver," said Charity.

Roxanne looked back and forth from Elizabeth to Charity. "Well, he didn't take me to dance with the Elves—"

"Oh, I'm sure he will, someday," Charity broke in.

"Charity," Elizabeth reprimanded.

"Your pardon, Mistress," said Charity. She smiled. "I like Varden."

"Obviously," said Roxanne. *And your feelings are returned*, she thought. "He was worried about your bad dreams, and he wanted to help. He mentioned that he had helped you once before ... years ago. Before Andrew found you."

A shade crossed Charity's face, and Elizabeth, who had begun kneading once again, stopped. "I can't remember anything before Father found me," said the girl. She started to shake. "I've ... tried to, sometimes, but I can't. If Varden says that he helped me, then he did, but I ... I ... I can't tell you anything of it."

She was telling the truth, Roxanne knew. It was obvious that she could not remember. But it was equally obvious that Charity was not *supposed* to remember.

The witch looked at Elizabeth. The woman's face was calm, but guarded. If Elizabeth was keeping silent, she had her reasons, and much as Roxanne hated working without full knowledge of the circumstances involved in the matter, she had to respect them.

"All right," she said. "Can you tell me anything of your dreams, Charity?"

The shade did not leave her face. "I ... I can ..."

"There is no shame in a dream, Charity."

"They're so real. I feel like ... like I actually do those things ..."

"Roxanne," said Elizabeth gently, "is this really necessary?"

The witch bit her lip for a moment. "I wish I knew some other way, Elizabeth."

"It's all right, Mother," said Charity. Elizabeth did not look convinced, but the girl straightened her shoulders as though preparing to face some punishment. "I do ... terrible things in my dreams, Roxanne. I hurt people—people I know—like Francis the smith, and Svengard the herder. In my dreams I like doing it ... I don't know why. I feel very lonely in the dreams, and I want to cry. But I can't. Father is in my dreams, and he wants to help me. And then I'm trying to hurt him too, and when I can't stand it anymore, I wake up screaming." She looked away, ashamed despite Roxanne's reassurance. "I usually don't know where I am for some time. My sister Mary sleeps with me, and she holds me until I come to myself."

"How do you hurt them, Charity?"

"Somehow, Roxanne. I just hurt them. That's all I know."

Roxanne felt as though she were grappling with shreds of fog. Varden had as much as said that Charity's dreams were caused by her memories of a former state, but if an old hatred for the smith or the herder was, in fact, responsible, Roxanne was sure that she would have sensed it.

She looked into Charity's eyes, saw nothing but lake-blue innocence. She could link mentally with Charity, but she did not like the idea: it would be an intrusion ...

"It's all right, Roxanne." Charity nodded slowly. "If you have to."

It took Roxanne a moment to realize that Charity had read her thoughts. The girl had talent. With training, she could do much good in the world. Inwardly, the witch sighed. An empty house. And the Elves were fading, too. "Are you sure, Charity?"

"I am."

Roxanne could not but admire her courage. Much good, indeed. With a twinge of regret for all that was fading, all that was already lost, then, she offered her hands. "Take my hands and close your eyes. Try not to think of anything in particular."

Roxanne's mother had trained her well, and in half a minute she was in trance, mentally linked with Charity. Methodically, she sorted through the images of day-to-day living: baking, washing, taking care of her little brother. Soon, she found dim memories, and she followed them into Charity's dreams. The scenes unfolded before her.

There was a little, squalid hut, lit by a meager fire and by a candle, and a pair of old hands that stitched a piece of leather. There was loneliness, and pain, and an iron brace on a leg, and the surety of dying alone.

The images shifted, and she saw the charred hands of Francis the smith. There was satisfaction at the deed. She saw Svengard's flock decimated, saw the herder penniless and hungry. Satisfaction again.

And Roxanne remembered the Leather-woman. Years before, the old hag had lived at the edge of town. Crippled and evil-tempered, she had mended and made bits of harness and tackle for a living, and she had practiced some of the more malign forms of magic against those who had angered her. She had attacked Francis' hands and Svengard's flocks.

But what did Charity have to do with her?

More images. Andrew was reaching across a fire, holding something shining in his hand. Amid a rising roar, as of a great wind, Roxanne saw the shining thing grasped by the old hands and dashed to the ground. The scene erupted in a blast of white light.

Her body went stiff as the light slammed her back in her chair, tearing her hands from Charity's. For a moment, before she came to herself, she saw the night sky again. But etched against the darkness in lines of glittering starlight was a web, a lattice that, she knew instinctively, formed a bar and a closed door capable of holding apart worlds . . . or lifetimes.

A cool cloth touched her forehead, and she opened her eyes. Elizabeth and Charity were standing over her, their faces pale. "I'll be all right," Roxanne managed. "My fault, really. Don't worry, Charity."

Varden came to her house that night, tapping softly at her door well after the sun had gone down. Roxanne had been expecting him (she had been working her loom with her mind only half on the weave), and she let him in. "Welcome to my home, Fair One," she said formally.

"I am honored," he said, bowing. He did not belong within stone walls and among pieces of wooden furniture, but he nevertheless entered and sat down cross-legged before the fire, his back to the flames, his hands resting on his knees. "Tell me," he said.

"I would think that I should be the one to speak

those words." Roxanne stood before him. "Tell *me*, Varden: what happened before Charity came to Saint Brigid?"

"Why do you ask?" His tone was guarded.

"I linked with Charity this afternoon, and I saw some unpleasant things that had to do with the old Leather-woman. Then there was a great light. I do believe my head dented the back of Elizabeth's best chair."

The Elf dropped his eyes. "So that is what I felt."

Roxanne sat down on the floor facing him, arranging her skirts as best she could. Despite the idiocy inherent in any thought of a human attempting to soothe an Elf, she tried to make her voice gentle. "Varden, if I'm supposed to help Charity—and if you're supposed to help me—maybe it would be best if you share what you know."

He shifted uneasily. "Best for whom? Me? You? Charity?"

"Don't give me riddles, Varden, please."

"I am not," he said. "You are speaking of what is best, and that is precisely what I am concerned with. Charity's past is buried, save in her dreams, and in those dreams it comes to her only darkly, in an obscure fashion. She is shielded from much horror by that. For this reason, it would not be good for her if anyone knew of what went before."

"Anyone," said Roxanne, "except for Varden of the Elves."

He rested his gaze on her, and Roxanne suddenly felt the absolute otherness of Varden. She had been speaking to him as though he were a man, forgetting that he was no more like her than peas were like crickets. But: "Roxanne," he said softly, and she heard a plea in his voice, an element of supplication for understanding that bewildered her, "this is part of what I am here for, part of what the Elves are here for. Healing and comfort. Aid. In this time of fading, we realize how much our human cousins need us, and, despite persecution, despite atrocity, we reach out to them. And sometimes it seems as if we mar as much as we make. Five years ago, I helped Charity, and unfortunately, because of my ignorance, I did not shield her from her past. No, Roxanne, I will not say all that I know about Charity, for I fear that so doing would harm her even more than her nightmares. I will tell you what I can. I beg you, for Charity's sake, to accept that limitation."

She stared at him. He was an Elf. Immortal. Powerful beyond belief. And yet . . . he begged her. "Varden . . ." She searched for words. "I . . . I didn't realize. I'm sorry."

"There is no need to be sorry, Roxanne. The responsibility is not yours. I can tell you this: Charity's life before she came to live with Elizabeth and Andrew was one of great hardship and pain. The task of living each day was too much for her, and yet it was beyond her will to end her life. Andrew took pity on her, and I aided him. Charity remembers nothing now, save in her dreams. I regret my error. Elves do not sleep. Our understanding of the phenomenon is cloudy."

Hesitantly, she reached out, laid her hand on his. "Varden . . . I sleep. I understand something of it."

"And you are a witch, Roxanne. You can indeed help." He hesitated, as though now afraid to ask. "Will you, then? Knowing as little as you do?"

She looked past him, looked into the fire that burned on the hearth. She loved Charity. Everyone did. The nightmares, she knew, would only grow worse. Charity would cease to be able to sleep at night. The flower would wither, trampled by dreams.

She felt Varden take her hand. "Will you shield me in my work?" she said.

"I will."

"Then I'll do whatever I can."

His grip tightened for a moment. "What *we* can, Roxanne. The hand of the Lady be on you."

Maybe it was that she was becoming more used to him, and maybe it was that she was holding hands with him, and maybe it was that the concern she shared with him had bridged the abyss of immortality that separated them—regardless, Roxanne could see the depth of love and compassion in the Elf, could feel it stretching off into distances that she could only vaguely comprehend. She could not help but love in return. Trembling, she leaned forward, reached out with her free hand, drew him to her, pressed her lips to his.

"Merry meet, Varden," she said, shaking now half at her audacity, half in profound joy.

He smiled softly, his face shadowed by the firelight, but lit with the radiance of the stars. "Merry meet, Roxanne."

Her hand lay still on his shoulder, half about his neck. She was inclined to leave it there, and the Elf did not seem to mind. "I take it, then, that you do not wish me to pry into Charity's past on my own . . . in Circle."

"I would wish otherwise, it is true."

"How am I to help, then?" She saw the radiance about him even more clearly now, as though her eyes were becoming used to seeing such things. She could not be sure, but she seemed to be partaking of it herself, her skin flickering ever so faintly with lambency.

"When you linked with Charity today, did you see anything besides the images of the Leather-woman?"

"I saw the stars at the very end. As I did in the forest. They seemed different, though: there was a web among them. It seemed to be some kind of barrier."

"It is indeed a barrier, Roxanne. A closed door. Andrew helped Charity, and I set a seal on his work. That was what you saw. It bars Charity's memories."

"Save in her dreams."

"It is so. You must help me reconstruct that web, adding to my work your knowledge of sleep and dream."

She thought about what she had seen. It was obvious that the energies comprising that barrier were immense: lifetime tensioned against lifetime, memory counterpoised by innocence. She quailed at the thought of putting her hands on such power in such an unfamiliar form. She was human. How could she possibly consider working with the magic of the Elves?

Varden's eyes shone. "Fear not. I will help you."

"Master Elf, I am mortal. Are you—"

She stopped, realizing that he was looking at her hand, at the light that, now distinctly, played over it. "Mortal, Roxanne?" he said. "What is mortal for a witch may be quite different from the usual meaning of the word."

She snatched her hand away, examined it closely. The light had changed it, added deep and obscure qualities to it, as though her slightest gesture would now be fraught with meanings that would extend far beyond the world.

"What . . . what did you do to me, Varden?"

"I did nothing, Roxanne. You are a witch, you work with magic, you manifest your Goddess. You are not so unlike my people. It may be that you see yourself now as we see you, but I did nothing save give you a vision of the stars. Your being appears to be sympathetic to such energies. Perhaps you should be careful: continued intercourse with Elves might lead to . . . alterations."

She stared at the light. It was different from that which shone about Varden, and yet not exceedingly so: the cool radiance of the moon rather than the crystalline shimmer of the stars. She reached out, touched him. As she did, radiance and shimmer flowed, merged gently. Varden's eyes flickered . . . or maybe they twinkled.

Retreat or go on, the decision was hers to make, but she knew, as surely as she knew that an immortal sat inches away from her, that the Goddess had brought about this meeting, had called Her priestess to duty, had touched her with enough of the essence of the Elves so that she now partook of their vision. She felt the smile spreading on her face as though she stood once again before the dawn, thirteen and new-initiated, lifting her arms in an instinctive embrace of the Infinite. *Whatever, My Lady,* she thought. *You call, and I answer gladly. Wherever You lead me . . .*

"When shall we work, Varden?"

"Tomorrow night," he said. "You should rest well: the link you had with Charity has shaken you, and we will both need all our strength. We may well have to partly disassemble the barrier, and if that is the case, we will have to hold Charity's past away from her. That will take much power." His brow furrowed. "I was quite serious when I spoke of alterations. Channeling so much starlight may affect you profoundly. I do not know in what fashion."

He looked at her carefully, much as she herself might examine a bolt of new-woven cloth: searching out the quality of the weave, the way of the pattern.

She saw him to the door, and before he left, he kissed her in farewell. She smiled shyly, as did he. "Merry part, Varden."

"Merry part," he said. "And merry meet again."

In her dreams that night, Roxanne saw the stars blazing brilliantly in a night sky. Their light was a palpable presence, and as though she floated in deep water, she felt its currents, drank in its energy, let it flow through her. Once, just past midnight, she awoke, not from any disturbance or discomfort, but more because, with the soft light still playing over her skin, waking and sleeping were not so very different from one another. She went to the window then, and looked up at the nearly full moon and at the stars that mirrored those of her dreams. For long minutes she stood, watching, before she at last returned to bed and to that inner vision.

And the next morning she awoke just at dawn, refreshed, alert. She did her morning housekeeping, and it seemed to her that there was, in the touch of the simple implements she used—broom and mop, brush and rag—a tranquillity and a joy that she had never felt before, for the wood and cloth in her hands were now just as much an intimation of the divine as her own flesh.

For a moment, brushing out her hair before the glass, noticing that, yes, her eyes held a radiance as though a touch of the full moon had gathered there, she stood still, contemplating herself. "I am a witch," she said softly, and it seemed to her that at that moment the statement was more true than it had ever been before.

But a soft knock roused her, and she went downstairs to find Elizabeth standing at her door, her face creased with worry and fatigue.

"It was . . . very bad last night, Roxanne," she said. "Charity was beside herself, and we could not bring her to her senses until nearly dawn. Will you come see her?"

Roxanne felt a pang. Her intrusion into Charity's mind the day before had more than likely brought this about. She grabbed a shawl and, after hesitating a moment, her ebony-handled knife, and went with Elizabeth through the streets of the village.

"Did she say anything this morning about her dreams?" Roxanne asked.

Elizabeth shook her blond head. "Charity never says much about them," she said. "But you can tell how bad they are just by looking at her. Oh, Roxanne, she hurts so . . ." Her voice broke then, and the witch put an arm about her shoulders as they walked.

When they reached Elizabeth's house, Charity was not there, but Mary was, and the older girl wiped her hands on her apron. "Charity left a short while ago," she said. "She said she was going to the church."

"You let her go?" said Roxanne.

"My sister is strong, Mistress Weaver," said Mary. "Stronger than most people think. She said she wanted to go alone, and I saw no reason to stop her."

Roxanne looked out at the street. It was late morning, but the day was still cool, and the light breeze wafted the odor of Francis' forge—hot metal and burning charcoal—throughout the town, mingling it with the scent of the forest. In the distance, someone was laughing. Closer was the sound of Andrew pounding a wooden peg into place. The day, she realized, was perfect. It was exactly as it should be. Everything was blending together in an intricate pattern, like a tapestry with not a stitch out of place. And even the church was fitting into it all, and not just because of Charity. There was more to it, as though she were being guided . . .

Half dazed by her knowledge, she patted Elizabeth's shoulder. "I'll go to her there, Elizabeth. It will be well." It could not, she knew, be otherwise, and she pulled out of the vision only enough to turn away and hurry up the street, her shawl about her shoulders and her knife stuck in her belt.

Facing the town square was the church, the one built by Alban, the last priest. It was overlarge for the village—Alban had had pretensions—but it was well made. Next to it was the priest's house, also overlarge—Alban had liked comfort. Kay, the new priest, the son of Francis, usually laughed about his predecessor, and he made a habit of living simply, frequently opening his extra rooms to travelers or to the homeless.

Kay, however, was not in the church when Roxanne entered and made her way up the dark nave, and that was just as well, for Roxanne felt that her kind, descending as it did from stone circles in the forest and from knives raised in honor of old Gods, could not but be an intruder in a church. There was no place for her before this uncomfortably plain wooden cross. True, survival might dictate that she conform outwardly with regards to weekly mass attendance, but body and soul, mind and spirit, she belonged to her Goddess.

And yet ... and yet her presence here was a part of this day, too, and, as such, it also was perfect. The pattern was becoming clear to her, as though she were approaching a shrine through a thinning fog, and, following that pattern, she turned away from the cross, turned toward the south, turned to where stood the strange statue of the Virgin. Before it knelt a young woman, her form indistinct in the soft twilight of the church.

Feeling keenly the gaze of carved eyes upon her, Roxanne drew closer to Charity, but just as she could see the girl more clearly as she approached, so she could also see the statue . . . and the faint light about it. More, though: she could suddenly see detail in it that she had never noticed during her compulsory hours in the church. The color of the statue was simply that of burnished wood, lovingly carved and smoothed, but Roxanne was suddenly seeing beyond the wood, beyond the surface, and she knew that Her robes were blue and silver, Her hair was dark, Her eyes gray.

Roxanne stopped a few paces behind Charity, staring in wonder. The Lady's belt was of carved emeralds and amethysts. A golden clasp held Her hair back on one side. Behind Her was the night sky, and the emblem of interlaced moon and star on Her breast was radiant.

The witch's heart was laboring, and she put her hand to her mouth, struggling with words that welled spontaneously to her lips, not in her own language, but in another:

"Elthia Calasiuove."

The whispered name hung in the air like a lamp. Charity looked up. "Roxanne . . ." She was weeping, and the witch was beside her in a moment, her arms about the girl. "It was awful, Roxanne. Much worse than before." She took a deep breath and swallowed, forced herself to stop shaking. "I . . . I had to come here. I thought she would understand."

"She does, child." Roxanne held her. "Varden and I are going to take care of your dreams tonight. Rest easy. I'm very, very sorry I've caused you this pain."

Charity wiped at her eyes and smiled weakly. "Roxanne, I trust you. I know you'd do me no harm. But I do hope that you and Varden can help me."

"We will, Charity. On my oath, we will. What can I do for you now?"

"I think . . ." Charity looked down the length of the nave, looked toward the open doors that gave out upon the sunlit street. She dried her eyes, took a deep breath, straightened. "I think I'd like to take a walk in the forest with you, Roxanne. I think that will help me today."

"Anything."

Charity got to her feet and took another deep breath, letting it out slowly as if dispelling the last of the night's phantoms. Roxanne rose and turned toward the light, but Charity held her back. She studied Roxanne for a moment, then nodded in the direction of the statue.

"She's your Goddess, isn't she?"

Roxanne looked into Charity's face. She could not lie to her. "Yes," she said. "She is."

"Varden has told me a little about Her, but he won't say much. He's an Elf, he says, and his ways are different."

Roxanne looked up at the gray eyes that watched her. Different? How different? The pattern grew a little more. Something was about to happen. Something wonderful.

"I saw her . . . last night," said Charity. "Just at the

worst. She came, and she helped me. I saw her . . . just like I see you now." She struggled with the words. "She called me her daughter. And . . . and . . ."

Roxanne waited. She felt it coming, and though she knew what it was, and what it meant, she would not speak. No prompting. No questions. Charity had to ask on her own.

The young woman glanced at the statue, then turned again to the witch. "I love her, Roxanne. I want to learn about her. Will you teach me?"

Roxanne was still held by the calm, gray glance. Deep in the depths of those eyes, she saw a flicker. Starlight. And moonlight. "Yes, Charity," she said. "Yes, I will." She took Charity in her arms, held her tightly. "Yes, I will. Blessed Be, my child."

Charity laid her head on Roxanne's shoulder. "Blessed Be, Roxanne."

Roxanne did not hear Varden's approach: she felt it. She was already at the open door when he rounded the corner, and he stopped when he saw her. Standing in the spill of firelight, a bundle in his hand, he bowed.

"May I enter?"

"Need you ask?" She took his hand and drew him in. He handed her the bundle.

"We will be in the forest tonight," he said, "and I am afraid that skirts will not do for such travel." He indicated the bundle. "I took the liberty."

Curious, she set it on the table and unfastened the gray cloth wrapping. It proved to be clothing much like Varden's, but cut along more feminine lines. A pair of soft boots was included, as was a belt.

She looked at him, met his eyes, and he smiled almost shyly. "We have time," said the Elf. "Charity is not yet asleep."

She picked up the tunic. The cloth was smooth and light, closely woven. Fine work. An embroidered border of flowers was worked into the hems. Masterful stitching. "I . . . I'm honored," she said, and then she gathered it all up and climbed the stairs to her room.

The garb fitted her perfectly. Sitting on the edge of her pallet, she tucked the breeches into the knee-high boots, then rose and belted the tunic loosely, as seemed proper. But when she lifted her head, her glance fell on the oaken chest containing her wedding clothes. She had carelessly let her gown fall on top of it, and the dark blue garment lay crumpled on the wood like a discarded chrysalis.

And when she looked into the mirror that hung on the wall above the chest and saw her face shimmering softly in the candlelight, her eyes filled with the radiance of the moon, her dark hair falling in waves to her shoulders and spilling across the green tunic, it seemed to her that she might well have been facing one of the Fair Ones instead of a glass. Slowly, since she had first touched Varden in the forest, she had found herself taking on something of his nature; and though she was priestess and witch, now, standing before this mirror, wondering at herself in elven garb, she would not have been much surprised to find that she was, yes, Elf too, as though the one nature inferred, even demanded, the other.

It occurred to her that she should perhaps have found this disturbing. But it was not disturbing at all. She had followed her Goddess through the years of her life, serving Her with perfect freedom, loving Her with as much of her being as she could call hers ... and now it seemed that the path she had been following led a little farther on. True, it branched off and took her away from the well-trodden road, but it was, unmistakably, her path, and she thought that, off in the distance, she could see a Woman waiting for her, a Woman robed in blue and silver.

Silently, Roxanne reached down, picked up her gown, folded it, and laid it carefully on the chest. For a long minute, she paused with her hand on the garment—and on the wood beneath—and then she turned and left the room without looking back.

Varden was waiting, and he nodded slowly. "It is well."

But Roxanne stopped at the cupboard and opened it. Her ebony-handled knife she thrust into her belt, and she dropped a necklace of acorns over her head and arranged it under her tunic collar. She turned to face the Elf. "Where do we go tonight, Varden?" She was not speaking of the forest.

He understood. "We will go among the stars. To the Door that you saw."

"And what shall we do there?" she said formally.

"We will take it apart and make it anew."

She felt the light in her face, in her eyes. "And what will that do to me?"

Varden watched her carefully. "I do not know for certain."

"I think I do."

"Are you willing?"

She fingered the acorn necklace. "This afternoon, I spoke with Charity. She wants to learn about the Goddess. She asked me to be her teacher. I said yes. In doing so, I took on responsibility for her. I will defend her to the death . . . could I possibly quail at fighting unto life?"

The Elf was silent.

"Since we first spoke at length last week," the witch went on, "I've felt the touch of a Hand. I've thought that only my actions were being guided, but now I think I know differently. She's guiding you also, Varden. And there's more here than Charity's nightmares."

Varden said nothing. The fire was behind him, and his face was shadowed. Only the gleam of starlight in his eyes told Roxanne that he was watching her.

She met that gleam, moonlight for starlight. "I love you, Varden."

He stirred, closed his eyes, took a deep breath. "I love you, Roxanne."

She looked at her hand. For all the light that pulsed through it, it was still mortal flesh and blood. "Would an Elf take a human for a lover?" Her voice was low, almost a whisper.

"It could be." Varden's voice was almost as low. "And it could be that there would be much pain on such a path."

She crossed the room to him, reached out. He gave

her his hand. "I've made my choice," she said. "Will you consider it?"

He did not falter. "I will consider it, Lady. I am honored by the choice, but I must look into my heart for guidance. Humans . . . humans are . . ."

"Humans are weak creatures. I understand," she said. "But I'm a little less human these days, it seems. I'll wait."

She let go of his hand and stood back. He bowed deeply to her, went to the door, and opened it. Together, they stepped out into the night.

Beneath the thick canopy of leaves, the forest paths, Roxanne knew, were dark, but tonight they did not seem overly so to her eyes. Rather, she saw everything—branch and trunk, water and stone—in shades of blue and gray, but though she did not have to take Varden's hand for guidance, she did anyway. His grip was gentle, and he had obviously guessed at her newfound ability, for he did not hesitate to point out to her sights that she could not have seen without it: a fox engrossed in its hunting, an owl sweeping noiselessly through the branches above them, meadow mice tumbling at the roots of a tree.

The path rose toward the forest highlands, and the full moon was nearing the zenith by the time they emerged from the forest and entered a broad expanse of meadowland that was thickly carpeted in grass and ringed by trees. Near the center was a rectangular block of stone that looked to be made of granite—smooth and polished, glinting in the light—and, like

David's statue, like everything touched by the Elves, it seemed to possess an inner radiance of its own.

"This place is cherished by my people," said Varden. "I suppose one could say that it is sacred, though such a distinction does not exist in our language."

Roxanne inhaled sweet air that was laden with the odors of the forest and of the night. Sacred, profane ... any such distinction, she felt, was meaningless. Standing in this meadow, she was in the presence of the Goddess. She went down on one knee. "*Elthia Calasiuove*," she said aloud. "My Lady. You call, and I come gladly."

When she rose again, Varden was staring at her. "It is not often that a mortal calls Her by that name."

"It's the name I heard."

"You have seen Her?"

"I saw enough: in the church this afternoon ... in David's statue."

He leaned forward, kissed her lightly on the forehead. "Hail, Friend," he said, and, taking her hand, he led her forward to the stone slab. "Here we will work, if it please you, Mistress Witch. I understand that it is the way of your people to cast a magical Circle before such operations. Such is not the case with my folk, but I will bow to your customs should you deem it necessary."

She could not but marvel. She was a mortal witch, essentially an intruder into this place, and yet Varden was willing to yield to her wishes.

She had been taught always to work in Circle, but, looking from one side of the meadow to the other, stretching out her awareness and examining the lay of the land, the growing grass, the life in the soil, she could not but feel that a Circle would be superfluous. This place was already consecrated and hallowed far beyond anything she could hope to achieve.

Bending, she touched the earth, and when she straightened, she was dizzy with starlight. "There is no need. She is here."

They sat down before the granite block, holding hands, their knees almost touching. "Are you prepared?" said the Elf.

"I am," she answered. "But I can't get there by myself, Varden. You'll have to help me."

He nodded. "Fear not. You will learn, I am sure. For now, close your eyes."

She did so, settled herself, turned her awareness inward. She felt something change . . .

. . . and then she was looking at the stars.

"We are here," she heard the Elf say, and as she watched the stars, she saw strands shimmer into view, glittering blue-white against the black sky. Turning, she saw that they joined with a complex web. It looked familiar. "Is that the Door?"

"That is Charity."

Tentatively, she reached out to it, and she sensed for herself the truth of what he said. The web was Charity. Charity was the web. The strands were aspects of her life, real and potential: interactions, changes, qualities, talents.

"You see now as do the Elves," said Varden. "When I healed Francis the smith, I saw him in this fashion. I reached among the strands and altered their pattern: I took away the future of blighted hands and death and gave him health."

Roxanne was awed. "Your power is great."

"Great, and yet not so great. I attempted to help Charity, and I erred. Charity has suffered as a result. Now, perhaps, you see why Elves are barred from touching human life."

Together, they followed a group of strands that led off into the starry void, strands that joined eventually with another lattice that took shape ahead of them. This time Roxanne recognized it clearly: the Door.

"Here our task becomes difficult," said Varden. "Are you still willing to work without knowledge of Charity's past?"

Could she do otherwise? "I am."

"Then, if you are, stay on this side of the Door. If you venture beyond it, you will know more than you wish."

Dimly, through the interstices of the lattice, Roxanne could see another. Strands from it entered the barrier, merged with it briefly, then reappeared on the near side, reaching out to join Charity's life. "All right."

With Varden's help, she laid her hands on the webbing, felt the energies it contained, the potentials, the possibilities. She felt also the life that was Charity and felt its consubstantiality with the other life that lay on the far side of the Door. Slowly, she grew accustomed to the lattice. Slowly, she searched through it and found the deeper levels of memory and pain that manifested as nightmares. But though she found the pain easily enough, Roxanne found also innocence and beauty, and well-nigh limitless love, and once again she found herself bewildered by the connection between Charity and the long-vanished Leather-woman. Little enough love the old hag had given . . . or received.

Let it lie, she told herself. *Charity doesn't need any more grief.*

Hours passed as she examined the Door and learned its ways. She marveled at its complexity, at the skill with which it had been constructed. The continuity of the girl's life had been unaffected, but memory and thought were carefully blocked, and delicate balances were maintained between recollection and identity. It was as though Charity had undergone a second incarnation in the same lifetime, completely bypassing death and rebirth.

And then, in what must have been the early hours of the morning, she came upon the strand she was looking for. In appearance, it was much like the others, but when she touched it, she could feel the memories rising up unblunted. She saw again the old hands working leather, the interior of the squalid hut, felt loneliness and despair deep enough to blast a world to sorrow.

She jerked her awareness away with a cry. Varden was beside her instantly, and she felt his energies merge with hers as though he held her in his arms. "This is the one," she choked. "This is it."

"You are certain?"

She fought for balance, reached out to the stars, gathered strength from them. She felt her link with

Varden grow stronger. "I am. This is memory and dream both."

"This is not good," he said. "Notice how this particular strand depends upon the major braid of Charity's life. It connects fully with her continuing existence. We will have to work with great care. I . . ."

She read his tone. "You're not sure it can be done."

"True. But it must be done nonetheless. I will not have Charity suffer any more."

They spent the next hour repositioning portions of the web, finding alternate balances for the energies so as to take the strain off the nightmare strand. The lattice would not hold for long in this configuration, but it did not have to: by morning, if all went well, the Door would be once more in place, and stable.

And as she worked, Roxanne felt the starlight flowing through her, felt her sympathies altering, felt slow changes building in her heart. She had already gained the vision of the Elves, and now she was acquiring more: something of their being, maybe, or of their awareness. She was not frightened at the prospect. Rather, it seemed a thing of joy, beckoning her. She would defend Charity to the death, and she would indeed fight for her also unto life.

At last, the nightmare strand was clear, and Roxanne and Varden drew back, evaluating. "It will have to be rebalanced," said Roxanne.

"Damped, actually," said the Elf. "We must find a way to neutralize it. What does your intuition say to you, Mistress Witch?"

She let her mind range about. "We could push it

farther down," she said. "Bury it. But then there is always the chance that it would rise again, particularly when Charity begins training with me. Something is liable to be stirred up."

"That would be undesirable."

"We'll have to break it."

Varden started. "Do you realize what that might do?"

"Yes. But I think it's the only way. Otherwise, in a year or so, you and I will be out here again."

She outlined her idea. Energy flowed evenly not only throughout the lattices on either side of the Door, but through the Door itself. Currents could be joined together and set in a counterflow that would be absorbed by the whole structure. Uncontrolled, this would lead immediately to disaster, but if the Door was properly linked with the surrounding stars, any resonance or instability would be drained off.

"It would last until a star burned out," Roxanne said. "And by then, Charity would be well into another lifetime, and she'd have death and rebirth between her and the other side."

"There is the problem of time."

"I gave my word that we'd take care of it tonight. On my Oath."

"Then let us start."

There was merit in the idea, and the structure of the web lent itself naturally to Roxanne's plan. Gradually, Elf and witch freed the energy of the nightmare strand, allowed it to be absorbed by new strands that they stretched out and joined to the stars. When they finished, only a slender strand remained, and Roxanne took hold of it, braced herself against the pain and loneliness, and edged it slowly toward the nexus of intersecting probabilities that she had created. The light strained in her hands as though it were a taut cable, but, little by little, it yielded. Slowly, it approached the connection where the last of its energy would be dissipated.

"Roxanne," Varden said suddenly. "Hold."

She stopped. "Varden?"

"There is some instability in the lattice. I am holding one life apart from the other, but the pressure is increasing, and the imbalance we have caused is adding to it."

"I can't move this strand without that imbalance."

"True, but if we are not careful—"

Incredibly, horribly, there was an audible *snap*, as though space itself had fractured. The strand that Roxanne was holding broke, dissolved into fragments. The Door began to disintegrate.

"*NO!*" she screamed, but the sound of her thought was hollow, and she saw the lattices of the two lives draw toward one another. "Varden!"

"I am not holding them successfully, Roxanne," he said. His voice was tight, but calm. "You had better get away from the Door. If this collapses, you may be crushed."

She was already reaching out to him. "And what about you, Varden? Do you think I'll leave you in there?"

"Roxanne, please take yourself to safety."

She ignored him, joined with him, added her energy and her abilities to his. She felt the cool power flowing through her, felt, now even more, her heart changing and widening as they slowed the convergent rush of the lattices. The flow of starlight was incredible, but Roxanne held on, her heart laboring with its breadth.

Hold . . .

It was not Varden's voice she heard, but she held regardless, and, about them, the last traces of the Door faded, leaving her and Varden afloat between Charity's two lives. Nearby, the massive strands of continuity tugged at the lattices seeking to merge the two.

And if that happened, then full memory would come to Charity.

Roxanne's giddiness increased, and, pulled by the starlight with ever-increasing urgency, she felt herself slipping away from her own identity. She scrambled for a foothold, looked for something against which she could brace herself, found nothing. She slipped farther, and then she understood: it was a question of her or Charity. Defending to the death.

"Varden," she said, her voice a sigh. "Farewell . . . I'll hold it . . . myself. Whatever . . ."

And then she let go, and then the light took her, whirled her away as though she were a cork in a flood. Her heart widened until it tore, and the universe rushed in through the rent, filling her, straining the walls of her soul with its immensity.

She held the two lifetimes apart without effort now: there was nothing left of her identity to hinder the flow. Silently, she floated without thought, her mind blank save for a vision of calm gray eyes.

They came closer.

Child.

The voice, soft though it was, reverberated through her. She stirred.

Roxanne.

Her name. Yes, hers. She was Roxanne. She had that much. The starlight still flowed, but she had that much. The gray eyes held hers, and she suddenly felt the touch of energies that made the rush of starlight seem but a trickle.

Hold.

She held. Strength flowed into her, then, and knowledge. Her heart mended. Her soul eased. She suddenly realized to whom the gray eyes belonged.

Call Me, Child, said the voice. *You know My Name now. Call My Name, and you call Yours. Call Me. You know Who You are, and You know what You can do.''*

Lady . . . I'm not an Elf.

Call.

Something, she knew, would change irrevocably if she did so. She would close a door. She would follow her path, and behind her, gates would be locked . . . forever. There would be no going back. No more would she be the simple wise-woman and weaver of Saint Brigid. She might be called Roxanne still, live in her house still, eat and dance, sweep the floors, and stroll under the trees of Malvern Forest, but all that would be no more than appearance, for inside, she would be something else.

But she knew that, whatever she would be, she would be able to end Charity's suffering. She was a witch and a priestess, and she was also a teacher . . .

and perhaps she might be a lover. And as she called the Name that was both her own and that of the Goddess, she fused with her cry not only her magic, but her love and her loyalty too, and the stars shook with her power.

Silently, she floated between the two lattices, looked from one to the other, knew them both. Charity and the Leather-woman. One and the same. She was not overly surprised. Surprise was no longer something that was possible for her. "Thank you, Varden," she said softly. "You did your best."

"I failed." The Elf's voice carried a hundredweight of sorrow.

"No, beloved. You succeeded. But if you do not understand sleep, you understand death and rebirth even less. You did everything you could, Immortal, but now it's time for a mortal hand."

She seized the connecting strands, and, with full knowledge, with infinite power, she snapped the taut cables, felt the old life fade and the new life blossom, threw herself into Charity and let the energies of renewal and rebirth and starlight alike flow through her until the young woman's existence was whole and sound and stable.

There would be no more nightmares. The Leather-woman was gone. Now there was only Charity.

She came to herself in the grassy meadow. Her face was wet with tears, as was Varden's. Gently, and with reverence, he took her hand and pressed it to his lips. "Again I have erred," he said. "I underestimated you. Earlier this night I all but said that my mortal cousins were weak. I find that I have been wrong." He wiped at his eyes with the back of his hand. "Forgive me, Roxanne."

"I can't blame you, Varden," she said softly.

He dropped his eyes for a moment, but then he lifted them, met her gaze. "Perhaps not," he said. "But it seems that I have much to learn. Of sleep. And of death and rebirth. Will you be my teacher, Roxanne?"

She stared at him for a moment. "I will, Varden," she managed at last. "If you will be mine." And then: "Will you . . . will you be my lover?"

The tears ran down his face, but he smiled at her, and the radiance of that smile was unmatched even by the radiance of the just-rising sun that broke over the distant horizon in an arc of fire. "I will," he said as the light mounted in the east. "If you will be mine."

Now . . .

Elvenhome

Joan knew it was going to be one of her odd days when she drove to work that morning. The sun was too bright, the sky too blue, the fields on either side of the road too green for her to feel at all normal. Traffic about her and landscape unreeling past her windows, she struggled to keep her eyes on the road, to shut the warm, sweet air of midsummer out of her mind.

She could never say exactly what caused these days. If she tried very hard, she could push the whole question away ... for a while. The air was clearer maybe, the polluted Denver skies swept clean by mountain breezes; or perhaps some flower was in bloom, causing an obscure allergy to flare up. But such excuses smacked to her of dishonesty, and though she was quite willing to forget to mention a thing or two when dealing with a difficult applicant or a reluctant employer, she was quite unwilling to apply the same procedure to herself. And so, when (the Mercedes idling at a light) she found that on her right beckoned a small park, a carefully landscaped and mowed and manicured city park with an artfully sculpted pond in the middle and nothing natural about it save for the water and the grass and the earth, she nonetheless found herself staring at it hungrily ... and admitting that she *was* staring at it. Hungrily.

Green. And blue. And the fertile brown of good dirt, warm and gritty and all ready push the tender shoots of plants toward the sunlight. Joan wanted to do nothing so much as pull over, take off her shoes, roll up her Yves St. Laurent pants, and (admitting it again) go wading. And she wanted to reach down and touch the water and the earth, because ... because water and earth were what *mattered*, not things like managing employment agencies and clients who—

A horn blast startled her out of her thoughts. The light had changed. Flushed and cursing under her breath, she dropped into gear and pulled out quickly; and if her eyes were moist, she only clenched her jaw tighter, kept a more careful grip on the wheel, fought more grimly against the sunlight and the sweet air.

It was one of her odd days.

Excruciatingly conscious of her every thought, she managed, as usual, to fight down the urgings, and she was only a few minutes late when she hurried past the receptionist and entered her office. But even here, in a room full of synthetic carpeting and the subliminal flicker of fluorescent lights, her ordeal was not over, for her window looked out upon fields as yet untouched by the burgeoning construction of the suburbs, the tall grass speckled with yellow daisies and the gully just to the south supporting, even in the summer heat, a stalwart bunch of cattails.

Eyes averted, she closed the blinds on the scene, and then she sat down at her desk with a cautious glance through the window that looked out into the main office. To admit her problem to anyone was out of the question, but no one on the other side of the glass appeared to have noticed her distress. In any case, were she asked, she had a headache, that was all. Not an unusual thing for a woman who was trying to run an employment agency.

A tapping at her door. "Joan?"

"It's open," she said with more irritation in her voice than she wanted. Those fields, and particularly that pond, were still in the back of her mind. Why this damned desk? Why this stupid brown velvet blazer with the too-tight sleeves? Why anything at all instead of grass, and ponds, and . . . ?

Sandra, the receptionist, stuck her head in. "The counselors are waiting for you, Joan."

"What?" Joan fumbled with the papers on her desk. Headache. That was it. Just a headache.

"It's Wednesday. Staff meeting." Sandra peered at her. "Are you all right?"

The odd day. She had forgotten about the staff meeting. "Ah . . . ah . . . ah . . ."

What was it again?

"I have a . . . a headache. That's all. I'll be right in."

Sandra disappeared behind the closing door and Joan tried to put her thoughts in order. What was she supposed to talk about this morning? Sales technique. That was it. Selling people was just like selling

ballpoint pens. You had to know the tricks, the
dodges, the ways to finesse the disembodied voice
on the other end of the line and simultaneously gloss
up the flesh-and-blood client who sat at your desk.

But it was an odd day, and her thoughts were
jumbled, the sleeves of her blazer seemingly just a
little tighter than usual. She knew she could not
speak with coherency, and with a pang she remembered that the large room where the counselors
worked—where the meeting was to be held—looked
out, through a wall of windows, on the same scene
of fields and daisies as did her office. She would
never make it through a talk, but she had to, for to
admit that something was wrong with her—to admit
that something was *that* wrong with her—was . . .
was . . .

Grappling with her thoughts, she forced them to
slow down, forced herself to consider the matter logi-
cally. There was a way out of this. There always was.
Placing clients, collecting fees, giving talks during
odd days: all were just problems to be solved. And
she could solve them. In this case, if she could not
speak, then someone else had to.

Quickly, she looked through the reports on her
desk. Among them were breakdowns of placements
for the last month, and she noticed that two counselors, Rick Shane and Wheat Hennock, stood out mark-
edly above the averages. Wheat's performance was
particularly interesting, since she had joined the staff
only two months before.

Good. Rick and Wheat could do the talking, and
Joan could keep her back to the windows. The two

would, doubtless, feel rewarded by being singled out, and the other counselors would work all the harder in hopes of eventually garnering the same recognition for themselves. Managing people, managing problems: she could do it. She was Joan Buckland, and she could *do it.*

She paused at her door, pulled down the sleeves of her blazer, and composed herself before walking quickly out past the receptionist's desk and down the hallway to the counselors' room. Even as she approached, though, she could see the windows through the open door, and the lovely yellow light was spilling into the room. It was a hideous threat, and she kept her eyes firmly on the beige carpet— she was thinking, that was all—as she sidled in and sat down facing away from the view.

She looked up and forced a smile. "Okay, everyone. I want to talk about technique today. You've all had the basic courses in selling, but you've all got your distinctive styles, too. Some of those styles work, some don't. I'm not coming out against imagination, but if it doesn't make you money, you don't want to use it. Now—" She glanced at Rick and Wheat . . . and fell suddenly silent. Rick looked much as he did every day: gray suit, blue tie, pale blue shirt, polished shoes. The epitome of competence. Wheat, though . . .

She was a young, sweet-looking woman with cornflower-blue eyes and hair the color of dark honey. She had from the first reminded Joan of fields and daisies (a near-fatal recollection on such an odd day), but this particular morning, there seemed to be a nimbus about her, a delicate shimmer sparked with traces of silver that glittered like the stars on a clear winter night.

Joan stared, and she suddenly realized not only that she had been silent for considerably longer than was good for appearances, but that Wheat had met her eyes. There was no question in the young woman's glance, only a calm acceptance, and perhaps . . . perhaps a sense of wonder.

Joan shook herself out of it. Ignoring the fields, trying to ignore the nimbus, she plunged on. "Rick and Wheat have done extremely well this last month, and it . . ." The fields, the nimbus: they were somehow related. Though she had denied herself the pond that morning, she was sure that Wheat had no such qualms. Dawn might well have found her wading among the minnows, reaching down to touch a lily . . .

She realized that ten counselors were watching her: nine puzzled, one calm. "It . . . it looks like they've got some insights into what works," she said, stumbling through the words. Problems, solutions. She could do it. She *could*. "So I'm going to let them talk about what they do. I'm sure we'll find out a lot that will make us all better employment counselors. Rick?"

Rick stood up so that he could be heard better. One hand in his pocket, he looked at the floor for a minute to choose his words. "I think the first thing I realized," he said, "was that most people don't know what they want, even if they think they do. It's up to me to tell them. Usually they haven't thought much about it, so I've got the advantage, because I have. I work with what I've got . . ."

Joan lost track of his words. She went back to thinking about the fields, about the pond, about Wheat. The young woman was listening to Rick, but her cornflower-blue eyes were troubled. And there was still that . . . that nimbus.

Nimbus? What?

Rick went on for several minutes, but his thoughts were neither novel nor overly remarkable. Perhaps he used his training a little more effectively than did others, but Joan had already perceived that his superb performance this last month was more of a fluke than anything else. Control the conversation, convince the employer that he or she needed the client, convince the client that he or she needed the employer, and, most important, stay on top of whoever was responsible for the fee until the money came through. Next month, no doubt, Rick's performance would return to pedestrian normalcy. She began to worry that she would have to speak after all.

But after Rick finished and sat down, everyone looked at Wheat. Joan had marked her as shy from the beginning because she was usually quiet, but she showed no trace of nervousness when she rose . . . still surrounded by that odd shimmer that no one else appeared to have noticed.

"How do you do it, Wheat?" said Joan. She tried to sound hearty, but the back of her neck was prickling as though something were about to happen; and she knew, with a horrible sense of prescience, that Wheat's success had nothing to do with luck.

Wheat looked at all of them with that same calm acceptance. "It has to do with love," she said.

Joan could have sworn that everyone stopped breathing. Including herself.

"You have to look at the clients that come to you and love them," Wheat went on, "because they're people and they deserve it. You have to feel them, what they've been through, why they've come to you. I look at them, and I try to sense what they want. What's important to them. If I can't get that, I level with them about it. Maybe I can get them one thing but not another. But maybe what I *can* get them is more important to them than what I can't. Sometimes security is more important than a title, or a casual office is more important than money."

Rick snorted. Two counselors murmured to one another. Joan sat, stunned.

"And when I'm calling employers, I try to do the same thing. There are . . ." Wheat searched for words, as if translating from another language, seeking equivalents where there were none, looking for words that did not exist. "There are . . . energies in the world, and you can sense them over a telephone line just as well as if the person sat at your desk. I'm helping people. I help the client. I help the employer. That's what I'm here for. Aid. Comfort. I can't think of a better way of loving someone than to make sure that he or she has a job and is happy in it."

Rick exploded. "Oh, bullshit, Wheat."

She looked at him, that same calm expression in her eyes. "That's what I do," she said simply.

"Wheat," said Rick, "you've been through the

same courses as the rest of us. Are you telling us that all that is just garbage? What about those skills? Come on, Wheat! What's your secret? How do you clinch the deal? How do you go for the close?"

In Joan's eyes, the nimbus around Wheat flared a little, but the others still did not notice. Wheat gazed past her, out to the windows, out across the green and brown fields with their daisies and their cattails. "People," she said softly, "have a very precious thing. It's called free will. I never interfere with it. I level with my clients. I level with the employers. I let them make the choices."

"You're crazy." Some of the counselors were plainly confused. Some were thoughtful. Rick, however, surprisingly red-faced, was on his feet, and one or two of the other counselors looked as though they might join him in another moment.

Joan straightened. "That's enough, Rick. Sit down." She noticed Wheat looking at her and tried to ignore it. "Wheat should be congratulated. If that's how she does it, that's fine. She brings in money for the company and for herself. As we all know, the bottom line is what counts. You can't spend good intentions."

Wheat flinched.

Joan continued. "All right: if you've found something useful here, add it to your knowledge. I've been in this business for fifteen years and, heaven knows, I'm still learning." She glanced at her watch. "I'll let you all get on with your work. Wheat, could I see you in my office, please?" She kept her tone bland.

Wheat followed her employer back past the receptionist's desk and into the paneled office on the other side of the glass wall. The window blinds were still drawn. Wheat glanced at them in surprise but made no comment. Joan gestured her to a chair and sat down behind her desk.

Still the look of calm, the sense of wonder in Wheat's eyes. And that nimbus. Joan tried to ignore it. "You should be congratulated again, Wheat. Very good. Very good indeed."

"They all could do that, Joan," said Wheat softly. Her voice was pitched just loud enough to carry clearly, no more. "I'm sorry I upset them, though."

"They'll get over it." Joan found herself staring at Wheat, or rather, at the nimbus surrounding her. With chagrin, she saw that Wheat had, once again, noticed her stare, and she cleared her throat and shrugged her shoulders against the constraints of the brown blazer for what seemed the millionth time that morning. "You'll have to excuse me." She rubbed her forehead. "I'm not quite myself today."

Wheat looked concerned. "I'm sorry to hear that."

Whenever Wheat said anything, Joan noted, she seemed to mean it. While, on another's lips, the phrase *I'm sorry* might have been no more than a thoughtless courtesy, it seemed for Wheat to be an expression of sincere sympathy.

Wheat was like that. Even Joan had to admit that she had been a joy to have in the office these last two months. She was someone who honestly wished people a good morning and a good night, someone who had brought flowers to the receptionist after she had been sick, someone whose laughter sparkled in the air like a spray of water on a hot summer day. Joan wondered if that was what Wheat had meant when she had talked about love.

"Was all that true?" she asked abruptly.

"About love?" said Wheat as though she had picked up Joan's train of thought. "It was."

"Do you belong to some kind of religious sect? No offense, Wheat. I'm just curious. You don't have to tell me, of course: as your employer, I have no business asking."

"I have no particular affiliation, Joan." Calm, very calm, Much more calm that Joan felt. Much more calm, in fact, than Joan could have imagined feeling under any circumstances.

She fought with herself, with the fields and the daisies, with the nagging thought about what it would have been like to go wading that morning. Wheat knew. Joan was convinced that Wheat knew.

But she only rubbed her forehead again. "You've done well, Wheat. I certainly have nothing to complain about. But I'd like to ask you not to talk with the other counselors about what you do. It seems to upset them. You've obviously got a very personal method. Please, don't force it on anyone."

"Free will, Joan," Wheat said quietly.

"I'm glad you agree. OK, have a good day."

Wheat rose. Now she looked puzzled. "Joan . . ."

Joan had already made an effort to convey the appearance of starting on her paperwork, but she looked up.

"Did you understand anything of what I said back there?"

More than anything right now, Joan wanted to bury herself in figures, reports, percentages. Over the years of intermittent odd days, she had found that only dry numbers and sterile paperwork could hold at bay the urges that threatened to make her run out into the fields and roll among the blossoms. But she looked at Wheat and tried to be patient. "Wheat," she said, "you're a nice person, and you've got a nice way of looking at the world. Please be careful."

"I don't understand."

"Nice people get hurt."

"You think I'm naive?" There was no annoyance in Wheat's tone. It was a question, no more.

Joan only looked at her.

"I'm sorry," said Wheat, and again she sounded as though she meant it. "I didn't realize that you . . ." Her voice trailed off, and she reached for the door handle.

Unthinkingly, Joan asked the obvious question. "That I what?"

"That . . . ah . . . that you didn't . . . know."

"Didn't know? Didn't know what?" Joan looked up, straight into Wheat's eyes, straight into a reflection, a gleam, that was at once completely alien and utterly familiar. The oddness reasserted itself violently then, and she gripped the edge of her desk as if that were all that would keep her from bolting for the door. "What . . . what are you trying to say?"

The sadness was back in Wheat's eyes. "It's all right, Joan. Don't worry about it."

She left, closing the door behind her. Joan let her go.

Joan kept her eye on Wheat after that, ostensibly on the basis of her concern for office morale. But when she was honest with herself, she acknowledged that Wheat's words held a vaguely compelling mystery.

I didn't realize that you didn't know.

Didn't know ... what? Didn't know about love? What did love have to do with it? This was a business, for God's sake, not a hippie commune!

She tried to dismiss the subject, but it was not that easy. There was that nimbus, for one thing. And, for another, the familiarity she had glimpsed in the young woman's eyes. Maybe they were just side effects of the temporary and intermittent madness of the odd days, but if that were the case, then why had Wheat's words at the staff meeting corresponded with them with such disturbing exactness?

Who the hell was this woman who was working at Buckland Employment Agency?

She said nothing to Wheat, to be sure, but once or twice she pulled the woman's employee records and pored over them in her office. Joan was used to people fitting patterns, herself included. But Wheat did not fit. Anywhere. Given her background, she should have been a nice, quiet, Catholic girl who went to church on Sunday and who spent Saturday afternoons reading romantic novels. Certainly there was no intimation of someone who would take solitary camping trips in the middle of winter, create stained glass windows in her spare time . . . and give as an emergency contact a man—Hadden Morrison—whom she was neither related to nor cohabiting with.

I didn't realize that you didn't know.

"Right," Joan muttered as, once again, she closed Wheat's folder and slid it back into the files. "I don't know." And after a moment's consideration of her own chronic attacks of madness, she added: "And I don't think I want to, either."

A little less than a month later, the odd days struck once again, and, once again, desperately fighting herself, Joan drove carefully to work, parked, and hid in her office with the blinds drawn. Fortunately, there was no staff meeting that morning. Then, too, she had numbers to work with: budgets, salaries, commissions. All very banal, all demanding concentrated thought that would eventually do away with the . . . problem . . . entirely.

Or so it had been in the past. This time, near noon, her face dripping with sweat squeezed out by strain and tension, she realized that her usual tactics were not working. She was losing: the fact that she was separated from the sight of the fields outside by a fraction of an inch of opaque metal was all that was saving her from making a fool of herself.

Trembling, she got up and stumbled down the hall to the ladies' room, averting her eyes as she passed by the office windows. In the sterile, tiled whiteness of the lavatory, away from upsetting visions, she washed her face with cold water and redid her makeup, forcing herself to concentrate in what she knew was a vain attempt to banish the madness.

She did not know how she was going to get through the rest of the day. Going home was out of the question: she would have to cross the parking lot to her car, and she would lose control the moment she stepped outside. But her work was suffering severely—her work was, in fact, nonexistent—and it was pointless to try to continue.

Glancing at her watch, she realized that a half hour had gone by. She could not spend the entire day in the bathroom. She had to decide what to do.

The door opened and Wheat entered quietly. "I saw you leave the office," she said. "Are you not well?"

It was just the sort of thing that Wheat would notice, and just the sort of compassionate thing that she would do; but Joan had backed up against the wall, for once more there was an aura around Wheat, a nimbus of shimmering silver. "No," she managed. "I'm . . . I'm not well."

"Can I get you something?"

"No. There's nothing."

Gently, Wheat approached and peered into Joan's face. "How often do you have these . . . attacks?"

Joan shrugged. She did not want to discuss her bouts of insanity with anyone, particularly with someone who seemed to be so uncomfortably connected with them.

But Wheat, whether connected or not, held to her quiet and her compassion. Love? Yes . . . yes, it had to be love. "I think you'd best go home and lie down."

The honest words forced Joan to be honest herself.

"I . . . I can't make it," she admitted. She was on the verge of tears: she was sure now that Wheat knew of her weakness, and, frightening as that was, it was made doubly so by her suspicion that Wheat understood more about these days than she did herself.

"Close your eyes," said Wheat.

Wheat's tone was gentle, but her command could not be questioned. Joan felt Wheat's hand rest on her head for a moment—Oh, the temerity of it!—and felt something . . . change.

The oddness suddenly vanished.

All thoughts of temerity or touching fled in the rush of relief, but Joan was still weak and shaking, and Wheat guided her back to her office, helped her collect her things, and, despite the stares of the counselors and the openmouthed astonishment of Sandra, calmly escorted her through the outer office, down the hall, and out to her car.

"You need to go home," she said. "Lie down. Get some sleep. We'll see you in the morning."

Joan fumbled with her keys, dropping them several times before she got the door open. When she looked up, she saw care and concern in Wheat's eyes. Care and concern . . . and light.

Starlight. She knew it was starlight.

"Can you make it, Joan?"

"I don't know." Admitting again . . . cursing herself for her weakness.

"Do you want me to drive?"

Joan looked at the car. She could hardly insert a key into a lock. How, then, could she expect to drive? "I suppose you'd better."

"All right, then." Wheat helped her into the passenger seat.

And as the young woman closed the door and rounded the car to take the wheel, Joan watched her. Along with the nimbus, the familiarity was back again, and suddenly it did not seem at all strange that Wheat's employee records did not make sense. Why should they? Nothing else did.

Aside from telling Wheat where to turn, Joan spent the trip to her apartment in silence, slumped in her seat, watching the scenery pass. She had always driven herself to work and back, had never had the leisure merely to observe; and now, as they passed the small pond, she found to her surprise that although she could sense earth and sky and water with the same unnatural clarity of her odd days, she was more in control, able at last to stop fighting insane urges and appreciate what she was seeing. Yes, it was all beautiful, all just as it should be, but . . .

. . . but . . .

. . . but . . . *what had Wheat done?*

She glanced at the young woman. The shimmer about her was strong and, somehow, reassuring.

Wheat parked and helped her up the stairs and into her apartment. Joan paused only long enough to remove her shoes before she collapsed onto the bed. Wheat found a light blanket and covered her.

"Sleep," said the young woman. "I'll be in the other room if you need anything." She drew the blinds.

Joan hitched herself up on one elbow. "I appreciate

it." Her speech was slurred with strain and fatigue.
"I feel . . . strange."

"Sleep now."

Joan settled down and closed her eyes with a sigh.
"May I use your phone?"

"Uhhh . . . sure . . ." Sleep was pulling Joan along
a dark tunnel, and in the distance she could see a
faint gleaming. "Yeah," she murmured, half to
Wheat, half to the current. "Go ahead."

She heard Wheat leave the room, heard the faint
sounds of a number being punched in on the phone.
"Hadden? Hi. It's about Joan. I . . . don't know what
to do." A pause. "You don't either? Oh, dear . . ."

Well, that made three of them, Joan decided as she
let the current take her . . . and then she was floating
on a deep, quiet sea, the light of a thousand stars
above her. Something was flickering on the far borders of her memory, something to do with Wheat . . .
and with others. The memory was up in the stars,
but it would not come.

The waves laved her gently, the stars shone down.
She gave up on the memory and was content just to
drift, to float, to feel the movement of the waves as
they buoyed her up.

And when she awoke just at twilight, the dream
of floating stayed with her, bringing with it a sense
of lightness and well-being. Rubbing feeling back
into an arm that had gone to sleep, she tottered to
the window and opened the blinds. The mountains
were edged with the warm glow of sunset, and
Venus glittered brightly above the rooftop of the
apartment building across the street.

Peaceful. Very peaceful. The world seemed hushed, quiet, and for the moment there was no traffic to break the silence. Leaning her head against the window frame, Joan shut her eyes, feeling the tranquillity.

A rustle from the living room told her that Wheat was still there. "Bless her," she murmured, opening her eyes. Venus glittered again. "Maybe she's right."

She went to the bathroom and removed her smudged makeup, splashed her face with water, dried off. She felt good, better than she had in a long time. In the mirror her gray eyes were calm, her ash-blond hair tousled and artless.

Putting up her hands, she rubbed her face for a moment, then slid her fingers back through her hair. Her ears were tingling, as though she had slept oddly, which, she realized, was probably the case. Everything seemed to be happening oddly these days.

She found Wheat curled up in the overstuffed chair in the living room, a magazine on her lap. She was not reading it, though. Her eyes were on the window, and, in fact, she seemed to be looking past it, maybe even past twinkling Venus and the first stars.

"Wheat?"

The cornflower-blue eyes flicked to her. Joan saw the light in them. It was stronger now, closer to recognition. Wheat smiled. "Feeling better?"

"Much. I wanted to thank you for putting up with me."

"No problem. That's what I'm here for." Wheat smiled.

Joan smiled also. She had never before asked of an employee such a favor as she had asked of Wheat that day. It was unprofessional. It was simply not done. But Wheat was different, Wheat did not fit categories, and Joan was not at all disturbed by the fact that she had ignored her own rules. Love? Well . . . maybe. It obviously worked for Wheat. It made a charming person of her, a joy, a delight, someone who could bring comfort, seemingly, through the touch of a hand. Joan was willing to go as far as to admit that much.

The light in Wheat's eyes flashed. "By the way, you look very well."

"I'm a mess." Joan was lying: she felt wonderful, and she knew that she looked it.

Wheat set the magazine aside and stood up. "I guess I'd best be going."

"Look," said Joan. "I've probably really loused up your schedule today. I'd like to take you out to dinner to make up for it."

"No need," Wheat said quietly. "You've repaid me already."

"I have? How?"

"By being you. That's all."

"I don't . . ." That far. But no farther. Joan felt a chill. "I don't understand . . ."

"Don't worry." Wheat checked her watch. "I really have to go, Joan. I'm late for an appointment."

Joan drove her back to the agency parking lot to pick up her Toyota. Near their destination, Joan's curiosity about Wheat flared again. "Who's the lucky fellow?"

"Hmmm?"

She groped for the name she had heard when Wheat had made her phone call. "Hadden?"

"Well . . . he'll be there. Family, I suppose you'd say."

Joan glanced at Wheat. In the half light of the street lamps, the shimmer about her was even more pronounced. What had she said during that call? Joan could only recall the first few words. She pulled into the parking lot and stopped beside Wheat's car, and, unthinking, she shut off the engine. She smelled the grass in the field, heard the chirping of crickets. Wheat thanked her and reached for the handle of the door.

Then Joan remembered. "What did you need advice about me for, Wheat? What's Hadden got to do with all this?" Joan suddenly remembered that Hadden was the man listed on Wheat's employee records as an emergency contact.

"Hadden's a friend, Joan. A good friend." Wheat had turned to face her, and the starlight gleamed in her eyes. "I ask his advice about a lot of things. And he asks me."

"And what's going on?"

Wheat sat back for a moment as though weighing the question. Her next words surprised Joan. "Do you know anything about Elves?"

Joan blinked at the sudden change of subject. "Yeah. They're fairy tales. What's going on?"

Wheat watched her for a moment. "I'll see you tomorrow," she said. She swung open the door.

If this woman knew something about her odd

days, if she had anything at all to do with her hours of torture, Joan wanted to know what it was. But Wheat was already at the Toyota when she found her voice. *"Dammit, Wheat, what's going on?"* Her ears were burning. She was doubtless flushed: she had never treated an employee so rudely, never left herself so exposed, so open.

Wheat had opened the door of the Toyota, but she half turned. "I'll see you in the morning, Joan. Just give yourself some time to rest. Good night." She was not agitated. She was, in fact, completely calm. Joan's outburst, while perhaps unexpected, was obviously nothing to worry about. Joan shook with frustration and embarrassment as Wheat got in, switched on, and drove away.

She hesitated only for a moment before restarting the Mercedes and following.

Why the hell am I doing this? She waited at a stoplight a few cars away from Wheat. *I've got to be crazy.*

She peered into the night. Ahead and to the left she could see Wheat sitting relaxed at the wheel, apparently unaware that she was being followed. Agitated, Joan ran a hand back through her hair. It was none of her goddam business who Wheat was seeing that night, or why, or where. But she was following nonetheless. The same compulsion that caused her to stare at flowers and trees, that forced her to stand, shaking, before fields and the rising sun, had focused tonight on Wheat. There was, she felt, a connection. Wheat had as much as admitted it. Suddenly and inextricably, reality and her obsession had apparently twined themselves together.

The light changed, and Wheat pulled away and headed up the freeway on-ramp. Joan followed, her tires screeching slightly as she rounded the corner in pursuit of Wheat's taillights.

I-25 north, then Highway 6 westbound, towards the mountains. The valleys and ridges were invisible against the darkening sky, but there was enough twilight left to outline the topmost peaks. They passed Golden, the road wound into the foothills, and the last light left the sky as the two cars followed the twisting asphalt through tunnels and cuttings. There was no other traffic, and Joan began to suspect strongly that Wheat knew of her pursuit. But Wheat was keeping her speed constant, taking the turns and rises evenly, smoothly, and Joan pressed on after her.

Am I crazy? Her world, already touched with madness, had contracted to a pair of red taillights on a mountain road. What good was her fancy talk of sales technique now? Control a conversation? Control a client? She could not even control herself! Jaw clenched, mouth dry, she was following one of her employees into the Rockies. And what would she say to Wheat tomorrow at work? What could she say now?

Minutes went by. They had been on the road for close to an hour when Wheat suddenly slowed and took a turnoff. As the lights of the Toyota faded up along a dirt road, Joan pulled to a stop just off the highway and shut off her engine.

She was shaking. The madness had at last caught

up with her. The odd days, the compulsions, and now this. She had no business harassing her employees. Wheat had given her no real indication of any connection with her personal problems. Why, the woman had probably realized early on that she was dealing with a madwoman, and had only wanted to get away with a minimum of fuss.

Joan got out of the car and leaned on the warm hood. She had been sick for a long time. She realized that now.

The stars blazed down at her, and a glow to the east indicated the presence of the moon. Crickets chirped, small animals rustled in the brush, and a soft wind sang through the pine needles.

She put her face in her hands. Tears were running down her cheeks, and she could not stop them. But maybe tears could cleanse the sickness from her brain. Maybe that way she could go home and leave this compulsion here, at the entrance to a small dirt road.

But, through her grief, the persistence of a particular sound finally caught her attention: a motor running. Looking up, she noticed that Wheat's taillights were still in view, and that, though they were a good distance away, they were not moving.

Wheat was waiting for her.

She stared at the lights for a long moment. Once again, reality was mingling with her obsession. Silently, she got behind the wheel, restarted the Mercedes, and turned onto the dirt road.

Wheat flashed her brake lights a couple of times and started off once again, leading Joan along a narrow track that wound deep into the surrounding mountains. Fifteen minutes ... twenty minutes. Still they traveled, crawling in low gear through the starry darkness.

The road rose slightly, then fell and widened into a pancake of bare dirt. At the crest of the rise, Joan could look down and see, in the moonlight, Wheat's Toyota parked at one edge of the clearing. There were two or three other cars there also, but no sign of Wheat or anyone else.

Joan took a deep breath, and then she eased down the slope and parked among the other vehicles, shutting off engine and lights with the feeling that she was holding a loaded pistol to her head. What could she say to Wheat tonight? It seemed she was going to find out.

Silence. Even the wind had died. She waited a few minutes before she stepped out onto the hard-packed earth, but the door slipped out of her hand as she closed it, and it slammed loudly, the sound echoing off the trees as she turned around with a gasp.

"Hello, Joan."

She stared into the darkness under the trees. There was a shimmer among the trunks.

"Welcome." It was Wheat's voice.

She flushed with embarrassment, her ears burning as though touched with a glowing coal. "Hello, Wheat."

"I was kind of hoping you'd follow ... but ..."

"You were ... ?"

"... but ... well, I thought it would be best to leave the decision to you."

The moon had cleared the treetops fully, and by its light, Joan made her way through the parked cars. Near the edge of the dirt, though, she stopped, startled, even frightened, for Wheat had stepped out from the trees, and now she was standing a few yards away. She was barefoot, there was a wreath of flowers on her head, and about her was a shimmer as of starlight and moonlight wound together.

She smiled and extended her hands to Joan. "Be at peace."

Joan stayed where she was, steadying herself against a powder-blue Volkswagen. The engine was still warm. "What's going on here?" she demanded, her voice loud in the quiet night.

Wheat lowered her hands. "Going on?"

"What is this place?"

"Elvenhome." Wheat gestured at the surrounding trees. "This is it. I mean, we haven't actually *built* it yet, but that's what it is."

Joan let go of the Volkswagen reluctantly, half fearing that her legs would give way under her. "What are you talking about?" Fear was creeping up on her, and it made her voice harsh. "Elvenhome? What the hell does this have to do with Elves?"

She approached and stopped a few feet away from Wheat. Starlight and moonlight wove about the young woman. Radiance seemed to play over her.

"Wheat, what are you talking about? Elves? *Elves?*"

Wheat's eyes were calm. "We're coming back, Joan," she said. "We disappeared centuries ago, but there was a lot of intermarriage with humans over the years. Most people have some elven blood now. It's starting to wake up in some. If you're lucky, you recognize what's happening to you. Some people don't. They need to be told."

Joan felt numb, but she began backing up, moving in the direction of her car. "I don't know what you think you're saying," she whispered, "but I'll tell you this: I thought *I* was nuts. But you're even more of a fruitcake than me."

Wheat took a step forward. "Joan . . ."

"Stay away from me!" Turning, Joan fled back to her Mercedes. Panic made her fumble at the door for a few seconds before she got it open.

In a minute, she had slewed the car around and was heading back up the dirt road, tires clawing for purchase on the sharp turns, headlights bobbing like will-o'-the-wisps. When she reached Highway 6, she turned east and floored it.

She awoke before dawn in her own bed, hardly remembering how she had gotten there. The clock said four-thirty, an hour before she usually rose, but she could not sleep any more. Feeling her way in the semi-darkness, she slipped into a robe and wandered into the kitchen to make coffee.

She remembered clearly—too clearly, in fact—most of what had happened the night before. Up until she had dashed for her car, the events were, in fact, well-nigh burnt into her mind. But she had only dim recollections of her mad drive back to Denver that had, doubtless, broken every speed law in the state of Colorado . . . and, equally doubtless, most of the other traffic regulations as well. After that, her apartment. And after that, sleep. Dead, dreamless sleep.

She pulled the carafe out of the coffeemaker and replaced it with her cup, filling it as the cycle was just beginning. The brew was strong and hot, and while it cleared her head a little, there was, nonetheless, some residual fuzziness that would not go away, and her hands, gripping the cup, seemed not quite to belong to her.

Later on, in the shower, she sat down in the tub and let the water cascade over her as though she could let the previous night rinse off her like a layer of dust and grime. The water was hot, the steam warm and comforting, pressing close about her. She sighed, relaxing, half dozing off with her head resting on her drawn-up knees.

A minute later she started awake with a cry and hauled herself to her feet. She had seen a sea of stars spread out before her, glittering against a black sky. Trembling, she steadied herself against the tile wall and washed thoroughly, trying to erase the vision with soap and shampoo.

Outside, the sun was just breaking the horizon as she finished drying off and stepped to the mirror to comb out her hair. A shaft of pink and gold slipped in through the window and dazzled her for a moment. She closed her eyes and continued to work out the tangles, but behind her closed lids she saw a gleaming. Stars . . .

And still that fuzziness. Giddiness, actually. No . . . just . . . generally . . . feeling . . . odd . . .

The sun moved, the beam disappeared. She opened

her eyes, comb poised to flick her hair back over her ears.

Her ears.

She shrieked, the sound ringing through the apartment, and she fled into the living room, her hands pressed to her head as if trying to deny what her eyes insisted was the truth. It could not be. Such things did not happen.

But the touch of her fingers only confirmed it, and, after nearly an hour of hiding, she finally mustered the courage to go back to the mirror.

Her face, she realized, had also changed. She looked younger, less strained, and there was some alteration in her cheekbones that made the ears fit more naturally. There was a familiarity about herself now, the same familiarity that she had seen in Wheat. She still could not name it, but she knew it.

Too shocked to be frightened, she managed to finish getting ready, blowing her hair dry and arranging it so that it covered her ears completely. It was an unusual style for her, but it seemed to be flattering enough. She prayed no one would comment on it.

The world looked different that morning, different and yet . . . quite normal. She knew instinctively that what she saw was, for the first time in her life, what was really there. Sun on grass, blue sky patched with white clouds, the mountains to the west piling stone on stone and tree on earth. Sometime in the course of the night there might well have been a new creation, for everything sparkled as if only hours old.

At another time, she would have called it one of her odd days. Not now. It was not odd. It was, instead, perfectly reasonable, perfectly acceptable, and, after having passed by the small park with the pond every day for the last five years, she finally pulled off the road and went down to the shore for a few minutes.

On an impulse, she sat down on a bench, removed her shoes and hose, and rolled up her slacks. The sand felt good under her feet, and as the morning grew in brilliance and clarity, she waded like some graceful water bird, minnows darting about her. A light breeze ruffled her hair, and she self-consciously lifted a hand to smooth it. Her fingers brushed her ear, and she reddened at the physical reminder.

Knee deep in water, she stopped, her hand to the side of her head. The pond rippled, the rushes bent and waved, and, out in deeper water, a fish broke the surface for an instant. Somehow, she had stumbled into a perfect morning, and it was all hers.

If only it could always be like this, she thought. And it occurred to her suddenly that it could. Forever. She had only to accept—

Accept what? Madness? What had she done last night?

She swung back to the shore, wading hurriedly and nervously, her movements furtive and small. The mood was shattered, gone. The calm, the quiet . . . it had all been no more than a matter of numbing shock. She was mad, crazy; and she had always been so.

Quickly, she pulled on her stockings and shoes, pausing only long enough to work the sand out from between her toes with shaking hands. As she buckled on her heels, though, she heard someone call her name.

She nearly cried out, and furtively, and with a sense of flustered guilt, she looked around. She saw no one. She was alone. Again, though, there came the sound of her name, and it finally occurred to her that the name she had heard was not Joan.

It came once more. *Ash*. She felt suddenly cold. Her name, and yet not . . . and yet it bounced around in her ear, ricocheted inside her skull, and finally settled into some niche meant for it.

The wind ruffled her hair once again. She felt her ears in fear and stumbled to her car.

She was fairly nauseous with fright by the time she reached the agency parking lot. Everything was too bright, too clear, too new, and she gave everyone no more than a quick nod as she entered and all but ran into her office. She wished that the door had possessed a lock—or, better yet, a bar. All she could do, though, was close it, but she looked at the filing cabinet for a moment or two before deciding that it was too heavy to move.

Blinds closed, lights on. Silently, she sat down, put her head in her arms, and wept. She did not want to be crazy. She had not asked for it. She would have liked to have been normal, like everyone else. It was not her fault. It—

A soft tapping at her door. "Joan?"

Her head snapped up and she stared at the knob in fear. She could hardly tell Wheat to go away, but she did not want to talk to the young woman. She did not want to talk to anyone.

"Joan?" Wheat's voice was calm, betraying nothing. She might have been any employee with a problem or a question for her superior, but Joan heard clearly the unspoken part of her sentence: *For your sake . . . you can't afford to hide from me . . . please . . .*

Several seconds went by. Joan stared at a spot of brightness on the wall where a sunbeam had found its way in through the blinds. Wheat was leaving it up to her. She could speak, or she could remain silent. Free will.

Free will. Of course. She could make an attempt to get help, or she could hide and go silently mad. The choice was hers.

It has to do with love, she remembered Wheat saying. *That's what I'm here for. Aid. Comfort.*

She wiped the tears from her cheeks. "It's . . . it's open."

Wheat slipped in and closed the door behind her. "I'm terribly sorry about last night," she said softly.

Joan forced herself to speak evenly. "What . . . what . . . what's going on?"

Shutting her eyes, Wheat sighed as though she were almost as embarrassed as Joan. But she took a deep breath and let it out slowly, and when she opened her eyes again, there was something more in them than cornflower blue. "Did . . . did something happen this morning?"

In reply, Joan raised her hands and, very deliberately, pushed back her hair.

Wheat's voice was still quiet and calm, but Joan heard the awe in it. "It's all right, Joan. You're fine. I . . . I guess I should have warned you about that."

"Warned me about *what*? Dammit, *what*?" Joan dropped her hair and covered her face.

Wheat's voice was gentle. "Do you remember what I told you last night? There's some of the old blood in a lot of people. It wakes up sometimes, and ... well ... it ... it prevails."

Joan looked up numbly. "What are you saying to me?"

Wheat shrugged with embarrassment, but her eyes were kind. "You're an Elf."

Joan stared, then exploded. "But I don't want to be an Elf!" She gasped and clapped a hand over her mouth, her eyes going to the closed door.

Wheat looked, at once, amused, affectionate, and concerned. "Oh?"

"It's ..." Joan turned away, clenching her hands as if trying to drive her nails through her palms. "It's not right. It's crazy. It can't be happening."

For a moment, Wheat was silent. Then, suddenly: "What's your name?"

"Ash," said Joan. She realized in an instant what she had said and started to cry again. "Oh, my God ... I don't even know my own name anymore."

"But you do," said Wheat. "Many of us wind up with a new name when the blood awakens. Please, Ash. You can't deny it. It's really happening."

Joan got up, went to the window, pulled the blinds open so violently that she nearly brought them down. The field outside leaped into her, filling her with yellow sun and yellow flowers. She caught her breath. "I ... I think I need a drink."

"Ash," said Wheat behind her, "what you need is some time to think. Take the day off."

"I can't take off two days in a row."

"Yes, you can. You're the boss. Take the day off, go home, and think. Tonight, I want to take you—"

"Up into the mountains, right? To meet the rest of the loonies, right?"

"Ash—"

"Don't call me that." She closed the blinds almost as violently as she had opened them. "My none is Joan." She went back to the desk and began shoving papers into her briefcase.

"Your hands are shaking," Wheat ventured.

"I know, dammit. I know."

"Are you going home?"

"I'm going where I want to go, and it's none of your damn business." Joan picked up her purse and turned to Wheat. "Stay away from me. Just stay away."

"Ash . uh . . . Joan . . . I . . ."

"You heard me." She felt her hair catch on her right ear and freed it with a vicious shake of her head. The unfamiliar style brushed against her cheeks. Wheat offered a hand, but she knocked it away. "Back off."

She glared at the young woman, but wound up looking into her eyes, finding there . . .

. . . stars. Shining. Twinkling whitely in the firmament. A nebula glowing softly at the edge of sight.

With a small cry, Joan pulled away and ran for the door.

"Joan!"

She did not stop. Muttering something to the receptionist about an emergency, she swung the plate glass door open and made her escape.

When she reached her Mercedes, she threw her purse and briefcase into the back seat, heedless of how they might fall. She gunned the car out of the parking lot, but she was not going home.

As the mountains grew around her and the trees thickened, she realized that she had made a mistake. Her plan had been to return to Elvenhome, to confront it in the bright daylight, to do her best to stare it down. She had thought to be free in that way, to leave Wheat and her friends to their lunacy, to return herself to her occasional days that were odd but controllable.

But the impending confrontation was doing nothing to lessen her symptoms. On the contrary: it was increasing them. The trees, the sky, the mounting spires and walls of rock that now hemmed in the highway—everything was drawing her farther and farther away from what she had been. Now her hands shimmered on the steering wheel, and when, briefly, she closed her eyes, she realized that the stars were with her now, burning clearly in the firmament within her.

But she pressed on. She had no choice. The call was irresistible, and it kept her foot on the gas, her hands on the wheel, her eyes on the road that turned and twisted into the hills.

This was not confrontation. This was capitulation. She knew the turnoff instinctively, and her wheels were on dirt almost before she was conscious that she had arrived. When she reached the pancake of bare earth, it was only by an effort of will that she kept herself from getting out of the car after switching off the ignition.

About her, the trees stood straight, the ground beneath their branches shadowed. They were calling her, and it was simply a matter of how long she could hold out against their call, of how much resistance she had left.

Her hand was, in fact, already on the door release, but she heard the sound of an engine on the dirt road as a light-blue van crested the hill and descended. She slumped in her seat.

The van stopped a short distance away, and two men in Levi's and work shirts got out, opened the side doors, and began removing what she vaguely recognized as surveying equipment. One of the two waved at her, and when she gestured weakly in return, he set down a metal box and approached.

"Hello, good morning," he said, leaning his elbows on the edge of her open window. His hair was black, with hints of silver peeking through, his eyes sea gray. His smile was open, frank, gentle. "My name is Hadden."

She nodded at him nervously. "Hello."

"I . . . don't recognize you. Have you been here before?"

She shook her head abruptly, then caught herself. "Uh . . . last night. Just for a minute." She noticed that his hair was long enough to cover the tops of his ears completely.

"Can I ..." He smiled as if he understood her confusion, as if, indeed, it was something he had himself experienced. "Can I ask what your name is?"

"Ash—" It was out before she could think. "I mean ... Ash is ..."

"Ash is a lovely name," said Hadden. "It suits you."

She nodded vaguely, wondering if she would ever answer to anything else now.

"Feel free to wander around, Ash," he said, straightening up. "There's nothing here that will hurt you. Web and I are going to be doing some elevation work, so we'll be around."

"Elevation work for ... for Elvenhome?"

"Elvenhome of the Rockies, yes," he said. "The first we've had in centuries. We all put up the money to buy the land. We'll do the building ourselves, of course."

"Elvenhome of the Rockies," she murmured softly. The name was comforting, as though it filled some long-neglected need.

Hadden smiled. "We're finding ourselves again. We meet up here almost every night, just to get the feel of the place. Just to enjoy it."

Without invitation, he unlatched her door and swung it open, reaching gallantly for her hand. She looked at him for some moments, hesitating. "I ..."

"I know. Wheat told me. It's a little scary sometimes."

"You came up here for me?"

"No. We have work to do. Do you want to call it Fate?"

"I . . . believe in a Deity . . ."

Another smile. "Call it that, then."

She gave him her hand, and a moment later she was standing on the hard earth. The wind sang through the pines, the sun shone golden, and the shade under the trees was inviting. "I . . . I think I'll take a walk," she said. Bending, she removed her shoes and stockings, then dropped them on the driver's seat. Barefoot, she looked at Hadden and faltered. "I really don't know what's going on, you know."

The wind caught her hair for an instant and flipped it back. Instinctively, she grabbed it. Hadden grinned sympathetically.

"You're not going through anything that the rest of us didn't," he said. "We all had to take our walks."

She turned to face the shadows beneath the trees. She felt a hand on her shoulder.

"Be at peace," said Hadden. "Like I said: we'll be around. If you need us, just call. After all . . ." She heard the smile in his voice. ". . . we certainly should be able to hear you."

She giggled nervously, though what came out was halfway to a sob. "I . . ." She turned around to find that he was walking back to the van. "I'd just like to know what the hell's going on," she said to the empty air. But it was a foolish question, she admitted, for she knew exactly what was going on.

She moved in wonder through the forest. All about her was the delicate interplay of plant and earth, root and stone; and not only did she feel it, but she felt herself to be a part of it. She saw the patterns in the bark of trees. She saw their mirrorings in the interlacing of branches and the veins of aspen leaves. The pine needles and moss seemed to be particularly soft here, as though they were meant for the comfort of bare feet, and she glided, elven and silent, among the shadowed trunks.

With her eyes closed, she saw stars, and with them open, she saw the forest, and she did not know which awed her more. Inside and out, she had changed. She was Joan Buckland, and yet she was Ash, and, whoever the latter was, she found herself wanting more of her.

She stretched out her hand, and a bluejay alighted on it, stared at her curiously, then hopped onto her shoulder and peered through her hair for a moment before saucily tapping her ear with its beak. She laughed and blushed, and the bird craned its neck at her once more before it flew off.

Everything . . . *everything* was different. The compulsion of the odd days had fled—forever, she now knew—to be replaced by a sense of surety and calm. She sat on a fallen log, and chipmunks came to play at her feet. A raccoon waddled up and nosed her hand, wordlessly demanding to be petted. A young sparrow hawk seemed to keep watch over her from a high branch.

Green-gold, gold-green, the sunlight flashed through the pines and the aspens as she rose and made her way up a slope. She waded through a stream, the water icy and pure. It rippled through the shimmer that surrounded her, rippled through her body and mind. For a moment, she was the water itself, stretching unbroken from snowpack to sea. It swirled through her and swept her even farther away from the person she had known as Joan Buckland.

Joan Buckland. Who was that, anyway? Married, divorced, no children, running an employment agency. Controlling her business, controlling her counselors, controlling herself with a steel grip. It seemed very sad.

Free will, Wheat had said. Free will, and love, and aid, and comfort.

She stepped out of the stream and stood at the edge of the water, remembering, forgetting. With a hand to her forehead, she stared at the damp ground. *Who am I?* Her life seemed hazy, obscure, as though, with a book before her, she had forgotten how to read.

And she suddenly looked about her with eyes that were seeing everything for the first time, and the wonder that possessed her then blended with her new-found innocence and left her reeling.

"Ash." It made sense, absolute sense. Ash. Of course. Joan was in the past. Joan was gone. She was Ash. Definitely. And it ... it *was* a lovely name.

Dizzy, she climbed away from the stream and sat down at the base of a pine, content for the moment just to look at the forest. A large root arched up from the ground next to her, and she leaned against it, resting her head on her arm.

When she opened her eyes, it was dark.

Night sounds. Starlight filtering down through branches. Cool wind on her face. She was not dressed for a mountain night, but she was surprisingly warm, and it was only moments before she discovered that something large and furry had placed itself between her and the cold. Something large and furry . . .

. . . and alive.

With a gasp, she pressed back against the root. The animal was moving. Even in the darkness she could see every detail of the massive head that swung around to peer at her with two large brown eyes.

"Uh . . . hello, bear," she said.

The bear rumbled in its throat and sniffed at her. It appeared to be deliberating.

She recalled Hadden's words: *There's nothing here that will hurt you.* She wondered if he had included bears in the guarantee.

The brown eyes regarded her with curiosity, and she dropped her head inquiringly.

"Friend?"

The bear rumbled again, snuffled for a moment, then touched noses with her. Slowly, it got to its feet and prepared to move off. As she watched it, though, she realized that she had no idea where she was. She appeared to be able to see well enough in the dark, but that did not alter the fact that she did not know the way back to her car.

"Wait a minute . . . please," she called. The bear stopped, and she knelt before it. "Can you take me to Elvenhome?" she said. "I'm lost."

The bear considered, then touched noses again and walked toward the stream. She followed, her hand resting lightly on its back. Beast and Elf, they traveled through the forest together, silent, unafraid.

A shimmering came into view ahead, and the bear stopped, nosed her gently, then turned and departed into the brush. In a minute, she stood alone in a dark silence that was broken only by the drift of quiet conversation from the direction of the shimmer.

She breathed softly, taking it all in: the night, the trees, the light of moon and stars shining down through the branches, the animals. There was light about her, and stars within her, and she realized—admitted—that it could be like this forever. *Forever.* All she had to do . . .

"Ash?" It was Wheat's voice. "Ash, are you there?"

All she had to do was . . .

"Ash?"

She pushed her hair back, carefully settling it behind her ears. Yes, it could be like this forever, and with a quick glance at the stars within her, she took a deep breath and—

"Yes, it's me: Ash," she called. She saw Wheat then, barefoot, crowned with flowers. They stood looking at one another for a minute, and finally Ash smiled self-consciously and shrugged.

"I'm home," she said softly.

Please Come
to Denver
(in the Spring)

Interstate 210 in California starts off promisingly enough as a branch of the vigorous and well-traveled Ventura Freeway. It skirts the northern reaches of Burbank and plunges through the very center of Pasadena before it turns south. Route 66 continues eastward in its incarnation as Foothill Boulevard, dwindling into a two-lane street that cuts across a half-farm, half-city landscape, cow pastures interspersed with fast food restaurants: fodder for two species.

Interstate 15 heads north, leaving behind quiet and obscurely named cities—Duarte, Glendora, Azusa—and it spans the windswept Mojave Desert. You can stop for lunch in Barstow, if you wish. Lauri did. The sun was high and the twin ribbons of asphalt seemed too endless just then, and she pulled off at one of the roadside steak houses for a burger and a Coke.

The highway leads on, traveling up through Las Vegas, racing across Nevada as the shadows fall from west to east and buttes and outcroppings leave trailing fingers of darkness to prefigure the night. I-15 continues. It noses into Arizona, then tips north again into Utah. Like Lauri, you can spend the night in Saint George, the party sounds of the out-of-state hot-rodders come for a race the next day drifting muffled through the walls. If you manage an early start, you can link with I-70 by noon, on the arid plains of Utah.

And I-70 will take you through the deep-sculpted desert of that state, eerie and colorful both, and will speed you into Colorado, climb the Continental Divide, and at last, amid the pines and the aspens and the eastern foothills of the Rocky Mountains, it will bring you to Denver.

The highway continues on, of course, through Kansas and Missouri, and it, too, finally dwindles into a common street in Baltimore on the other side of the continent, where the Patapsco River mingles with the Chesapeake Bay. But if you are like Lauri, you stay in Denver, within sight of the mountains. You look for work. You try to sort out your life.

Lauri got into the office early that morning, partly because she had paperwork to catch up on, mostly because she enjoyed having her first cup of coffee away from her sparsely furnished apartment where, from across the pond that lay in the middle of the warrenlike complex, some idiot's rock and roll would already be blasting through the air, shattering the silence.

The office suite occupied by TreeStar Surveying was quiet. Carpeted in moss green and paneled in light wood, it possessed a peaceful solidity that was almost sylvan ... as though a section of sunlit forest had been scooped up and magicked into a home for a surveying firm. At times, Lauri half expected to see chipmunks skitter across the floor, and she let the pervasive tranquillity take the tension from her shoulders as she let the door swing shut behind her.

It was a small company, and, in addition to Hadden, the owner, who worked in the field with Lauri, there was Julia, the secretary, and Web and Michael, who formed another field team. Together, they were something of a family. The constant good humor demonstrated by Hadden and Web was highly infectious, and there were days when, yes, Lauri actually hated to go home.

But at present, it was still early—the rest of the family had not arrived yet—and she made coffee and settled down at her desk in the quiet solitude. Outside the plate glass window, the world was coming rapidly alive, trees breaking out in an April haze of green leaves, tentative shoots that would soon be flowers poking up above the ground. For a minute, she watched two sparrows fighting over something indefinite on the lawn, and then she turned to her work. But though the calculations before her were involved, they were not difficult, and before a quarter of an hour passed, she made her final notation, sat back in her chair, stretched out her long legs, and returned to her coffee and her window.

Trees, flowers. The land out here on the southern outskirts of the metro area was still relatively undeveloped, and though office complexes, shopping malls, and houses were making incursions, there were still many places where the softness of undulating plains was broken only by fantasy folds of sandstone and granite upthrust by the local geology. By this time next year, Lauri might well be looking at a grocery store, but for now she had an uninterrupted view of the rolling land and, rising to the west, the mountains.

For a moment, though, she recalled—even saw—another window . . . one from which she had gazed months before. It was in Los Angeles, and it had granted a view only of sun-bleached streets and the near-featureless stucco walls that were all that a combination of architectural sterility and simple parsimony had allotted to large portions of that city. Denver was still open, was still, in many ways, young.

Denver was, for Lauri, a refuge.

Her eyes left the scene of sunlight and returned to her desk. Maybe there were windows like this one in Los Angeles, but she herself had never found them. Maybe there was something there that one could shelter and call precious, but it had, apparently, escaped her. Carrie was—

Let it go.

She swallowed more coffee, concentrating deliberately on the bitter liquid in order to take her mind off the past. When she looked out the window again, she saw that Hadden had pulled up in his blue Datsun. He parked and stepped out onto the asphalt, then looked up toward the bright morning sun, stretched, and laughed.

Lauri smiled. It would be a good day. She would be in the field with Hadden, and he seemed to be in a fine mood. But she recalled that he always seemed to be in a fine mood.

Hadden strode across the lawn and took a moment to stop and admire the buds and the leaves before he continued toward the office door. On the ground, square in his path, the sparrows were still fighting, and though they ended their battle and looked up at his approach, they showed no fear. He stopped before them with a smile, and he said something.

The birds were attentive. Quite obviously they had no intention of flying off. In fact, they seemed to be glad of Hadden's presence, and when he reached down and actually petted them, they looked as though they enjoyed it.

Lauri stared, her cup halfway to her lips.

Hadden set down his briefcase and held his hands a few inches over the birds. They fluttered and fluffed themselves as though in a warm bath. After a minute, he stroked them again, picked up his briefcase, and headed for the office door. Lauri was still staring at the birds.

"I really don't believe," she murmured, "that things like that happen."

The door swung open then, and Hadden entered, his smile bright. "Hi, Lauri. Getting an early start?"

She glanced back at the empty lawn for a moment. "Uh . . . yeah. Hi."

"All ready for the Northridge job?"

Some people, she decided, had incredible talent with animals. Some people charmed snakes. Hadden obviously had a touch with sparrows. Lauri, on her part, attracted bees and wasps . . . usually with disastrous results when they found that she was not a six-foot-tall, black-haired flower. It was all a matter of vibes.

"Lauri?"

"Huh?"

"You didn't hear me?" Hadden sat on his desk and his open briefcase on his lap while he fished through the inner pockets.

"Hear what?"

"I asked you about the Northridge job and you went into a trance." He grinned at her.

As was usually the case when she was flustered, she did not know what to do with her hands. "I'm sorry . . . I—" She nearly spilled her coffee. "I was thinking . . ."

Hadden came up with a red pencil and stuck it in his shirt pocket. "No problems, I hope."

"Uh . . . no," Lauri said quickly. "What . . . uh . . . what did you do to those birds?"

"The sparrows? Oh, just gave them a little pat." Hadden sounded totally nonchalant. Such things happened every day. Sure they did.

"You have them . . . trained?"

"Hmmm? No, they were there, and they looked like they'd enjoy it."

"That's nice," said Lauri. "I wish I could do that."
One of the sparrows returned to browsing on the
lawn: hop, peck . . . hop again.

Hadden went to the windows and examined the
bird. "You might be able to learn."

"I really like things like that," she went on. "That's
why I like the field work. It's good to be able to stand
on the ground, feel the sunlight, breathe the air . . ."
She caught herself and laughed self-consciously.
"Listen to me, will you?"

"I am."

Something about his tone made her look at him in
surprise, and, as their eyes met, she saw something in
Hadden, something that shimmered, something that
gleamed in his eyes as though they were reflecting
starlight and moonlight and not simply the sun of
an early spring day. Hadden, she knew, was at least
forty, but he looked thirty, and, right now, in this
odd luminescence that seemed to be coming from
within him, he looked even younger than that.

He smiled. "Be at peace."

She blinked, and the vision was gone. But Hadden
was still smiling.

"I'm going to grab a cup of coffee," he said, "and
then we'll head on out. Should be a nice day today."

In accordance with the laws of whimsy that gov-
erned Colorado weather, the sky clouded up toward
mid-afternoon, and it was soon raining. Hadden took
the final readings while Lauri held her coat over the
theodolite: it was not pouring, not yet, but the clouds
looked very black out toward the mountains.

They were both thoroughly wet by the time they packed the instruments into the company van, and they stopped at a Burger King for coffee and a chance to dry off. Rain pattered on the roof and against the window. Hadden had pulled on a stocking cap when the wind had picked up, and he sat at the table, his hands wrapped around a smoking cup of coffee, looking like a pleasant-faced seaman examining a nor'wester kept safely behind glass.

"It's a nice day," he said softly.

Lauri glanced out the window. "OK. Whatever you say."

"Really," he said. There was a distant flash of lightning. "So . . . what do you think of TreeStar?"

The question caught her off guard. "What's . . . uh . . . what's to think? It's a great place to work."

"Enjoying it?"

"Yeah. A lot."

"Good." He swirled his coffee thoughtfully. "With many employers, there's a three-month probationary period. I don't bother with it, because my instincts are usually pretty good regarding the people that come on board. But I think this is a good time to let you know that I'm very pleased with your work. I hope you'll stay on with us."

"I wasn't planning to leave."

"Los Angeles isn't attractive anymore?"

She shrugged. "I think the only reason I stayed there as long as I did was that I was born there. There's . . . nothing for me to go back to."

"I wondered. I noticed your engagement ring

when I interviewed you, and since you hadn't been in Denver for long, I assumed your man was in L.A."

Lauri unconsciously let her left hand fall into her lap. "It's not an engagement ring. It's a promise ring. And it's ... uh ... it's from a friend."

Silence hung over the table for a few seconds. Hadden's eyes were kind. Not prying. Not predatory. Kind. "Forgive me," he said at last. "I didn't mean to intrude."

"It's OK." Maybe she should have stopped wearing the ring. But it was a link to something—someone—she wanted, and it embodied hope in ten-karat gold and a two-point diamond. And so she wore it. And so she was unwilling to discuss it.

"My apologies nonetheless," he said. "I should remember my manners."

It was not just a quick formula to gloss over an awkwardness in the conversation: Hadden sounded sincere. Lauri wondered if she was again seeing that elusive shimmer about him. "So, when are you going to show me how to pet birds?" she said, doing a little glossing of her own.

He grinned. "Next sunny day."

As she drove home that evening, she was conscious of the ring on her finger. It flashed intermittently in the light of the street lamps along Colorado Boulevard, and it caught in the lining of her coat pocket when she fumbled for the key to her apartment door.

It was all a matter of hope. She had made the long drive to another city, to another life, and she had found the courage to do it only because there was a faint possibility of a reconciliation. Sometimes people **had** to separate for a while, had to get their feet under them, had to recognize themselves as individuals before they could, eventually, return to a relationship and renew it. Carrie was in Los Angeles, Lauri was in Denver. If things worked out . . .

She cooked an omelet for dinner and ate it sitting on the floor, for she had no furniture save a mattress. Japanese flute music on the stereo competed unsuccessfully with the incessant hard rock from next door, but she had given up complaining. The telephone sat on the kitchen counter. She had not called in a month. Maybe she should try again.

She held out until bedtime, and the one-hour time difference ensured that there was no hint of desperation about the call. Carrie hated desperation. Everything had to be even, calm, *pro forma.*

Tension crawled into her shoulders in the interval between the last of the eleven digits and the click of the answer. She was a little startled: it was a man's voice. She swallowed and asked for Carrie.

Carrie was there in a minute.

"Hi, love, this is Lauri." She tried to sound happy.

"Oh . . . hello." Silence for several seconds. "What's up?"

In truth, nothing was up. It was the same day-to-day existence. Working. Eating. Long evenings spent staring out of a third-floor window at the twinkling and colorful lights of a young city. Sleeping alone. She could not say anything about that, though. *Pro forma.* "I just called to . . . to . . ."

She heard Carrie turn away from the phone for a

moment, "It's Lauri, Ron." There was a muffled response.

"I just called to talk," said Lauri when she was sure Carrie was listening again.

"About what?"

"About ... uh ... you. I just ... wanted to see how you are."

"I'm OK. Ron's over here right now. We're having a drink."

"Oh."

Silence again. Discomfort in both Los Angeles and Denver.

"Is your job all right?" said Carrie.

"Yeah," Lauri looked for words. At least Carrie had asked a question. "The boss told me I was doing fine."

"That's good."

"Have you ... have you thought at all about what I said last time I called?" It was a stab in the dark. She was not expecting much, but, really, she needed very little. Or so she thought.

"Last time? What was that?"

Lauri's mouth was dry. The conversation was going to hell, and there was nothing she could do about it. "About coming to Denver."

"Uh ... no. I hadn't."

"It's a nice city."

"I'm sure it is."

She might have been trying to climb a cliff of glass. "Well," she said when the silence had become too strained, "you might think about it. It'd be nice."

"Yeah."

"I'll . . . I'll talk to you later, then."

"Sure." Carrie hung up without saying good-bye. Lauri wondered what was going on, but felt, inwardly, that she knew.

The rock and roll faded out about midnight, and she crawled into bed. She stared at the light-stippled ceiling for several hours before sleep came.

The skies remained cloudy, and rain fell intermittently for the next week, so Hadden had no opportunity to keep his promise concerning the birds. But neither did he bring up the subject of Lauri's ring again, and Lauri was grateful for that, for it let her at least try to forget the whole sorry business while she was at work. By herself, in her own apartment, she could play by her own rules . . . and if she cried herself to sleep at night, that was, and would remain, her own affair.

But she could see that Hadden—and, in fact, everyone in the office—had noticed that something was bothering her. Fortunately, though, they did no more than speak, maybe, a little more softly to her. At least until Saturday.

The skies were clear that morning, and the sunlight sparkled on the small pond that occupied the center of Lauri's apartment complex. Lauri herself was just coming up the stairs from feeding the ducks when she heard her phone ringing. She took the stairs two at a time, missed the keyhole twice in her haste, but finally threw the door open and dived across the room.

"Good morning!" said Hadden. "I hope I didn't wake you."

"Uh ... no," she gasped. "I usually get up early ... even on weekends."

"Good! My lady and I are going up to the mountains for a picnic, and we want you to come along. How about it?"

She hesitated. "I ... don't want to intrude ..."

"Not at all. Ash wants to meet you. I've been telling her about my wonder assistant. And she's not even jealous!"

Lauri laughed in spite of herself. "Well, if you're sure."

"Of course I'm sure! We'll pick you up at nine. Don't worry about bringing anything except yourself."

And at precisely nine o'clock, Hadden's Datsun pulled up outside her apartment building. Ash turned out to be a slender, graceful woman whose blond hair matched her name. She smiled warmly and took Lauri by the hands when Hadden made the introductions. "Hello. Good morning," she said.

"Hi." Lauri wondered if she saw the same light in her eyes that she had seen in Hadden's. She looked for the shimmer, but the sun was too bright.

"Ash, do you mind taking the back seat?" said Hadden. "We have a tall lady here."

"It's quite all right," said Ash, who was looking at Lauri as though she were seeing something rare and wonderful.

"Uh ... thanks ..." Lauri could not think of anything else to say.

The drive to the mountains took them out Highway 6, and they chatted while they drove. Ash turned out to be the owner of the largest employment agency in Denver, but Lauri found it difficult to associate her quiet grace with that industry.

"You don't seem at all like the employment counselors I've met," she commented.

"I . . ." Ash smiled softly, as if looking within herself. "I did some growing up."

Hadden turned off at a small dirt road that climbed steeply at first, then rose and fell for twenty minutes or so until it opened out into a level area of hard-packed earth surrounded by forest.

Once Hadden had shut off the Datsun's engine, only the song of the wind sweeping through the tops of the pines remained to break the silence. The place reminded Lauri of TreeStar, and she wondered if the office decor had been inspired by it.

She stood at the edge of the clearing, hands in her pockets, looking up at the mountains. Ash touched her arm. "What do you think?"

"It's beautiful."

Ash had the picnic basket in one hand, and with the other she took Lauri's arm. "Come."

The three of them set off along a path carpeted with pine needles and the first blush of spring moss. Hadden and Ash had left their shoes in the car, and they padded silently along. Lauri's boots crunched an occasional twig.

The path led to a wide meadow open to the brilliant sky and studded with early spring flowers. Not ten feet away stood a deer, watching them placidly as they entered. Hadden waved at it, and it appeared to nod in return.

"It's nice to see the neighbors," he said as he spread a blanket on the ground.

Lauri was still staring at the deer. It had not moved. "First birds, now deer. How do you do it?"

Hadden grinned. "Innate talent."

And, while they ate, not only did the deer stay where it was, but they had other visitors as well. Another deer showed up, then two raccoons, several bluejays, and a sparrow hawk. The last perched on the branch of a sapling not three feet from Lauri, who, midway through a tuna salad sandwich, abruptly realized that she was involved in a one-sided conversation with it. And yet she would have sworn that the bird understood every word she said. She recalled again the sparrows outside the office, and she was not overly surprised when she turned around and saw that one of the deer was lying beside Ash, who was stroking its neck.

Lauri lifted her gaze, her eyes caught by a flash above the treetops. Beyond the trees on the far side of the meadow rose a white tower and the upper story of a building. Both were roofed in blue stone, but though the windows flashed as though polished up an hour before, she could tell that the structure was still at least partly unfinished.

She squinted against the bright sky. A filigree of silver tracery wound along just beneath the curving eaves.

"Did you want to learn about the birds?" said Ash.

Lauri's gaze came back to the clearing. The deer

was gone. And, yes, even in the sunlight, Lauri could see a soft shimmer about Ash, and there was light in the woman's eyes that was one with the cool, glistening mystery of the stars.

She was held by the vision, and it seemed to her then that she was looking beyond Ash, beyond the clearing . . . and into a realm of midnight skies filled with that crystalline light. The world dropped away. There was only the sky, the stars, the soft winds that blew—who knew from where? Sighing, she breathed the air, breathed, it seemed, the light, too; and she felt something within her respond to both, as though finally, after years of searching, she had come home.

"Yeah," she murmured, "that's nice. That's real nice."

"Good."

Ash spoke softly, but her voice brought Lauri back to the clearing. Lauri blinked. She had never really noticed how blue the Colorado sky was.

"*Killykillykilly*," cried the sparrow hawk. It had not left the branch of the sapling.

Ash grinned. "Stretch out your left arm," she said. "Invite the hawk."

Lauri was dubious. "That . . . uh . . . usually accomplishes very little."

Ash looked impish. "Try it."

Hadden was leaning back on his elbows, watching. Wondering if this were all an elaborate joke, Lauri put out her arm.

The sparrow hawk regarded her with bright eyes. "Would you . . ." Lauri felt a little silly. "Would you like to sit on my arm?"

The hawk seemed to consider, then, with a quick flick of its wings, it was perching just behind her wrist, gripping gently.

"You're . . ." The bright eyes met her own, unafraid, trusting. "You're very pretty."

The bird preened. Lauri was sure that it understood her. She looked at Ash and Hadden. "How is this possible? Things like this don't happen."

"You're a special person," said Ash. "The hawk knows that."

"Special?" Lauri's promise ring flashed in the light, bright as the eyes of the sparrow hawk. Carrie's eyes were bright, too, but the hawk's tiny eyes seemed inexplicably kind in comparison.

Gingerly, she extended her free hand toward it. "May I?"

Something about it indicated assent, and it suffered her touch.

"See?" said Ash. "It knows you won't hurt it."

It was true. How could she? After a minute, Lauri withdrew her hand. "Thank you." The hawk ruffled its feathers into place, flicked its wings again, and was back on the branch.

"Bravo." Hadden clapped his hands, and Ash dug through the picnic basket for the thermos of coffee.

In the tree, the hawk preened again. Lauri stared at it, seeing it as though through a haze of starlight.

She slept soundly that night, but her dreams were filled with the clear, diamond light of the stars. Rising before dawn, throwing open her bedroom window, she leaned out to see the first glowing arc of the sun blaze at the horizon in an aura of pink and gold. And when she went down to the pond to feed the ducks, she found them as trusting as the hawk, the newborns crawling into her lap and settling down as though in their own nests while their mothers looked on approvingly.

The colors. So bright. She had never seen colors before. Not like this. She was not sure what she had found, but she wished that she could show it to Carrie.

Lunch found her at her window, watching the pond as she ate bread and cheese and washed them down with a can of pop. Carrie, she thought, if you could only see this, you'd leave that hellhole in Los Angeles and come out here. If you could see this, we could patch everything up. You could get a job out here. We could . . .

She was already reaching for the telephone, punching in the numbers. She kept her eyes on the pond while the connection went through.

Ron answered again. He was a likable sort, but Lauri did not want to waste time. She asked for Carrie immediately, leaving Ron obviously baffled by her imperious tone.

"Hello?" came the familiar voice.

"Carrie," she said, "I want you to come out to Denver. I'll pay for it. Just . . . you gotta . . . you just gotta come out and see this place."

"I don't have time, Lauri. I'm busy." Carrie sounded maddeningly patient. She might have been explaining gravity to a child.

"It doesn't have to be next weekend. Next month,

maybe?" The pond was a mirror, reflecting the cloudless sky. "Don't blow off Denver out of hand."

"I'm not interested. Why . . . why do you keep calling like this?" There was a moment of stunned shock on both ends of the line. Carrie hastened to explain: "I didn't mean it that way. It's just . . . it's . . . uh . . ."

No, she did indeed mean it that way.

"It's . . ."

Lauri came out of her shock, sagged. "It's . . . it's OK." The pond was receding, turning from mirror into foul, algae-choked puddle. "Never mind. I understand."

But Carrie exploded suddenly. "No, you don't. You never understand. You take everything personally. You're always trying to turn yourself into a goddam martyr. I'm sick of it. If you don't want to talk reasonably, don't call."

"Carrie, I—" But the connection was broken. Feeling cold, feeling limp, Lauri drew the drapes. Martyr? Was that it? She was not sure. Maybe Carrie was right.

The pop went sour in her stomach, and she dumped the rest of the can down the drain and put the bread and cheese away. Stupid. It was, after all, just a pond.

And the hawk was just a hawk, and the stars were . . .

She was still, she realized, slightly in shock. Since she had left Los Angeles, she had always clung to a faint hope upon which she could hang a future. But hope and future were both gone now. Carrie had hung up. The receiver had come down with a finality that resembled the closing of a tomb.

She arrived at work ridiculously early the next morning, but she had not slept at all, and she saw no point in fidgeting through an additional hour in her apartment. Once in the office, she made coffee, but she gulped down a cup of the brew without being aware of it.

Three years . . . more than three years. More like four. It was always Lauri and Carrie, Carrie and Lauri. Maybe it had not been all good, but surely it had not been all bad either. They had gotten on each other's nerves upon occasion, and they had fought upon occasion—just like any two people who had decided to live together—but they had also shared joy and laughter. Right now, Lauri was remembering the joy and the laughter. It did not seem right that all the joy and laughter could be negated by the click of a broken telephone connection.

Why do you keep calling like this? It seemed that, in an unguarded moment, Carrie had let the truth show through, and Lauri recognized it as surely as a jeweler could tell diamond from cut glass.

And so that was it. She was alone now. Her hope had been a thread that had tied her life to another's. It was broken now, and she was adrift. Denver suddenly seemed strange, alien.

She did her best to calm herself when the others arrived, tightening down the bolts on her despair, keeping her voice even. She and Hadden went out into the field, but the interior of the van was a study in silence during the drive up to Northridge.

Hadden's face was grave, and he watched her carefully throughout the morning. Around noon, he called her over. "Want to get lunch?"

"I don't really feel like eating."

"You need to put something in your stomach."

"I'm afraid I'll throw up."

They were in the middle of a field, and there was no one else about for hundreds of yards. "Do you want to talk about it?"

"I can't." A hornet buzzed by, and she flinched, but the insect circled once and left her in peace.

Hadden shoved his pencil into his pocket and pushed up his sunglasses. "Lauri, I'm your employer. I'd like you to consider me your friend too. I don't invite just anyone on a picnic with my beloved."

"I ... I just can't talk about it, Hadden." She turned half away. She felt cold, but she could not tell if it was the wind or the lack of food. Hadden sized her up, frowning slightly.

"Is it because you're gay?" he asked suddenly.

She stiffened. "How did you know? I thought I played the straight game fairly well."

"Feelings. I pay attention to them."

"When do you want my resignation? Or did you want to fire me?"

Hadden capped the theodolite before he spoke. "I thought you knew me better than that, Lauri. I want neither. I want a fully functioning employee. I find you in the office looking like one of the living dead and you insist that nothing's wrong."

"What is this? Charity for the lezzie?" she said with bitterness. Yes, she knew exactly why Ron had been answering the phone.

"Whatever it is that's hurting you, Lauri, you're going to have to let it go. You can't live like this."

"Hadden, it's no one's business but my own. I'm not going to pester everyone in the world with it. I'm not some kind of whining fluffball."

"I know you're not." Hadden's eyes were, once again, reflecting that light, intimating the stars. "But sometimes we need a little help." He spread his hands. "That's why we're here. To help each other."

She snorted nervously. "Now, I suppose, you want to tell me about Jesus."

Hadden stared for a moment, then laughed. "No," he said. "I'm going to buy you a bowl of soup."

"I don't want to talk about it."

"That's OK ... fine ... but try the bowl of soup, please."

Hadden found a coffee shop about ten minutes away that was not overwhelmed by the noon rush, and he politely but firmly asked the hostess for a quiet booth in the back. Lauri did not say much of anything, but sat down, ordered a bowl of vegetable soup, and buried her face in her hands.

"I'm sorry, Hadden. This is ridiculous. If I can't handle my personal life better than this ..."

"We all have our breaking points," he said simply.

And in spite of her reluctance, she told him a little about what was happening. About Carrie, the four years, the small, shabby apartment in Hollywood ...

"So I came out to Denver when it really started to

fall apart," she finished. "Trial separation, if you want to call it that. I thought . . . well . . . I *hoped* that Carrie would join me here after a while."

Hadden nodded. "And yesterday she told you to forget it."

"Yeah." The promise ring glinted mockingly. She had not been able to bring herself to take it off.

The waitress brought their order, and when she had left, Lauri stared at the bowl of soup as though it were an enemy. "I can get through it," she whispered.

"I know you can."

Despite her words, though, the sorrow overwhelmed her, and she choked, bending her head, clenching her eyes shut. But Hadden took her hand, and after a moment, in the darkness behind her closed eyes, Lauri suddenly saw a shimmer . . .

. . . and then the stars came out.

She stared at them for what seemed many minutes, drinking in their clarity, their calm, their strength. It was only after she had, with their help, fought down the sobs that she asked: "What am I seeing, Hadden?"

"The stars."

"Where am I?"

"Within yourself."

She opened her eyes. "What the hell are you doing to me?"

Hadden shook his head. "I'm not doing anything to you. It's just happening. Maybe it's happening a little faster than usual because you've been around me and Ash, but we've been doing nothing except waiting."

"Waiting for what?"

He watched her for a moment as though weighing his words. "For you to see the stars, Lauri."

"OK. I see them. What's going on?"

"You're growing."

"Don't play games with me."

"I'm not. I told you you're growing. Everybody does in one way or another. Some people take a different turnoff than most, that's all."

She recalled the turnoff that Hadden had taken on the day of the picnic. She had not even noticed it until he was already off the highway. And it had led to . . .

"And what turnoff am I taking?" she said.

He pursed his lips, thought for a moment, then: "Eat your soup," he said. "Look how your hands are shaking."

"My hands are fine." But when she looked down and saw that Hadden was right, she relented and picked up her spoon. "I am an adult, you know."

Hadden's eyes twinkled. "Really? My sympathies. It must be terrible."

At least he had taken her thoughts away from Carrie. And, in fact, he continued to do so, for while they ate, he kept the conversation on simple, immediate things so that Lauri could, at least for the time being, avoid thinking about her former lover. But even when her thoughts managed to stray to Carrie, the starlight that continued to gleam just at the borders of her inner sight made them easier to deal with, and that grace allowed her better to accept its luminous presence without questioning Hadden further. It was a good thing ... whatever it was. She would figure it out later. For now, she contented herself with her newfound stability and calm.

When they left the coffee shop, Hadden pulled the company van out of the parking lot and headed in the direction of the freeway. Lauri looked at him curiously. "Aren't we going the wrong way?"

"In case you hadn't noticed," he said, taking the on-ramp, "we finished the job before lunch. I'm going back to the office."

Lauri settled down and watched the buildings pass by. Having said, in spite of herself, more than she had wanted to, she was disinclined to talk. Hadden and the stars had pulled her out of her shock, true, but now she felt alone. She supposed that it was something she would have to get used to. Funny, though, how four years of companionship made it difficult to contemplate a lonely future.

But she had survived before Carrie, and she would, somehow, survive now. The stars were nice. Something to fill the emptiness, something—

"What do you know about Elves, Lauri?" Hadden said quietly as he drove through the mid-afternoon traffic.

She continued to watch the passing buildings, the other cars. "Not much. They're either little and magical and sit on mushrooms, or if you like Tolkien or fantasy games, they're tall and whack people with swords."

He laughed. "Yes, that's the general opinion, isn't it?"

"Something you know that I don't?" She turned to face him. Hadden stepped on the brake and slowed the van a good three seconds before a convertible darted across two lanes directly in front of them. "Nice."

"Thanks. Innate talent."

"That's what you said before. But ... what about the Elves ... ?" Suddenly, it seemed important that she ask.

"They really existed, Lauri. Right alongside humans. For thousands of years. That's how all the old stories got started. They were, well, sort of magical, but they didn't sit on mushrooms. And they didn't usually go around whacking people, either."

"How ... uh ... how do you know this?" Lauri was puzzled. Hadden did not seem the sort that was given to bouts of fantasy.

"Research. Experience."

Experience? "So ... what happened to them?" Playing along with him. It was the least she could do, she supposed. "Did they die out?"

"Sort of. Most of them faded during the Middle Ages. But some ... well, some had intermarried with humans."

"Yeah. OK. Interesting theory." His conviction was making her uncomfortable. She rather wished that he would drop the subject.

"It gets even more interesting," Hadden continued. "The gene pool is a convoluted thing indeed, and, by now, everyone in the world has a certain amount of elven blood. Recently, it seems, it's started to wake up in people."

This was going well beyond Lauri's ability to maintain even a courteous suspension of disbelief, but as he had been kind to her, so she contented herself with, "Hadden . . . you're weird."

He grinned at her. "Isn't it great?"

When they finally arrived at the office, Hadden sent her home. The day's field work was finished, and he could easily take care of the paperwork himself. Lauri did not argue: the food had dealt with a part of her weakness, but she needed sleep, too. Hadden took her out to her car and made sure she could drive herself home.

"Wait a minute," he said after she had started the engine. He pulled a business card out of his wallet and scribbled on the back. "Here's my home phone number, and Ash's, too. If you need help, call us."

She looked blearily at the numbers on the card. "You think I'm having some kind of breakdown? I'll be all right. Really."

"It's not that. I'll feel better knowing you can reach us if you have to."

"Yeah . . . sure . . . well, whatever you say." She slipped the card into her pocket and pulled out of the lot.

Winding through the upper-class housing developments with their careful landscaping and ironclad covenants, the drive home was uneventful save for an occasional sports car driver who wanted to get somewhere—anywhere!—ahead of everyone else; and when Lauri got into her apartment, she threw off her clothes and crawled into bed. Most of the other inhabitants of the complex were at work, and she drifted off without a rock and roll accompaniment.

The stars surrounded her immediately, washing her in gleaming luminescence. Strangely, though, she knew she was asleep. She had perfect, lucid consciousness of her condition, but she decided that, for now, dreams were infinitely better than reality, and so, wherever she was, she put her hands behind her head and stretched out as though she were sunbathing. As before, she felt the light soak through her. As before, she responded to it, and she was content.

She might have been in that other place for many hours when, faintly, she heard a sound. She opened her eyes. She was in bed, and the phone was ringing. The clock said that it was near midnight, but the phone continued to ring, and she hauled herself up and ran for the kitchen.

"Hi, sweetheart," came the voice. It was Carrie.

What? The stars swam around her, and she realized that she had not turned on the lights. She wondered if she were still dreaming, but dismissed the thought. "Uh . . . hi . . ."

"I wanted to see how you were . . . how you were doing."

"I . . . uh . . . OK. What's going on?"

"I didn't mean to yell at you the other day."

What?

"I'm sorry I can't come out to Denver. I'm really busy at work. I can't take the time."

Can't take the time? Lauri had asked about a weekend. Diamonds and cut glass. Diamonds and cubic zirconium.

The stars hung in the dark room, blazing at her when she closed her eyes, shimmering faintly when she opened them. She was not groggy, but she was not exactly conscious either. "I understand," she said quietly. "It ... sounds like you've got something going now with Ron, and ... that's just the way it works out. Or doesn't work out, depending on where you are." There was no accusation in her voice, no despair. It was calm understanding. It was the starlight.

For a moment, there was silence from Los Angeles, then: "What kind of a crack is that? What did you expect, running off to Denver like you did?"

"Running off? Sweetheart, we talked about it. We agreed on this kind of separation, and you thought it would be good to join me here if we patched things up."

"I only said that because I knew you wanted it." Carrie was being maddeningly patient again.

"Wanted it? I wanted to stay with you."

"I *like* Los Angeles."

"Then why did you agree—?"

"I just told you."

Lauri fumbled. They had agreed. It had seemed so straightforward at the time.

She felt confused, flushed. Her face and her ears were burning. She bit her lip. "I ... I didn't see it that way," she managed.

"Well, if you can't handle reality, I can't help you.

I ran interference for three years, and I'm not doing it anymore."

"What do you mean running interference? I supported you for half that time while you went to school!"

"You're going to have to get used to this, Lauri."

Anger balled itself into a hot coal in her brain. "Look," she said, "I'm flying out to the coast. I want to talk to you. No more of this telephone crap. Just you and me. We've got to settle this."

"What?"

"I'll be out tomorrow. I'll come by the apartment after you get off work."

"But—"

"See you then." She hung up without waiting for an answer. She knew Carrie would be there when she arrived. It was not like her to run from a confrontation. At least not physically.

She called Hadden from the airport the next morning and explained that she would not be in to work that day. She also told him why. "I'm sorry," she said. "I've got to do this. If you can't keep me on at TreeStar, I understand."

"I'll see you in the office when you get back," was his response. "Don't worry about the time. There's no problem. Good luck."

United Airlines had been obliging enough to have a seat available, and she had put the fare on her credit card without even considering what it would do to her budget. She did not care. She was at the gate three hours early and sweated through two arrivals and departures before her flight came up.

When she had boarded and buckled in, though, she realized that, during the last several hours—since, in fact, she had hung up on Carrie—she had missed the stars. As the plane taxied, therefore, she sighed and closed her eyes, turned inward, looked for them. Faintly at first, but then flashing into full brilliance, they appeared.

She relaxed. She had been angry, agitated, and she had lost them. Or rather, she had ignored them. They seemed always to be present, now ... if she was willing to look.

She kept her eyes closed as the 737 picked up speed. The stars soothed her, comforted her. She laughed quietly at Hadden's story about the Elves. She was sure that he had made it up to take her mind off her worries. What a guy. What a boss! Hadden was one in a million. And so, she was certain, was Ash. Lucky people they were to have found one another.

Airborne. Wheels up. The plane climbed, banked, and climbed again. Lauri kept her inner vision on the stars, and, lulled by the quiet light, sank into a half trance. She could feel her body, the plane around her, the moving currents of air that rushed past the fuselage. She could even feel the earth beneath her, the earth that was by now thousands of feet away, the earth that was rolled and convoluted in the forested wilds of the Rocky Mountains.

Wood, stone, water. And about her, the rushing air. And within her, the stars. She was picking out variations now: an oddly shaped cloud, a hawk—maybe a sparrow hawk—flying below, a particular lake and a whitewater river flowing toward the lowlands. For an instant, among the stars, she saw it clearly, in perfect and precise detail. Curious as to what she could see physically, she opened her eyes, leaned toward the window, and looked down past the gleaming wing. She froze, then, and her clenched teeth barely contained her cry.

It was all there, just as she had seen it among the stars, but now there was more. Much more. Infinitely more. The starlight mingled with her physical vision, and she was suddenly connected with what she saw, as though, like the stars, it were within her. She had contemplated the stars, had touched in friendship a sparrow hawk, but now she was abruptly one with an immense expanse of land and water. The sun warmed her, rivers flowed across her, and she was aware of the imponderably slow changes wrought within her by the days and the years. Her trees rose up, lifting sun-warmed branches toward the skies. Within her, deep within, at the dark, quiet roots of her mountains, there was life, and growth, and she knew the eternally renewed potentials that she could manifest.

The vision overwhelmed her in an instant, and tears were running down her face by the time she pried herself away from the window and closed the shade.

There was no one in the adjoining seat to notice, but a steward was passing by just then. "Can I get you something, miss?"

She looked up at him, and, just for a moment, just for a microsecond, she really saw him, total stranger though he was, and she knew him. She saw his life as a unit, as something whole and complete, and she knew the sorrows and the joys that wove through it—the college degree he had given up because his girlfriend had become pregnant, his grief when the child was stillborn, the small apartment in Idaho Springs—knew everything, and looked through his eyes and saw herself in tears at something she could not understand . . .

The vision faded. She blinked at him.

"Maybe . . . maybe some coffee," she whispered.

The coffee—hot, bitter, homely—grounded her into a more conventional reality. She finally looked out the window again to find that the landscape was now landscape and no more, and she realized that it had been the stars that had given her that small glimpse of infinity, that, in fact, she could repeat the experience if she wanted to.

Hadden had said that she was growing. But growing into what? Hadden . . . Ash . . . both of them bright with some undefined radiance, the light of the stars shining in their eyes. Web too . . . she had seen it in Web. She was *sure* she had seen it in Web.

She was still shaking. Deliberately now, she closed her eyes, found the stars, and let them calm her, but this time she kept her awareness to herself. Whatever was happening, it appeared that she could control it to some extent. Opening her eyes, she stared at the back of the seat ahead of her, sighed.

Burbank Airport was small, compact, and reasonably efficient. By midmorning, Lauri was on the familiar Los Angeles freeway system in a rented car. Carrie would be at work—she had six or seven hours to kill—and after grabbing an early lunch, she headed up the coast.

Eleven o'clock on a Tuesday morning: traffic was light. She cruised along the coastal highway until the beaches were isolated and sandstone cliffs and scrub formed a backdrop for the road. Eventually, she pulled off onto the gravel and climbed down the incline to the sand. The place was familiar: she had been there before. Which argument had it been that time? Money? No, too common. Careers? That was more likely. Something abstruse, something about which one could vent one's anger delicately, *pro forma*, without getting too involved.

She remembered that there was a hollow under a rock outcropping that was dry at low tide. She had curled up there once, wondering what it would be like to let the waves come in, little by little, the water rising higher . . .

But it was high tide, and so she sat on the warm sand and watched the breakers. Yellow sun. Golden sand. Blue water. They all looked slightly different from what she remembered. The colors were brighter, more intense. Details were sharper. She looked at a tangled strand of kelp and saw the intricacy of the pattern it formed as it sprawled half in and half out of the water. The stars were still with her, she realized, and she could not but wonder what would happen to her now if she let them take her as far as they had on the plane.

Her hands, resting on the sand, tensed. She might not come back. It was frightening ... but it was tempting, too.

But she was not going to run away. She would confront Carrie that evening, in the living room of the shabby apartment they had shared for forty-three months. There had to be a distinct ending to their partnership. Even a corpse needed a signed piece of paper and a funeral to qualify as being legitimately dead.

The wind came in, warm and fresh and smelling of salt, and Lauri was strongly tempted to discard her clothes and plunge into the water. But she stayed where she was, knees half drawn up, hands clasped around her legs, hair tangling in the breeze. She had not been to the coast in months, and she was drinking it all in, just as, even now, she was letting the starlight inundate her, little by little, rising higher ...

Her face and ears were burning again, and she shut her eyes, dropping into the night sky that she now carried within her. The ocean flowed, the stars shone, the wind roared.

Inundating her, rising higher.

When she became aware once more, the sun was blazing into her eyes, the horizon on fire with the reds and golds of sunset. She gaped at it. Had she been asleep? Hastily, she checked her watch, and it confirmed that she had lost the entire afternoon. Thinking back, she could remember the stars, and that was all: one long, continuous dream of starlight.

She got up, less stiff than she expected, and made her way along the beach, up the stony incline, back to her car. Her steps were firm and sure, but she felt odd, as though she were not quite at home in her own body, and when she slid behind the wheel and closed the door, she looked at her hands. They were exactly what she expected ... but not quite. She could not say what it was at first, but as the sun set and the shadows fell, she saw, faintly, a soft shimmer. And it did not stop at her hands.

Growing ...

She drove south to Malibu, stopped at a gas station, and used the rest room. The fluorescent glare brought with it a harsh sense of reality, but it did nothing to mask the shimmer that had, seemingly, become one with her flesh. And as she washed up, she noticed that she looked younger, less strained.

Less strained? What the hell was going on?

She found the pay phone outside, fed it coins, and dialed Hadden's home number, grateful now that he had given it to her. He caught it on the second ring. She could have sworn he was expecting the call. Perhaps he was.

"Hadden? Lauri here."

"Yes?" How did he manage to put so much reassurance into a single word?

Confronted now with actually having to talk about it, she nearly collapsed into blubbering, but the stars upheld her, and her voice was, even to her own ears, surprisingly controlled. "What's ... what's happening to me?"

"Talk to me."

"I just blanked out most of the day staring at the goddam ocean, and now I'm *glowing*."

Silence for a few seconds. Then: "It's a little hard to talk about it over the phone—"

"Well, you're going to have to, because I can't teleport back for a guest appearance in Denver. At least not yet. Give me a few more days." She held up her hand. The streetlights were making the shimmer more distinct. She suddenly worried that people might notice. But no: she had not noticed Hadden or Ash. At least not before.

Before? Before what?

"Relax, Lauri. You're fine."

"Fine. Sure. I've got enough stars inside my head to keep Palomar busy for a year, and you say I'm fine."

"Are you frightened?"

"Ask me when I'm not so scared."

More silence. She could almost hear Hadden weighing his words.

"Lauri," he said at last, "do you remember what I was saying about the Elves?"

"Yeah. What about it?"

"It was true. I wasn't joking."

The words spun in her head. "Tell me exactly, Hadden," she said. "Try to keep it simple. I'm not thinking too clearly right now."

"OK. Close your eyes. Find the stars."

She did so. Her thoughts slowed, calm returned. "Right. It was true. So tell me."

"Lauri," he said softly, "you've got the blood. It's

waking up in you. When it wakes up, it takes over. It's changing you."

She stared through the glass walls of the phone booth. Traffic. Bluely glowing streetlights. Glistening ocean.

"Lauri?" Silence. "Lauri?"

"I'm ... I'm here. I'll be all right." She found the stars, breathed deeply, was surprised that she was not shaking. "Is there anything I should ... like ... do?"

"Just be gentle with yourself. Stay calm. You'll probably notice some ... physical changes along the way."

She felt her smooth face. "I have. I look about eighteen."

"There will be more. If you run into trouble, find the stars and let them settle you. Call Ash or me at need." He paused. "I wish I were there with you."

"It wouldn't help," she said, still watching the traffic. "I have to go it alone."

"Have you seen Carrie yet?"

"I'm on my way there now."

When she had hung up, she went back to the rest room and brushed out her wind-tangled hair. It was then that she saw that Hadden was right about the physical changes. She stared for a few minutes, heart beating in fear, and then she found her stars and finished her hair, arranging it so that it covered her ears completely.

Time—even six months—gives perspective, changes viewpoints; and when Lauri turned off Old Cahuenga Boulevard and onto the dark side streets that wound, maze-like, into the Hollywood Hills, she found that what had once been familiar and common was now laden with a sense of distance. She did not live here. She was but a visitor, one who would stay for a few minutes and then depart, taking these same dimly lit streets down to the bright thoroughfares once again ... going off to wherever it was that she called home. And when she parked and stepped out onto the dry grass that divided the street from the sidewalk, the feeling became even more distinct: the apartment building, the cars, the scrubby trees—everything about her was trapped somewhere between the familiar and the strange, as though she could neither claim it as her present nor let go of it enough for it to become mere memory and nothing more.

She shook her head at the sensation. Above, the stars were almost washed out by the city lights and the smoggy air, but they were burning brightly within her.

She used her old key to let herself in through the security door, and she padded up the hall, her footfalls all but silent. As had been the case on many other nights—nights now months past—she smelled the dinner of the old Korean couple in the front apartment. Fish, garlic. Whether she lived in Denver or L.A., whether an ancient blood had come alive in her or not, this life would continue.

Before she knocked on the door, though, she paused, head down, thinking. This was her past. This was only her past. She lived in Denver now, in a different climate, among different people, leading a different life. And now those differences had been augmented infinitely. Did she have any business here at all? For her, Carrie was gone. It did not matter anymore.

But Carrie had, it seemed, sensed her presence, and she opened the door while Lauri stood pondering. She was dressed casually, and her light hair was caught back on one side with a cloisonné comb that Lauri did not recognize.

After looking at her for a moment, Carrie turned and went back into the apartment. She left the door open behind her. Lauri hesitated, then followed.

The odor of fresh paint hung in the living room. Furniture had been moved around, and there were two new pieces of art on the wall.

Carrie stayed on the far side of the room. She was regarding the rug as though burning words into it. "Well, now that you blew a bunch of money coming out here . . ."

The stars were bright . . . and growing brighter. Lauri could see the shimmer about herself plainly. In an instant, she felt the apartment, how it had changed: the different bedspread in the other room, Ron's suits and ties hanging in the closet, the rack of elegant wines in the kitchen. She felt tranquil, and that surprised her . . . or maybe it did not. Odd how the stars changed things . . .

Carrie was glaring at her now, and Lauri found that she had to laugh softly. "I didn't blow anything."

"It's not going to help. I gave you my answer. I won't let you interfere with my life."

Lauri took an experimental turn around the room, noticing the difference the starlight made. True, it was a shabby apartment, but it had its points, and she could, even now, remember the joy and the laughter that had, at times, filled it. "I think you can take a few minutes for me without calling it interfering."

"I'm not coming out to Denver."

"That's all right. It's not necessary."

Carrie stared. Lauri wondered if she had seen the shimmer, but decided that it had more likely been her tone of voice. Factual. Exceedingly *pro forma.* "Then why the hell did you come out?"

Lauri's world grew. She could sense the apartment building with its rooms and its people, the street outside where her rental car was parked, the vast, sprawling, pulsating city that tumbled down the mountains and stopped only when it reached the sea . . .

She let the awareness pass, focused instead on Carrie. "I came here to say good-bye. That's all. It was nice while it lasted, and we were good for each other for a while, but I know, and you know, that it's over. And I just wanted to let you know that I understand. And if I caused you pain, I'm sorry. And that's all."

The stars shone. Lauri watched Carrie struggle with the words, and while she watched, she suddenly saw her and knew her just as she had seen and known the steward on the plane. It was an intrusion, she knew, and she pulled out of the vision immediately, but not before she had felt the fear in Carrie, and the need for security, and the deep sense of isolation that a lesbian relationship had inflicted upon her.

Carrie had clenched her fists in preparation for an outburst, but then she appeared to change her mind. "I . . . I didn't know what you wanted."

"I don't want anything."

"You've . . . changed."

"I guess so." Lauri shrugged. She was thinking longingly of Denver, of the mountains and the pines and the aspens, and of a certain meadow surrounded by trees . . .

She remembered the sparrow hawk. Unafraid. Trusting. Its eyes had been as bright as the promise ring that now burned on her finger.

Slipping the ring off her hand, she laid it on the coffee table along with her old keys. "So, I'll see you later," she said. "Take care."

For a moment, Carrie looked at the ring, and then she bent, picked it up, held it in her palm. Lauri crossed the room in silence and let herself out, but she paused for a moment at the open door. Carrie was still standing by the table, the ring in her hand, her slender figure seemingly a part of the furniture and the pictures and the books: a memory—only a memory—of a time when there was no starlight in the world.

The Shadow of the Starlight

August was hot, as was typical for late summer in Denver. In the morning, the sky was blindingly blue, with a yellow sun climbing above the flat horizon that looked out onto Kansas. The sun raised the temperature, and it raised also the tall thunderheads that would, come mid-afternoon, bring a foretaste of steaming dusk to the city and leave it simmering as though under the lid of a pot.

And as Lauri pulled the company van into the parking lot outside TreeStar Surveying, she discovered once again that Elves did not sweat.

She parked the van and ran her fingers along her hairline. Not a trace of moisture. Just the soft shimmer of starlight that was one with immortal flesh, visible only to immortal eyes. It was unnerving. She wondered if she would ever get used to it.

She wiped her dry fingers on her Levi's out of old, human habit, and, with a flick of her head, settled her dark hair over her ears, covering them for the benefit of the new secretary. Amy had been with the company for only a few weeks and did not yet know that she was working with a myth. It was somewhat difficult to decide on a way of telling her.

Lauri swung open the door into the air-conditioned office, glad that she did not have to worry about that particular problem. That was Hadden's department.

Hadden owned the company. He, too, had to keep his ears covered.

Amy was blond, with blue eyes, and as usual, she was fighting with the computer as Lauri strode into the room. Lauri waved to her on her way back to Hadden's desk.

Hadden looked up at her approach.

"Bloomfield's happy," she said.

"Good." He leaned back in his chair. "How was the drive?"

"You will notice," she said, fluttering her work shirt, "That I am . . ." The fluttering was doing nothing. She was dry. And reasonably cool, too. She had perceived the heat, she realized, but it had not affected her. ". . . uh . . . that I would be sweating under . . . uh . . . other circumstances."

Hadden smiled.

"A lot." She fluttered her dry shirt again. Very unnerving. "When do we get the air in the van fixed?"

Hadden's gray eyes twinkled: a just-perceptible flash of starlight. "It's a pretty old van. You think we really need it?"

Lauri made a wry face. The phone began to ring, and Amy picked it up. "Probably doesn't matter," she said. "But please: no more two-hour trips."

"Shouldn't be necessary. Bloomfield has his elevations, right on schedule, and that should settle it."

"We could skip the air and put in a stereo," Lauri offered. "Honestly, the boredom will kill you faster than the heat. That is, if the heat ... uh ..." She looked chagrined. "Well ..."

"Lauri," Amy called. "It's Mr. Bloomfield. Line one."

Hadden gestured at his telephone. "Be my guest."

Puzzled, Lauri punched in the line and picked up the handset. "This is Ms. Tonso," she said. She listened for a minute, her lips pursed. Then: "I'll take care of it immediately, sir." There was an edge to her voice that even she could hear, and when she hung up, Hadden looked at her curiously.

"Problem?"

The drive out to Golden and back had been long and tedious, and the heat, though it had not produced any sweat, had nonetheless shortened her temper. Lauri did not like it. Not at all. Closing her eyes, she took a deep breath. There was a sky full of stars within her, and she could see them now, surrounding her, floating in the velvety blackness. She took their light in along with the air she breathed, let them calm her, let the anger seep away.

When she opened her eyes, the edge in her voice was gone: "The graphs and tables were missing from the report. Now, I saw them first thing this morning, just after Amy got through printing them. I suppose they're around here somewhere."

Amy approached, a folder of papers in her hand. "Is this what you're looking for?"

Lauri took it, riffled through its contents. "Yeah. But what are they doing here?"

There was an embarrassed smile on Amy's face. "I thought ... I thought we were supposed to keep them here. File copies? So I took them out of the report."

Silently, Lauri looked at her, then at Hadden, then down at the telephone, then finally at the plate glass windows that gave out upon the sizzling parking lot.

"Did I do something wrong?" asked Amy in a small voice.

The young woman was frightened. But two weeks on the job, and she had fumbled badly. Nor was this the first time: there had been misfiled pages, missent letters, checks and bills that had, seemingly of their own accord, crawled off into other dimensions. Lauri figured that Amy fully expected to be fired on the spot.

But: "I'll just run out to Golden again and give Bloomfield the pages," she said. Her voice was calm and firm, almost cheerful. She met Amy's eyes. "Easy there."

Amy's blue eyes were moist.

"It's OK, Amy," said Hadden. "We'll handle the rest. Just check with the field team in charge of the measurements before you take anything out of one of their reports."

Amy was still staring at Lauri. A single tear was winding down the side of her nose, leaving behind it a streak of mascara.

Without thinking, Lauri reached out and laid a hand lightly on Amy's shoulder. The young woman flinched as though she expected to be struck. "It's all right," said Lauri. "Really. No problem." The stars were still with her, leaching away any anger she might have felt, and she suddenly noticed that the blue of Amy's eyes had deepened.

Something flashed there, just on the edge of sight. Lauri caught her breath and quickly removed her hand.

"I'll . . ." Amy fumbled for words, wiped at her eyes. "I guess I'll get back to work. I'm sorry. I'll try to do better."

"Be at peace," said Hadden as she went back to her desk.

Lauri was still wondering what she had seen. "I don't understand."

"Now you know how it happens," said Hadden softly, and Lauri, startled, looked at him . . . and met eyes that flashed starlight.

Now you know how it happens. The words were still with her ten miles later when she took the on-ramp to westbound Highway 6 and headed out to Golden. She had not asked Hadden what he had meant, but she suspected that she knew.

She herself had not always been elven. Four months ago, in fact, she had not yet closed her eyes to see the stars shining in the darkness. Four months ago, she had been human. But there had been old blood in her veins, and it had awakened, and it had transformed her.

It had awakened, yes.

That flash . . .

Highway 6 wound on toward the foothills, a ribbon of concrete that split the scrubby landscape and passed through urban sprawl where outlying condominium complexes rose boxy and new from the arid ground. Still, Lauri was not seeing with her old eyes, and the condos were pretty in their own way, the sunlight glinting pleasingly from freshly washed windows and glowing on cedar shake roofs. And, regardless of their rectilinear presence, the land beneath them still lived, fertile and rich, wanting only the touch of water to bring it to bloom and fruition. And if people needed a place to live in the growing city, and if they therefore claimed the open land for themselves, why, many of those same people also had old blood in their veins, and someday it might awaken in some of them . . .

. . . and Lauri wondered again about Amy. The elven blood could wake up in many ways: spontaneously, by the presence of others in whom it had awakened . . . or it could be triggered outright. Lauri had been half among the stars when she had touched Amy, and the effect had been electric. The deepening blue of the woman's eyes. That quick flash.

"What the hell did I do?" she mumbled out loud as the van rattled into Golden. "And how far did I stick my foot in it?"

She was warm—not hot—but completely undrenched when she got to the Bloomfield offices, and she grinned as she handed the papers to the contractor.

"You look cool as iced tea," he said, eyeing her

above his half-glasses. "You must have the air conditioner from hell in that truck of yours."

"It's the best," she said truthfully.

On the road again. Lauri donned her sunglasses and settled back in the seat. The inbound traffic was light, and she thought back to the incident at TreeStar. Amy had been afraid. No, not afraid: terrified. At the thought of being fired? Well, possibly. But the job market certainly was not that tight, and Amy had good references.

Nervousness would have been understandable. But that fear . . .

It was not the job, Lauri decided. It had to be something else. She replayed the event in her mind, watched, once again, that mascara-stained tear creep down the side of Amy's powdered nose, watched again that almost subliminal flinch with which the young woman had reacted to a comforting hand.

It was late when she got back to the city—past closing time—and she simply took the company van to her apartment. When she got home, she opened a can of pop, sat down in her living room, and called Hadden.

He caught it on the first ring. As usual. It was as though he had been expecting the call. As usual.

"All right," she said. "What did I do?"

"I think you know," he said. His voice was calm. It was always calm. Lauri had noticed the quality in her own voice since she had changed, but Hadden had it down to an art.

"I woke up the blood, didn't I?"

"Yup."

"Is this what you did to me?"

Hadden laughed, and the sound was clear and bright even over the telephone. "Not exactly. You were already coming around when Ash and I reached out to you."

"So what do I do now?"

"Keep an eye on her. If she runs into trouble, try to be there. It's been only four months since you changed . . . so you should remember how it goes. Try to show her that you care."

Lauri hesitated. "That's going to be kind of rough. Amy already has me pegged as some kind of bitchy libber . . . and she's pretty much right. I doubt if we have much in common."

"Ah, but you have a great deal in common: you're an Elf, and she's going to become one."

"Yeah." Her tone was doubtful. "But there's one other thing. Did you feel how scared she was this afternoon?"

"I did."

"That wasn't just about maybe losing her job."

Silence on the other end of the line. After a while, Hadden said: "I think humans have a lot of fears. Some of them we understand, some we can't. I don't know what to make of it. Maybe she'll lose it as she changes. I hope so."

But Lauri hung up feeling vaguely dissatisfied. She could not shake the feeling that Hadden had missed something in his evaluation. She tried to salve her thoughts with his comments about Amy's eventual change, but when she got into the office the next morning and found that Amy had a black eye, she was not reassured.

It was not a bad injury, and Amy had attempted to conceal it with makeup. Lauri centered herself among the stars. "Hi, Amy. How are you doing?"

" 'Lo." Amy hardly looked up. She was hunched over the computer keyboard as though expecting to be flogged. She did not seem at all inclined to talk, but Lauri waited by the reception desk until she finally met her gaze. Again, she saw the deepened blue, the slightest trace of a gleaming.

"Have a good day, kiddo."

Amy only looked frightened. "Uh . . . thanks."

"Yeah . . . take it easy." Chagrined, Lauri retreated to her desk.

She was out in the field with Hadden that day, and she had already decided to take the opportunity to talk further with him. She did not say anything, though, until they had broken for lunch. They had found a quiet park, away from main thoroughfares, and had sat down in the shade of a tall locust tree.

Lauri opened her lunch and bit into a ham and cheese sandwich. "Amy has a black eye," she mumbled.

"I noticed." Hadden was busy with tuna salad.

"What do you think? Did you ask her about it?"

"I did. She didn't want to talk. I didn't want to pry."

"Something's wrong," said Lauri. "I feel it."

A sparrow lit on her knee and looked at her expectantly. She reached out, stroked the bird absently, then fed it a bit of bread.

Hadden grinned. "Remember back when you wanted to pet birds?"

The sparrow was joined by two others. Lauri fed them also. They stayed, waiting.

"They want more than food," said Hadden. He reached out and scritched one of the birds. "Here, let me show you." He beckoned, and a sparrow flicked over to his hand. "You always know that we're a soft touch, don't you?" he said to it. He glanced at Lauri. "Find your stars, breathe in their light, and let it flow into your hands. Watch."

He cupped his hands beneath the bird and closed his eyes. Lauri watched the shimmer in his hands grow stronger, and the sparrow chirped with delight and fluttered and fluffed as though it were in a warm bath. It seemed willing to stay right where it was indefinitely, but Hadden finally opened his eyes and told it not to be greedy. With another chirp—of mild indignation—it flew off.

"Your turn," said Hadden, sitting back against the tree.

Lauri found her stars, gathered the remaining two birds, and let the light flow. When they had taken wing, she looked up. "Did you and Wheat just figure these things out as you went along?"

"Sort of. I imagine we have all sorts of talents that we don't know about yet. All we have to do is figure them out." A pause. "Did you know that Ash healed one of her neighbor's boys the other day?"

"She healed him? That's pretty good stuff." Lauri went back to her sandwich. "What did he have? A cold or something?"

Hadden was looking off into the distance . . . and perhaps farther than that. "Leukemia," he said quietly. "His mother was just taking him off to the lab for a second round of tests, and Ash looked at him and saw it. Somehow, she managed to . . . to whatever. She doesn't know what she did. But when the test results came back, they were negative."

Lauri had not moved since Hadden had named the disease. Ash was a slender, graceful lass, the owner of an employment agency, and Hadden's lover. A healer? Leukemia? Lauri looked at her hands. "That's . . . that's . . ." She could get no farther.

Hadden's voice was close to a whisper. "I wonder if we can't all do things like that."

"Kind of . . ." And she had worried about not sweating! ". . . kind of puts a different light on this whole thing."

"It does. It's not all singing and dancing in the firelight." He glanced at her, smiled. "Stop shaking, Lauri."

She laughed nervously, closed her eyes again, and let the starlight calm her. "It scares me, I guess," she said after a time. "I've looked at all this as just . . . a different way of living. I never thought . . . well . . . about having some kind of power."

Hadden did not reply for a minute. Then: "What do you think happened between you and Amy? Isn't that power?"

"I never thought of it that way. I . . . I guess so."

They got back to the office just as Amy was collecting her things. She looked up as they entered, and Lauri was relieved to see that some of her smile was back. "Mr. Bloomfield called," she said. "He's delighted."

"Good," said Lauri. "It was worth the trip, then."

Amy blushed. When she turned away, though, Lauri wondered whether she sensed the barest hint of a light about her.

"What are you doing for dinner tonight, Amy?"

The question seemed to jar Amy. Lauri sensed that some scenario was playing out in her mind ... sensed, too, another surge of fear. "I ... I ... I have to get home."

"OK." She kept her tone casual. "Some other time, maybe."

"Right." Amy nodded, gave her a quick smile, and hurried for the door.

But she paused and turned. "Uh ... maybe tomorrow night?"

"Sounds good to me."

Amy darted out. Lauri stood, hands on hips, watching her get into her car. "For a minute there I thought she was worried that I wanted to get in her pants or something."

Hadden shook his head. "I doubt that she even knows you're gay."

"I've never tried to help anyone through the change. I'm out of my depth."

Hadden put an arm around her shoulders. "It teaches you a lot. Worried?"

Lauri considered, letting the question hang. Though she had no definite idea what Amy's problem was, a faint suspicion was beginning to form in the back of her mind, one that she did not like. True, she could have reached out among the stars, linked with Amy, and read the woman like a book, but that would have been a violation, like rape, and if her suspicions proved at all correct, then Amy had already been violated ... was, in fact, being violated almost constantly.

"Yeah," she said at last. "I'm worried." She gestured at herself. "I've only been this way for a few months, so how the hell am I supposed to be qualified to do anything? Maybe you should take over."

"No." Hadden shook his head. "This is something you have to do. Consider it advanced training."

There was humor in there somewhere, but Lauri was too preoccupied to find it. "I'll try to remember that."

"Try something else, too," said Hadden. "Remember who you are. And remember what you are." He took one of her hands and held it up before her. It was shimmering, silver and bright.

The next day, Amy's eye was still ugly, but she was smiling again. Lauri, who had paperwork to do, now and again took a moment to watch her. Yes, something about the blond woman had indeed changed, at least to elven eyes. Lauri was fairly sure that Amy herself was not yet aware of it.

After work, they went out to a Pizza Hut and chatted over a mushroom and pepperoni with extra cheese. Amy seemed open and cheerful, and laughed at Lauri's tales about her downstairs neighbor and his billion-watt stereo.

". . . so I finally went down to complain," she said, "and he took a swing at me."

"He tried to hit you?" But there was a sense of apprehension beneath Amy's laughter. "What did you . . . what did you *do*?"

Lauri shrugged. "I pitched him into the lake. Everyone laughed. He kept the volume down after that."

Amy giggled nervously and nearly spilled her Coke. "You're tall enough . . . I didn't realize you were that strong."

"I've studied Tae Kwon Do for a few years. It comes in handy."

Amy set down her drink and looked at her as though for the first time. Her face was a mixture of awe, puzzlement, and a touch of fear. "You're very brave."

Lauri laughed, trying at the same time to read Amy's expression. "Nah . . . I'm just one of those horrible feminists you're always hearing about."

For a moment, Amy's thoughts seemed to turn inward. "Sure . . . OK . . . I guess so," she said slowly. Lauri had the impression that another scenario was playing out in her mind. "It must be interesting."

They were definitely an unmatched set: Amy in her Gunne Sax dress and impeccably applied makeup; Lauri in denim and denim, her hair a black mop and her face bare of any color except a suntan. Still, they could talk, and there was, moreover, a bond between them of which only Lauri was conscious so far, a bond that was growing steadily. Eventually, Amy would be finding stars behind her closed eyes. Eventually, Lauri would have to figure out how to explain what was happening to her.

"How do you feel about the mountains?" Lauri asked. "You want to take a lunch up there this weekend?" She admitted to herself that it would be a definite novelty to see Amy in Levi's. Unless, of course, she wore calico and a bonnet on such trips.

"Well . . ." Amy seemed uncertain. "Rob . . . that's my boyfriend . . . usually likes me to stay home with him on weekends." She paused, staring at the ice melting in her cola. "But . . . but he's going out with some friends. I . . . I guess I could."

"You live with Rob?"

She did. And it turned out that they kept an apartment together only a few minutes from where Lauri had thrown her neighbor into the lake.

"Let's do it, then," said Lauri. "You can get those pesky men out of your hair for a while."

Amy giggled and nodded; but she looked at her watch, then, and she gasped. "Ohmygod, I gotta get home. Rob will—"

The fear. Panic, really.

Amy caught herself. "Can we pay up?" she said quietly. "I really have to go."

Lauri looked at her for a few moments, sizing her up. "No problem. I'll pick you up on Saturday."

Amy was relatively error-free the rest of the week, her only mistake being a minor one regarding the admittedly simple filing system used at TreeStar. Hadden caught it on Friday afternoon just as they were closing the office. "Don't worry," he said. "You can fix it on Monday."

Amy stammered an apology. Hadden dismissed it with a wave of his hand. "Go home and have a good weekend. Monday is early enough to worry about it."

Amy looked grateful, and she picked up her purse and headed for the door.

"Don't forget about tomorrow," Lauri called. "Nine o'clock sharp."

A giggle. "Ron will still be in bed."

"Hey, all the better!"

"Tomorrow?" said Hadden as the door closed behind Amy.

"We're going up into the mountains for the day," said Lauri.

"Sounds like fun. Ash and I are going up to the Home. Why don't you drop in?"

Lauri watched through the window as Amy got into her car and pulled out. "We'll be up there," she said, "but that might be rushing things. Amy doesn't even know that Elves exist, much less that we're building a rec center off Highway 6. Of course, why should that bother her? Happens all the time, right?"

Hadden laughed. "I wouldn't exactly call it a rec center. But . . . well . . . you know these mortals . . ."

"Mortals. Hmmm. Not for much longer." She glanced at the street, then at Hadden. "This may be rough."

"Oh?"

"Her black eye. I think her boyfriend beat her up. I think it wasn't the first time, either."

Hadden sat down in a vacant chair and rubbed his chin thoughtfully. The blood had taken his beard away, but the habit persisted. "I was afraid that was going to be it. It does explain a few things." He looked sad. "You're right. It could be rough."

"Yeah. Rough. Real damn rough." Lauri was aware that the starlight in her eyes was shining brightly, even dangerously.

Forty minutes west of Denver, there was an odd little exit from Highway 6. Lauri turned her Bronco onto it and dropped back a gear for the dirt road and the steep grade.

Amy watched the trees and the hillside crawl by. "I never noticed this turnoff before," she commented. "I've been out this way too. Rob and I used to go out to Idaho Springs."

"It's kind of hard to find unless you know just what you're looking for," Lauri said. "But there's a nice place for a picnic out here." The road was rutted from the heavy loads of stone and wood that had been hauled over it, and Lauri made a mental note to suggest some smoothing: the area was starting to look too much as though there was construction going on. In fact, there was, but there was no sense advertising it.

The road wound into the mountains, rising and falling for twenty minutes or so until it descended and dead-ended in a flat puddle of bare earth.

"State park?" said Amy.

"Privately owned," Lauri answered. She did not mention that she was part owner.

There was one other vehicle there: Ash's Mercedes. Lauri pulled in beside it and shut off the engine.

There was a breeze that day, and it sang in the trees, the rustle of aspen blending with the sigh of pine. A deep feeling of peace lay upon the land here, and Amy must have sensed it, for Lauri saw that she was staring out of the open window as though she had never seen trees or mountains before.

Lauri got out and took off her shoes. Amy looked at her curiously.

"You don't need them here," Lauri explained. "This place is safe. There's nothing here that will hurt you."

Amy looked unbelieving, as though there were indeed no place in the universe like that, but she got out of the car and, after a moment of hesitation, even went so far as to remove her shoes. "I'll . . . take your word for it, Lauri."

"Good enough." Lauri reached into the back and picked up the picnic basket. "Let's walk. There are some nice meadows around here."

She offered her hand, recalling as she did a time, now four months past, when Ash had reached out to her. At the time, the action had seemed fraught with meaning, as though it would reshape her entire life. And, indeed, it had, for when, after a moment, she had taken Ash's hand, that gentle woman had led her into another world, just as she herself hoped to lead Amy. The blood had awakened, and it could not be denied. But the trauma could be eased, the uncertainty done away with. Healing. Comfort. Yes, that was it.

But though Amy grasped her hand and willingly

accompanied her toward the path, she moved stiffly, as though in pain. "You aren't well?" said Lauri.

"I'm OK." Amy dropped her eyes and turned her head away.

Lauri sighed. "Come," she said quietly. "You can leave it behind you here."

Amy, startled by her tone, looked up, her eyes deep blue now with the awakening of the blood, the shimmer a faint presence about her body. "What?"

She stared at Lauri, and the Elf knew that Amy was sensing the starlight. But just then a sparrow hawk skimmed by over their heads, swept up and away and, wings beating, hung as though beckoning above the clearing that Lauri knew was ahead.

"Hello, old friend," said Lauri.

"What?"

Lauri laughed. "It's the welcoming committee!"

Their steps took them into the trees and along quiet paths where the moss and pine needles seemed especially soft. Lauri padded silently. Amy stepped gingerly. The sparrow hawk had doubled back, and it flitted from tree to tree above their heads, keeping pace with them, now and then peering down, head cocked to one side, curious.

The meadow opened before them like a green chapel, surrounded by trees, bordered by a stream that tumbled among smooth stones. The sparrow hawk flicked out over it, circled, and with firm wing beats, mounted into the sky. Amy shaded her eyes, looking after it.

The grass was thick and soft, the sun warm. Lauri

spread the blanket while Amy wandered first down to the water, then up along a patch of white flowers.

"Isn't this better than watching the tube all day?" Lauri called to her.

Amy turned around. She was holding one of the small blooms. The wind lifted her hair out and to the side, and though she was wearing designer jeans and a football jersey, she was, for that moment, timeless, as though this meadow and these flowers had always been visited by young, fragile women who knew what it meant to pick one and hold it in just this way, wondering at it.

"It's . . . it's beautiful here," she said, and her voice carried softly to Lauri. And it seemed that she had, in fact, left behind her what the Elf had hoped she would.

But at the same time, linked as they were in that instant, Lauri could sense the dark bruises that covered Amy's back, the reddened welts on her breasts . . . and she knew then why the young woman had walked stiffly.

She dropped her gaze, staring for the moment at the blanket, and then beyond, letting her stars calm her, settle her. As much as leukemia had silently eaten at Ash's little neighbor, so did a different, less tangible ailment gnaw at Amy.

And so, Lauri hoped, would it be dealt with by elven hands.

"What's that, Lauri?" Amy was pointing out over the treetops. There was a tower there. It was white, with a roof of blue stone, and a silver filigree wound along just under the eaves.

"It's a house."

"Who lives there?"

"It's sort of a communal-type place."

"That must be nice. This is a pretty place."

"I'll take you there sometime," said Lauri.

She opened the basket and began setting out the food. She had packed it herself—chicken salad, bread, wine, cheese—and while she had done so, she had felt the sacredness of her task, for this simple lunch could, as far as Amy was concerned, make all the difference in the world.

The sparrow hawk swooped down and alighted on her shoulder, then nuzzled through her hair at her ear. Lauri blushed. "Hey, come on, give me a break," she whispered to it. "You want the poor thing to freak?"

Amy was staring again. "How ... how are you doing that?"

Lauri offered the small hawk a bit of chicken salad. "Well, it's like this. Just like we're safe here, so are the animals. They know we wouldn't hurt them." The sparrow hawk gave up on her ear and took the dab of chicken salad politely. "It *was* you the first time I was here, wasn't it?" Lauri said to it. The bird eyed her wisely and busied itself with the food.

Amy wandered over and sat down, moving slowly, wonderingly. A deer bounded out of the forest and, leading a fawn, went straight to her. The fawn took one look at her, curled up beside her, and went to sleep. The mother looked on approvingly. Amy reached out and stroked the dappled fur. "I don't understand any of this," she said. Her voice was hoarse, her eyes moist.

"Just take it for what it is," said Lauri. She let the starlight fill her, feeling the cool wash of energy expanding within her until it reached out and touched Amy, who relaxed and rubbed her eyes. Lauri let her rest.

But, abruptly, Amy broke down, eyes pressed tightly shut, hands going to her face to hide her tears. Lauri put her arms around her, thinking: *It's not supposed to hurt. Dear God, it's not supposed to hurt.*

Locked as she was in a personal and physical grief, Amy was oblivious to Lauri's arms; and though the Elf could feel Amy choking and heaving, she could also feel more: the grief itself, the confusion, the frantic searching for escape.

Ash had healed her neighbor, but even Ash did not know how. Lauri herself had no healing to offer. She had, in fact, nothing to give but her presence and her arms, and she could only hope that, coupled as they were with the safety and peace of this place, the chosen valley of the Elves, they would not prove deficient. And, indeed, Amy's sobs gradually grew less frequent, wrung her body less. She had buried her face in Lauri's shoulder, her hands clutched into fists; but that was easing now, and eventually she quieted, her hands relaxed, and Lauri cradled her gently, letting her drift in peace.

"What am I seeing?" Amy said at last. "Are they stars?"

Lauri lifted her head. It was happening. "They are."

"Inside me?"

"Some people have that talent," said the Elf. "This place can bring it out. Breathe slowly. Pretend you're breathing the starlight."

Amy seemed to understand. She breathed, and a deep calm surrounded her. "Where am I?" she whispered.

"Inside yourself. We all have places like this inside us. We just have to find them. It's a place you can go to for quiet, or ... for ... well ... for strength. When you need to."

After a minute, Amy appeared to realize where she was and what she was doing. She shifted, opened her eyes, drew away from Lauri. She kept her gaze elsewhere. The fawn, still beside her, looked at her with concern. The doe watched.

"Rob likes to beat you up, doesn't he?" Lauri's voice was quiet.

Amy would not look at her. "I make him nervous," she said. "I twitch. He doesn't like that."

"That doesn't give him the right to hit you."

"It's my fault. He works hard, and he's tired when he gets home. He needs to rest ... and I get in the way. He gets so angry at me ..."

"And he drinks ..." Lauri was surprised at her certainty. "So he knocks you around." *Damn human ...*

Amy still would not look at her. Her blond hair, damp with her tears, straggled down on either side of her face.

Starlight or no starlight, Lauri could not understand. "Why the hell do you stay?"

Amy at last looked up. "I need him," she said. "I love him."

"It sure doesn't sound like he loves you."

Amy looked baffled. "Of course he loves me."

The next day was a Sunday, and Lauri was crawling across the blue slate roof of Elvenhome to caulk the flashing around the chimney. The slope was not great, but the stone was slippery, and she was not used to heights. She held the stars in her mind to keep her acrophobia at bay.

She reached the chimney and straddled the ridge. In most directions, she could see trees, pine and aspen, her view level with or above their highest branches. To the west, beyond the trees, were the mountains, clear and sharp against the unspeakably blue sky. Below her, beyond the eaves of the house, was the ground, forty feet down. She tried not to think about that. It was even preferable to think about Amy.

The picnic had ended on a better note, and Amy had been laughing again when Lauri had dropped her off at her apartment.

"I'll see you on Monday," Amy had said. "Thanks. I had a great time. I'd like to go back up there someday."

"Just name the time, Amy. I'll be more than happy to take you."

And Lauri, perched on the roof, recalled the faint nimbus that she had seen about Amy as the young woman had gone up the walkway and into the apartment building. Amy herself was probably not yet conscious of it, but it would still be a while before the blood would begin to manifest directly for her. Now, with Lauri's help, she could see the stars. Soon, they would be with her always.

But other recollections of that day made Lauri's hands tighten on the caulking gun. Her own attitude toward men had always been one of indifference. She had been gay for as long as she had known that there was something more between adults than talking, and men had never been anything more to her than friends or co-workers. While the affair in Los Angeles that had blown up and propelled her to Denver had been a maelstrom of conflicting emotions and psychological games, it had not contained even a hint of physical abuse, and she had, it seemed, forgotten about those kinds of love in which intimidation and violence played a part.

Those bruises, those welts: they made her blood boil. Worse, they made her feel helpless. How could she reach out to Amy, separated as she was from her by an abyss of conditioning, sexuality, and lifestyle, of which Amy's studied polish and femininity were only surface indications? And what, in any case, could starlight do against a raised fist?

Immersed and aggravated by her thoughts, she missed her footing as she inched back toward her ladder. In a moment, the caulking gun had gone flying, clattering down the roof and off into the air as she scrambled for a hold. The slate, though, offered little for her hands to grasp, and she slid rapidly toward the edge, following the path of the caulking gun.

She heard it hit the ground, a harsh *clank,* probably on the walkway and she hoped it hadn't cracked any of the flagstones and *dammit where the hell is a hold on this slate . . . ?*

Her body was off the edge before her fingers closed on the rain gutter. She was strong, and, thanks to a combination of Tae Kwon Do and starlight, her reflexes were good, and though she wound up dangling in the air, she felt confident that she could pull herself up. If the gutter did not give way.

As if in response to her thought, the gutter creaked, a masonry nail two feet from her deciding that it was not up to the added load.

"Lauri," she heard from below her. "Are you— oh, shit!"

The voice belonged to Wheat, and Wheat, she recalled (her mind pursuing with maddening efficiency her previous train of thought), had been Amy's employment counselor.

Petulantly, the nail continued to yield. The gutter creaked even more. Climbing back onto the roof was out of the question: any movement on Lauri's part would cause the nail to give way, would, in fact, more than likely pull out the entire section of gutter.

Lauri heard Wheat shouting for Hadden and Web. She forced herself to stay calm, turned inward, found her stars.

The gutter creaked. It was obviously not going to hold. Lauri could feel it pulling free, could imagine what a forty-foot drop would do to her. She stared at the nail, willing it to hold, seeing it through a haze of starlight.

The gutter sagged.

"Hold on, Lauri!" It was Ash. Well, Lauri reflected, in about half a minute a healer was going to be exactly what she needed.

That damned nail. She glared at the traitorous hardware, and in her mind, a blue star was blazing directly in her line of sight, the nail eclipsed by its brilliance.

Hold. Dammit. Hold.

And then she suddenly felt the ladder under her feet, felt it rise and steady until she could put her weight on it.

"You got it, Lauri?" Wheat called.

"Yeah," Lauri shouted back. "Yeah ... I got it." Her arms were suddenly rubbery. "Lemme ... lemme just rest for a minute before I try to come down."

As she steadied herself, though, she noticed the nail: it looked as though it had been partly melted. She looked closer, saw that it was, quite perceptibly, fused not only with the gutter but with the stone behind it. Remembering the star she had seen, she stared, swallowed, and then, slowly, inched down the ladder.

Hadden, Wheat, and Web all grabbed her when she came within reach, and they bore her bodily over to the bench under the big aspen tree that grew in the front courtyard. Ash pressed a glass of water into her hand. "Find your stars, Lauri."

"I've ... I've got them," Lauri panted, half from fright, half from the sight—and import—of the melted nail. Power. First Ash, and now Lauri. Nor did she remember how she had done it. "I'm . . . I'm . . . I'm . . . all right."

Hadden's face was grave. "What happened?"

She shrugged. "I got sloppy up there. I was thinking about Amy."

"Hmmm. How did it go yesterday?"

"We talked. The animals accepted her, no problem. We talked. I was right: her guy beats her up. But she thinks it's her fault."

Ash nodded slowly. "Yes . . . that's usually the way it is."

Lauri blinked at her tone. "Ash?"

Ash seemed to turn her sight inward. The starlight in her eyes flickered. "I was married years ago, and divorced. There were . . . reasons for that."

"And you blamed yourself for it all?"

Ash shrugged. "We grow up that way sometimes. I finally realized that nothing I did rated a beating from another human being. I ran. Eventually, he stopped trying to get back at me."

"He *what*?"

"I'd run away," Ash said simply. "I had to be punished."

Hadden rubbed at his nonexistent beard. "And Amy? What about her? The blood isn't going to wait. We need to be ready."

"She can stay here," said Ash. "One wing of the Home is finished. There is water, and the lights are working. We can put her up until her man gets tired."

"But then what?" Lauri felt the power that Ash

had once wielded, that she could possibly wield again.

As though looking back on a life that had taken an unexpected turn or two, Ash smiled quietly. "Then she is her own, to stay or go as she wishes. She will be a kinswoman."

It rained heavily most of the next week, autumn storms presaging the coming winter. Flooded streets mirrored the slate gray of cloudy skies, dirt lots turned into swamps, construction halted, and at TreeStar Surveying, field work was, by necessity, suspended. Lauri had paperwork to keep her busy at the office, but she made sure that she occasionally took time out to chat with Amy.

Yes, the young woman was changing. Now even Amy herself had noticed, though it was obvious that she did not know what to make of it. She moved with a sense of ease and grace through the office, and if she smiled, she smiled without nervousness or appeasement. Her mistakes dwindled. A potted plant appeared on her desk. There was a gleam of starlight in her eyes. On Friday afternoon, Lauri found her examining her hands in wonder.

"How's it going, Amy?"

"Fine ..." Amy's voice trailed off thoughtfully, then she caught herself and looked up at Lauri. "I think I might need glasses."

"Is my handwriting giving you problems? Don't worry: it gives *everybody* problems."

"No, honestly," Amy giggled, "I look like I'm glowing."

"Uh . . . well . . . maybe you are. Have you thought of that?"

Amy shrugged and shook her head. "I wouldn't be surprised if I was, with all the other crazy things going on."

Lauri shoved her hands into her pockets, sensing that she was going to have to do some fast thinking in the next few minutes, sensing that, as usual, she was not going to think quite fast enough. "Crazy things?"

Amy looked up, and starlight flashed in her eyes. "It's like when we were up in the mountains last weekend. I see stars when I sleep. And I think I see them when I'm awake." She blinked. "Am I nuts?"

"No more than anyone else around here." Lauri was conscious that, from across the room, Hadden was watching her. "How do you feel about it? Besides being nuts, I mean."

Amy gazed out the window, out onto the lawn that adjoined the office building. "I was sitting in the park today . . . eating my lunch. I wasn't paying attention to anything, but a robin came and sat on my shoulder. It . . . it let me pet it." She looked up at Lauri. "It wasn't just begging for a handout. It really seemed, like, glad that I was there. And then a squirrel curled in my lap. Just like the fawn did. A-and I feel like . . . like I'm them and they're me."

"Are you frightened?"

"No."

Lauri considered. She felt Hadden watching her still, and she knew what he was thinking. Getting close. Time to say something. Healing and comfort.

She ran a hand through her black hair, brushing past an ear. The change was profound. She was twenty-nine, but she looked almost ten years younger than that, and the set of her cheekbones and face had altered enough to make her ears fit in better, so that she looked complete, all of a piece. Even some of the inflections of her voice had changed.

She checked Amy. Physical changes? Not yet. Soon, though. Very soon.

"What do you know about Elves?" she said casually.

Amy looked startled. "Oh, my God ... we've got *them* around here too?"

Lauri was conscious that Hadden had turned away, shaking with suppressed laughter. She frowned. It was not fair. She had no idea what she was doing. "Well ... uh ... who knows?"

"Don't they sit on mushrooms?"

"I'm not sure." Lauri was watching Hadden. "Maybe they smoke them." He did not turn around.

"But what about Elves?"

"It's ... well ... like they really existed," said Lauri. She was suddenly terrified that Amy would laugh. "Right along with humans. They disappeared somewhere around the fourteenth century, but before that they'd, well, like, intermarried. Lots of people have some of the blood now, and it's waking up in some. Aquarian Age or something like that."

Hadden straightened, and though he was still facing away from her, Lauri saw his nod.

"Cute story," said Amy, who had gone back to

staring at her hands. "Maybe that's it. Maybe I'm **turning** into one."

Lauri chuckled. "Maybe."

"What happened to make them disappear, though? Didn't they have the Black Death in the fourteenth century?" Lauri looked at her, and she shrugged. "I majored in history."

"Yea . . . OK . . . uh . . . well . . . I don't think it was the plague. I think it was . . ." She recalled Amy's bruises, her scratches . . . her fear. ". . . uh . . . persecution."

"That wasn't a good time for a lot of people back then."

"No," said Lauri. "No, it wasn't."

Persecution. Lauri thought about it on her way home that night, wondering what it had been like to be an Elf in 1350. Though in one way she could see Amy's bruises as only a symptom of her society and her age, the brutalization of woman by man that made her glad that she stood apart from heterosexual relations, in another—and here she was stretching back in time, wondering—she could see it as simply one more episode in the story of what had become her people: piled on top of her anger at the wounding of a woman was her outrage at the thought of an Elf being struck by a . . . a *human*.

The memory of the gutter at Elvenhome and of the fused nail came back to her. If she, but four months an Elf, could wield power like that, what then could one born to the race do? And why, in that age of intolerance, inquisition, and burning, had that not been done? What had held her forebears back from reaching out among the stars and throwing greater-than-human energies at those who persecuted them? Was the power valid? Or did it fail in time of need? What good was power if it could not save one's race? What good was it if it could not even save one fragile woman from a beating?

She pulled into her parking space, switched off, and sat for a while, staring at the brick wall in front of her as the rain pattered on the roof and the engine ticked away its heat. She was still helpless. Much as she wanted to reach out to Amy, drag her away from the man who abused her, the action was not hers to take. Amy had to do it herself, or not at all.

Maybe ... maybe Amy even *liked* the way he treated her.

She got out and strode into the apartment complex as though stalking some evil destiny.

She drove out to Elvenhome the next day. The sky was like slate, gaps in the overcast yielding views only of more and darker clouds that increased her worry and the sense of oppression that accompanied it. She had forwarded her calls to the telephone at the Home, but though one ear cocked for the ring, she spent the day putting down the parquetry floor in the dining hall, it never came.

Ash and Hadden were upstairs, laying carpet. They all met over sack lunches under the trees.

"Do you feel it?" said Lauri. She did not specify. She did not have to.

Ash, in the middle of an apple, nodded. "I do. I've gotten a bedroom ready."

"She won't come. She loves him. She thinks he loves her."

"Who can say?" murmured the healer.

"How are you at broken bones, Ash?"

"I can try."

Evening again, and night. Lauri stayed up at the Home, sleeping bag unrolled under the trees, physical stars blending with those within her. The overcast had departed, the skies were cold and clear, and the trees seemed to whisper to one another, telling stories about the old times, the starlight, and about the Elves and their return. She wondered how her people had lived before ... before the Loss. The histories were silent, and racial memory gave her only vague and obscure images of firelight in peaceful clearings, warm embraces, and soft words.

And the stars. Always the stars.

There was something infinitely precious there: that peace, that feeling of wholeness and of completion. It was something worth fighting for, something even worth dying for.

And she wondered then if that was not what had happened. Persecution, intermarriage, fading ... but by that fading the blood had been spread throughout humankind, slumbering through the centuries, but waiting to awake, to bring something precious to everyone: human, Elf, one transformed into the other, a fighting through storm and strife to azure sky and blue water. Amy was finding her way now, and her path was painful, even dangerous, but Lauri now felt sure that she was going to make it all the way. The skies, the stars, the trees and stones would soon be hers. As could be the case with everyone. Even . . . even . . . Rob.

She had drifted far and long within herself when the darkness among her stars suddenly flamed red, blinding her, driving her through jagged spaces. She looked through holes in the sky into emptiness, and she came to herself screaming, clawing at the sleeping bag as though it were devouring her, hands clutching at the cloth, at the air. Somewhere inside her, an abyss had opened up and was pulling her stars into it, spiraling them into its maw, tugging at her mind . . .

. . . trees . . . bending over her . . . reaching . . . . . . eyes . . .

Far off, she thought she heard someone calling her name, but the roaring in her ears was drowning it out. The abyss had grown, stars vanishing into it, draining out of her consciousness.

She was still screaming. With her physical sight, she caught a glimpse of Ash's features, hovering ghostly as if in moonlight, eyes gleaming, lips pressed together.

Ash! Help!

And then she felt hands on her: soft hands, but bright with power. Ash's voice suddenly rang within her: *I'm here.*

Her fall ceased. The abyss still gaped, but the stars had halted their flight. From out of the red sky came a dull muttering.

Hadden. Ash again. *I need help.*

Here, beloved.

Light wove around Lauri like a down comforter,

calming her, easing her. She snuggled into it with a sigh, let it merge with her, fill her.

Breathe, Lauri. Gently now.

Slow and steady, she told herself. Just like with Amy. But then she had a brief, compelling vision of a sparsely furnished room, of a dark form that lifted a greasy hand—

The abyss gaped once again.

Lauri! Hold!

The words snapped her back to herself, and she searched among the stars for something with which to center herself. A hot blue primary burned in her field of vision, and she concentrated on it, clung to it as light poured down into the abyss, dragged its edges together, bound and sealed it with a tracery of starlight.

Her inner vision cleared. The sky was once again a field of gems, safe and calm. She shuddered and went limp.

She opened her eyes and managed to focus on Ash and Hadden. "I . . . I don't know . . . what . . ."

"Rest, Lauri." Ash passed a hand over Lauri's forehead, and strength came with the touch. "Give yourself some time."

Lauri worked her mouth soundlessly while she pulled her thoughts together. Then: "I can't rest. That came from Amy. I *know* it came from Amy. She's in trouble."

Despite Ash's protests, she stood up. Though she was unsteady at first, her bare feet felt the life in the cold ground and drank it in; and when, inside the Home, the telephone began to ring, she managed to sprint for the door. But she picked up the receiver just as the connection was broken with a loud pop.

"Amy? Amy!" Dead air. Dialing Amy's number brought nothing more than a ring . . . and no answer. Lauri slammed the handset back into the cradle. "I'm going out there."

Hadden was already pulling on his Levi's. "I'm going with you."

Four in the morning, the eastern sky paling faintly. Lauri and Hadden in the Bronco, traveling full-bore down the twisting mountain highway that led to Denver. Speed laws were things to be ignored. Time and Amy were all that counted.

Spurred to recklessness, Lauri did not slow down even when she reached the city limits, but the residential streets forced her to cut her speed, and her hands were tight on the wheel as they rumbled into Glendale and its clutter of apartments. She knew the way to Amy's building, but even if she had not, the dull oppression that glowed like a hot iron in her mind would have guided her. She double-parked directly in front of the building and flicked on her emergency flashers.

"I'm going in," she said.

"Do you want help?" Hadden was speaking calmly.

"I want to do this alone."

"He may be there."

She shrugged and started to swing out of the doorway, but Hadden detained her with a hand on her arm. He was looking at her meaningfully. "Hey," she said, "it suits me just fine."

"Healing and comfort?"

"I don't think that's a fair question."

"You might want to think about it, nonetheless."

She jerked her arm out of his grasp and ran for the stairs. Two flights up, down the hallway, and the oppression was burning in her face.

She listened at the door. Silence. But the lights were on, and a bare bulb formed a bright spot where a lamp was leaning crazily against the venetian blinds.

She called into the spaces between the stars. *Amy!*

Nothing. Not even an echo. Lifting a hand, she knocked softly. Then, damning all, she pounded.

A minute or two went by before she heard a stirring. A white face, streaked with grime and blood, peered out at her from between the blinds. Lauri had a feeling that it belonged to Amy, but she could not be sure, and when the door finally opened and she got a good look at the woman who stood before her in a torn nightshirt, she was no more certain. In truth, it had to be Amy, but the blood, the bruises, and, more than either, the dull, lightless eyes made Lauri hesitate.

"Hello ... Lauri ..." The woman's voice was mechanical, flat. It was as though a corpse spoke. The shimmer, the glow, the health ... everything was gone.

"Amy ..."

Amy went back into the room, leaving the door

open. "You might as well come in," she said over her shoulder.

Lauri entered and pushed the door closed behind her. The apartment was a wreck: papers, dishes, and furniture scattered as if tossed by a storm. "Where's Rob?"

"Out." Amy did not turn around. Her voice was listless, empty.

"What the hell did he do to you?" Physically, it was obvious, but at present the physical was of incidental concern to Lauri.

Amy turned around. Lauri might as well have looked into empty sockets for all the life that was in her eyes. "I got sick," Amy said simply. "I was seeing stars. Rob got mad."

Trembling, Lauri reached out and took her gently by the shoulders. "So what did he do, Amy?" she whispered. "Try to beat it out of you?"

"I'm better now . . ."

Lauri felt like screaming. Blood was still seeping from a cut in Amy's forehead, and most of her face was bruised and swollen. But her eyes were pits of emptiness, and oppression radiated from her.

Lauri's stars wavered, and she saw, in the distance, the abyss that had taken Amy away from herself. Amy started to shake, and she pulled away. "You better go. Rob'll be back any time now. He went to get some beer."

"So he can come back and finish you off? Over my—"

"He's got a gun, Lauri. You better go." Amy was leaning on the kitchen counter, the Formica top

stained with coffee and the dregs of an overturned
catsup bottle. She was still shaking. "I . . . I . . . wanna
. . . I . . . I can't . . . uh . . . uh . . ."

The abyss yawned. Lauri suddenly realized that,
not content with sucking down Amy's stars, it was
going to take the rest of her, too. Even physically,
though, Amy was collapsing, and before Lauri could
move, she lost her grip on the counter and dropped
to the floor, banging her head on an overturned table.
Lauri was beside her in a moment, cradling her head,
calling her.

The abyss widened. Elf and woman. Healing and
comfort.

She sensed that Amy was far ahead, well into the
pit that had opened within her. But though it was
dark in there, dark and cold, and though she shuddered at the thought of following, she had to follow,
and so she was already reaching out among the stars,
reaching out to the hot blue primary she had seen
before—looking for energy, looking for power, perhaps looking only for a simple glimpse of light that
she could take with her into the darkness—as she
plunged after Amy, saw through Amy's eyes, lived
with her through that last, soul-killing beating.

Cold, darkness. *Amy!* The blue star fed her,
strengthened her. Blazing far above her like a distant
electric arc, it nonetheless blasted down into the endless night below, splitting the darkness as the high
beams of her truck had split the pitch of the mountain roads.

Amy!

Faintly, a whisper in the void. It was unintelligible,

perhaps it was not even a word. A sigh, maybe. But it was something, and Lauri, well into the abyss now, the darkness all around, her stars infinitely far away, searched for whatever intangible thing it was that was Amy.

Again the whisper, but fainter now. Lauri searched. Somewhere . . . she had to be somewhere.

The blue star was barely a glimmer on the edge of sight when she felt something, knew it to be Amy, grabbed it.

Amy! Hold on to me!

It was as though arms were thrown around her neck then, a head pressed to hers. *Lauri . . . I'm scared.*

Lauri nearly laughed. Amy's fear could not have equaled one tenth the sheer, unadulterated panic that she herself felt. The blue star was nearly eclipsed by distance, the abyss seemed both infinite and absolute, and she was somewhere inside and yet outside of herself. She had no idea what to do, and now the life of another was in her hands.

I'm scared: the words were not even fractionally adequate to the situation.

She tried to rise, got nowhere, redoubled her grip on the stars, and tried again. Nothing. Her terror was like a hand about her throat, and Amy's trust was all that allowed her to fight it down.

Hadden! Ash!

Movement. Presence. The blue star flickered, and then she saw another night sky around her. It was not hers—she knew that she was still in the abyss—but she understood that Hadden and Ash were with her now, and the stellar fire of immense suns shone on her, yellow, blue, gold, green. The incandescence coursed through her, expanded to encompass Amy, grew in intensity . . .

. . . and then they were rising.

Amy was still clinging to her, and Lauri let the light flow into the emptiness that was there. Amy drank it in. *Lauri . . .*

You're OK. Really. Just breathe the light.

Amy was like an abyss herself. There was a hunger there, a void, a passionate yearning for something feared lost. Lauri felt as though she were spooning meat into the mouth of a starving child.

Rising . . .

Breathe, Amy.

More light. Lauri's own stars shone about them now. She recognized them, was sure of them. Below, the abyss closed, webs of light tightening over it, sealing it. Amy gasped then, and, with a whisper as of a breath of wind, Lauri's stars were joined by others, and they shone mightily.

For several minutes, they drifted together, holding one another in mind and in body, Lauri resting, Amy, she could tell, changing, making up for lost time.

"It's beautiful," she said, or Amy said . . . or maybe they said it together. Lauri could not be sure. She thought she detected a slurring, though, as of swollen lips, and she pried her eyes open and looked into Amy's battered face. Incongruously, despite the bruises and the blood, Amy was smiling.

"What is it, Lauri?" she said. "What do the stars mean?"

"It means, love ..." Lauri looked into eyes that were, once again, filled with light, stared at flesh that was, for all its marks of battering, suffused with a delicate shimmer. "It means that you're an Elf. You've got the blood I was talking about. It woke up. It's changing you."

Amy closed her eyes, sighed. "Rob asked me what was going on, and I told him about the stars. He got mad."

"How ... how do you feel about that?"

"I just want the stars. I tried to tell him that, but he didn't like it. He started hitting me. He didn't care about the stars ... and I realized then that he really didn't care about me, either. I ... I don't think he ever did." She opened her eyes suddenly. A flash. "I want the stars," she said fiercely. "I want them. I won't let him take them away again."

Lauri heard the door open. "Hadden?" she said. "We're OK."

But Amy's eyes had widened in fear, and Lauri turned around to see Rob framed by the doorway, his T-shirt greasy and his jeans stained with what she assumed was Amy's blood. He was holding a six-pack of beer, and he was staring at Lauri.

"What the—" He started forward, fist balled, face red. Lauri rose and set herself between him and Amy.

"She's a friend of mine, Rob." Amy's voice was husky. "Leave her alone."

"What the hell's she doing here?" he demanded. "She ..."

Lauri wanted no delays, no interference. "I came

here to save Amy's life after you nearly beat her to death. I'm going to get her out of here."

"The hell you are."

"Rob ..." There was a plaintive tone in Amy's voice, but she abruptly caught herself. Holding on to the counter, she slowly got to her feet. "You really hurt me, Rob." The plaintive tone was gone. It was a statement of fact. There was no pleading or apology in it. "You nearly killed me."

"Bullshit. You make me so goddam mad. All that shit about stars. You gonna start that again? What the fuck are you trying to do to me?"

"I'm not trying to do anything to you," said Amy slowly, evenly. "I just want out."

Rob eyed Lauri. "Get outta my way, cunt. I want my woman."

Perhaps he had chosen his words to anger her, but Lauri had her stars, and the light leached away the emotion. She was calm, centered. She had a job to do, and when Rob lunged, coming at her, swinging the six-pack like a club, she was ready for it. She ducked, allowed the momentum and the weight of the beer cans to spin him half around, then drove in.

A kick sent the cans flying, and she grabbed Rob by the shoulders and whirled him back as though he were a sack of cabbages. A second kick, a round-house, caught him square on the side of the head, and he went down heavily and lay still.

She turned around to face Amy. The small woman was staring at the inert body. "You didn't ..."

"He's just out, Amy. He'll be OK. Sorry about that."

Amy wavered, looked dazedly about the room.

"Get your things together, kiddo," said Lauri. "Clothes, personals ... whatever. We're getting you out of here."

"Where ... where are we going?"

"Home. We're going home. Up into the mountains. Where we were before. Remember the house you saw?"

In five minutes, Amy was dressed and had filled a duffle bag. When they came back out into the living room, though, Rob was gone. Lauri was startled: she had expected that the combination of alcohol and impact would have kept him unconscious for several hours.

"What are we going to do?" Amy was looking at the place where Rob had been.

"We move, Amy."

"Lauri, he's got a gun in his car."

The gun. Amy had mentioned it before, but Lauri had forgotten. She kept to her stars. "Then we move faster. Come on."

They got down the stairs and out to the street without incident, Lauri carrying the duffle bag and, partially. Their progress was slow, but the truck was still there, still double-parked and idling, and Hadden reached out to help Amy in.

Amy gasped. "Hadden! You?"

"To be sure," he said softly. "We're all in this together."

Lauri threw the duffle bag into the back and swung behind the wheel. "I had to fight him, Hadden," she explained. "I put him out, but he came to and took off when I wasn't looking. Amy thinks he's going for a gun."

"Well, then we'd better get out of here." Still perfectly calm. Yes, indeed: he had it down to an art.

"Right." The Bronco's tires screeched a little as Lauri pulled out, and she wove through the back streets, heading for Colorado Boulevard and the freeway on-ramp as fast as she dared. Above, the pale light of early dawn was filling the sky. Streetlights began to dim, buildings emerged as forms of gray and pastel. The clouds had departed: the sky that day would be of deepest sapphire.

Traffic was thin when she reached Highway 6, and she overtopped the speed limit as much as she dared. The urgency was not so great now, but she wanted to get Amy to Elvenhome.

Lauri stole a glance at her. Amy was curled up in the seat, dozing. The shimmer about her was bright, distinct, and, even through the grime and the bruises, Lauri could see that her face was softening, lines of worry and pain vanishing as the blood worked.

They were just entering the foothills when Hadden spoke up from the back seat. "Lauri, there's a car back here that's following us, I think."

Lauri saw it in the mirror. A red Mustang was in their lane, tailing them.

"He's been with us at least since we got onto Sixth Avenue," said Hadden. "You think it's the man?"

"Rob? Yeah, probably." Lauri's voice was flat. She remembered the gun. "I'm still going up to the Home. He'll be on our turf."

"Agreed."

The Mustang stayed with them as they wound through foothills that quickly rose into mountains. Hoping to lose it among the turns, Lauri put on some speed, but the Mustang accelerated, closing the distance. Peering into her mirror, Lauri thought she recognized Rob's features behind the wheel.

Amy awoke, looked back, caught her breath. "It's him!"

"Thought so." Lauri upped her speed a little more. If she could make the turnoff to Elvenhome quickly enough, with enough of a lead on Rob, he might miss it entirely and continue on out toward Idaho Springs.

"Lauri, you don't understand," said Amy. "When he's mad, he doesn't think. He's liable to try to kill you."

"He's going to find I'll argue with him." Lauri tried to sound confident, hoped that she had succeeded.

"Hold on to the stars, Lauri," said Hadden. "And you too, Amy. You're one of us now." Lauri saw him in the mirror. He was very calm, and the starlight was in his eyes. "Do what you need to, Lauri. There are some things worth taking risks for."

The last quarter mile to the turnoff was abominably straight, and as Lauri spun up onto the steep slope, she knew without looking that Rob had followed.

She gunned the Bronco, jouncing up the dirt road. "When we get there," she called to Hadden over the bumps and the engine noise, "you get Amy up to the house. I'll deal with Rob."

"What do you intend to do?"

"Jump him. I'm an Elf. I should at least be able to sneak up on him. After that, it's clobbering time."

Amy was terrified. "Lauri, don't. I can't let you do that. He's got a gun. Just let me go back to him. He'll leave you alone then."

Lauri felt her jaw clench. Rob himself could not make her angry, but the thought of what Rob had done to Amy . . .

"Amy," she said, "do you *want* to go back to him?"

Amy hesitated, looking first at Lauri, then at Hadden, then at the pursuing red car. Lauri felt the struggle. Starlight. Finally: "No. I don't."

"Then you goddam well don't have to. Hadden, can you warn Ash that there's going to be trouble?"

"She knows."

The parking area came into view as they crested the last hill. The fresh gravel was glowing in the morning sunlight, and the sparrow hawk flashed through the sky. Lauri floored the accelerator down the slope and slewed to a halt close to the path. "Everyone out," she yelled as she threw her door open. "Leave the bag."

The Mustang was at the top of the hill. Lauri judged distances, times.

"We can make it to the trees if we run."

Amy was unsteady. Hadden scooped her up and carried her, and Rob was just pulling up beside the Bronco when the trees closed about them. Glancing back, Lauri had enough time to see him get out, to see a bright flash of metal in his hand.

"Move!"

Rob did not know the paths of Elvenhome: that, Lauri thought, might increase their lead, might give Hadden and Amy a chance to reach the shelter of the house. And when they reached the meadow where Lauri and Amy had picnicked, from which Lauri could see, projecting above the trees, the white tower with the blue roof, she called out: "Go on ahead, Hadden. I'll wait for him here. I'm not letting him near the Home."

Hadden nodded and, still with Amy in his arms, started across the clearing. He was halfway to the shelter of the trees on the far side when Lauri heard a crashing of heavy boots on the path behind her. Rob was coming on, making better time than she had expected. She slipped behind a pine tree and waited.

Then he was there, passing just on the other side of the pine. Lauri moved, crashed into him, knocked him down, but the hour's drive had given him time to sober up, and he reacted more quickly than she had expected, lashing out and swinging the gun into the side of her head.

Stunned, Lauri rolled over on her side, fighting for clarity, fighting for the stars; but Rob was already on his feet, and he was taking aim at Hadden and Amy. The gun gleamed, a cheap, nickel-plated .38, and though Lauri struggled, she had only managed to get to her knees when Rob squeezed off three shots. They sounded trivial and faint in the open air, but she saw Hadden go down, falling half on top of Amy.

Rob turned to Lauri and leveled the gun. "Nice try, bitch."

Lauri tried to move, but her head was still spinning from the blow. With the muzzle of the pistol barely a foot from her head, she scrambled for her stars, saw, once again, the blue primary, and grabbed for it.

Rob's finger started to tighten.

A blur. The sparrow hawk swept down, streaked across the clearing, and, with an audible smack, buried its tiny talons in Rob's wrist. The pistol went off, but the shot went wide, kicking scraps of bark out of the pine tree.

In Lauri's mind, the blue star exploded into light, snapping her awareness back, tightening nerves, muscles, thoughts into a fine and intense focus. Rob was cursing, flailing out after the hawk with a bloody hand, but the hawk had already swept up out of his reach. Giving up on the hawk, then, he turned to Lauri once again, the gun still in his hand.

But Lauri was seeing him through the blue-white incandescence of the star, and abruptly, the light filled her, expanded swiftly, and lanced out at the man before her in a glowing pressure wave of energy. Struck, blinded, thrown back by the ephemeral but potent blast, Rob rolled over and over in the grass.

He had dropped the gun, and as he seemed more concerned with his dazzled eyes than with Lauri, the Elf was content to leave him that way while she went among the stars. She found that Hadden had been hit in the leg, that Ash was on her way. Lauri's thoughts were calm, even, the star still shining within her. She could feel Hadden's leg bleeding, could feel the shattered thighbone. Yes, there were things worth dying for. There were things worth preserving at all costs.

Within her, she heard Hadden's voice: *Finish with Rob. I can wait for Ash.*

Methodically, still with that terrible, incandescent focus, she got to her feet, picked up the gun, emptied it, and threw it away. Nearby, Rob was still struggling, thrashing, clawing at his face.

Dropping to one knee beside him, Lauri rolled him face up and grabbed the front of his shirt. His eyes were glazed, but he could now see well enough to recognize her, and he stared in fear.

Very deliberately, she shook her hair back from her ears and let the stars inside her blaze until she was sure that he could see the light in her eyes. "You've come to the wrong place, man."

He was stiff, rigid, terrified.

"You're not going to come here again, are you?"

Silence. His eyes were wide. He was seeing the light.

"Are you?" She shook him, the starlight lending her strength.

"N-no."

"Ever?"

"No. No. I swear."

"Human oaths mean nothing here. I'll give you a reason better than an oath." For a moment, her eyes bored into his, and then, in the same way in which she had grabbed Amy in the abyss, she seized him. Dragging him within himself, she rent the fabric of his existence and showed him the awful emptiness. He writhed in her grasp, but she held him, forced him to look, and only when he began to whimper in abject terror did she pull him back, seal the rent, and return him to himself.

She pinned him to the ground. "Know this, man," she hissed into his face. "That's where you put Amy. That's where you left her. What do you think I ought to do with you?"

He babbled. "Please ... lemme go."

"If you ever come here again, if you ever bother Amy or any of my people again, that's where you're going. Right back there. Forever. You can rot out there for all I give a damn."

"OK-OK-OK ..." He was thrashing again, blubbering like a whipped boy, gasping as though he was not sure that the world of sky and sunlight would not at any moment be taken away from him. Looking into him, Lauri saw the fear and knew with certainty that he would do as she wanted. But she saw something else too: dimly, faintly, she saw the potential for the starlight to take him. Even Rob. And who knew when it might happen? And would not her contact with him contribute to the eventual awakening of his blood?

She let go of his shirt and stood up, feeling sick. Even Rob might see the stars someday. Even Rob could find completion and rest. She would have to check on him. When the blood awoke, he would need help ... more help than anyone else.

For now, though, he was far from starlight. He was, in fact, all but witless with terror. Lauri looked down at him. "Get out. Go," she said, and she watched as he crawled to the trees, stood up shakily, and half ran, half stumbled back toward his car.

Drained, almost grieving, she turned and walked slowly to the others. Ash was there, and, impelled by the need before her, she had, once again, healed: Hadden was on his feet now, his leg sound, and he was watching as his beloved laid her hands on Amy.

In a moment, Lauri felt the energy, felt the surge of strength as Amy blossomed.

Amy's face was clear now, and though it was dirty, there was no trace of a bruise or a cut. There was, instead, a soft shimmer about her, and her eyes were bright with starlight. The tip of an ear poked out from her disheveled hair, and Lauri noticed that her cheekbones had changed. She looked complete, all of a piece.

She smiled at Lauri, the morning sun golden on her skin. "Lauri . . . I . . ." She hesitated, looking for the words.

"Welcome home," Lauri said. Her queasiness surged again as she heard an engine start up in the distance, but the sparrow hawk flitted over, dipped its wings, and rose into the sky, into the clear light, toward Elvenhome.

**Don't miss Gael Baudino's
fascinating new novel,
The Bournes of Life,**

set in a Southern town sometime not so long
ago. Alma Montague returns to her home-
town of Lee's Corners, to images of the past
and a present twisted around the tragedy of
forgotten memories. It is a town filled with
the bigotry and prejudice of our times, with
the anger and mistakes that always follow the
foolish. Here, the elderly Alma is drawn inexplicably into the town's gossip and slowly un-
ravels the mystery surrounding a strange
young boy called Magic and his obsessive
guardian, Mrs. Gavin. Into Lee's Corners
walks Mr. Dark, a colored man who appears
physically different to each person who sees
him, whose purpose seems custom-made for
the town's individuals wrapped in the mystery of Magic.

The Bournes of Life is a mysterious fantasy
and a reading wonder to enjoy while
sitting on the porch, sipping a cool iced
tea on a late summer evening. . . .

Death was not what she was looking for, though she did not know it at the time.

The railroad station at Lee's Corners, like the library, like the city hall, like the power plant and even the new fire engine, was a product of the perennial and acrimonious rivalry between the town and what, to the nonlocal or perhaps objective observer, could easily have been its twin just across the county line, Magdalene: a bitterly polite, internecine war of status, appearance, and acquisition that had been waged for decades, even centuries, and that, even during the glorious years of the Great Folly, had seen the two towns vying for supremacy first in the number of men and boys made available for slaughter, then in the valor of their defense against the invading Yankees, and finally, in the depth of their misery when those same Yankees, triumphant in the end, had settled in to divide and to despoil both the towns and the choice bottomland that surrounded them.

As such, therefore, the station had a rawboned, defiant, fist-in-the-air-and-jutted-chin sense of ad hoc vulgarity about it, as though it had been thrown together on a moment's notice, not because Lee's Corners had needed it (it had not), but rather because word had arrived that Magdalene was building a railroad station, and nothing would do, therefore, but for Lee's Corners not only to have one first but to have one that was bigger, better, and more expensive than Magdalene's, no matter how much bigger, better, or expensive Magdalene had originally planned for its own station to be.

And, true, it was indeed well known in Lee's Corners that at some undefined time in the past, a presidential candidate, suitably impressed with the grandeur of the station, had actually called for his train to make an unscheduled stop in the town, though it was equally well known that the story in Magdalene (a story obviously concocted out of a mixture of whole cloth and blatant jealousy) was that the candidate had actually made a *scheduled* stop in Magdalene, and that the unscheduled stop in Lee's Corners was only for the benefit—and comfort—of his dog. But then, what else would one expect of Magdalene?

Over the years, the train station had changed little. Yellow from paint and gray from weather, its high-backed wooden benches as comfortless when the agent turned the lights on for the northbound 3:05 (A.M.) from Biloxi as when he turned them off after the passing of the southbound 8:07 (P.M.) from Memphis, its windows powdered with clayey dust in dry weather and streaked with clayey mud in wet, its wooden floors resounding to the tread of debutante and drummer and football team alike, it was, like the bottomland itself, like the rivalry that had engendered it, an unchangeable feature of the town, to be removed or renovated only at the Last Trump. Or when Magdalene decided to make the corresponding change.

Alma Montague, seventy-seven years old and waiting, remembered the station perfectly. Almost fifty years had passed between her departure from Lee's Corners and her return to it, but the station was the same: still defiant (though, admittedly, the trains had grown fewer over the years), still shaking its fist at its Magdalene counterpart (which was, to be sure, shaking its fist right back), still a mixture of the tawdry, the vulgar, the ad hoc.

Alma herself, though, was not the same. Human stuff being less sturdy than wood and brick and considerably less renewable than dust or coats of paint, she had left Lee's Corners with an angry spring to her step, but she was returning wrapped in shawls against the mild April weather, her joints twinging from the damp and from a miserable night spent on the train, her feet throbbing from . . .

. . . well, from age. Simple age. Millions of footsteps, the stupid, mechanical wear that was the result of bearing even a skinny female frame through so many years of locomotion.

Funny, she thought. *You treat a hundred patients for hemorrhoids and arthritis, and there it is right in front of your face; your future. But you miss it. You just miss it. And you keep missing it until, one day, you wake up, and now it's your hemorrhoids and your arthritis, not to mention the fatigue and wrinkles and the tiresome busi-*

ness of just getting through another day until you finally—

"Miz Montague?"

And there was the colored porter, standing before her, bowing and smiling, one hand on the brim of his cap. Here was another changeless part of the station: his dark, smiling features imprinted on the gestalt of the building as the black faces and black hands of others were imprinted upon the very clay of the landscape, like thermonuclear shadows seared into concrete.

"The driver will be around with the car in a minute, ma'am," he said. "He's loading your baggage now."

"Thank you."

"Where shall I tell the driver he will be going, ma'am?"

Every syllable enunciated, every smile, every bow a perfect gesture of pleasant and genial goodwill; and she had seen the sign herself the day before, at the limits—the limits that hardly warranted the term *municipal*—of some nameless village:

NIGGER . . . DON'T LET THE SUN SET ON YOUR HEAD.

"Please tell him"—

She heard herself say *please*. It sounded, perhaps, a little too loud, a little too strained. Or maybe she only thought it did.

—"that he'll be driving me up to Montague Mansion."

The porter's face actually registered puzzlement.

"Montague Mansion place, ma'am? I . . . I'm afraid . . . I don't right know where that is."

Alma smiled, nodded. She had expected it. "It's outside of town. The mansion."

Enlightenment. "Oh! The mansion! On the hill! I'm sorry, ma'am, it clean—"

"No offense taken, I assure you," said Alma. "There's no reason for you to remember Montague Mansion. It's been deserted for years."

A commotion came echoing along the arched ceiling. With the exception of drummers and livestock agents, few travelers boarded or left trains in Lee's Corners, but this morning there appeared to be a number of people gathering at one end of the station. Alma was first aware of a sallow youth with black hair, then of a parsnip-colored man, then of a portly, middle-aged woman in furs and diamonds. All three—and others too—were converging upon some fixed point . . . though Alma could see nothing particularly remarkable about that point until, straightening up and peering intently, she discovered that there was a young boy of perhaps six or seven years standing there in the company of the conductor.

"That's Mrs. Gavin," the porter said in a voice that still betrayed nothing but genial goodwill, but Alma heard the distinctness—and the status—of the honorific. "She's the widow of Mr. Gavin, the banker." He paused as though the mention of the name would bring a word of recognition from Alma, but hearing nothing, he continued. "She does appear to be in a hurry today."

Indeed. The portly woman was almost running,

and though the parsnip-colored man (there was a parsnip-colored woman with him, too, Alma noticed) had a noticeable head start, he and Mrs. Gavin reached the point . . . the boy . . . almost simultaneously, while the sallow youth suddenly hung back, shrugged, pulled out a cigarette and slouched against a nearby wall, smoking.

"My dear little boy!"

Yes, it was the portly woman, sweating and heaving in her furs and her diamonds. She was down on her knees before the boy and had put her arms around him while the parsnip-colored couple stood motionless, the set of their heads providing the only clue that their gaze was not only upon the boy but also—hostilely—upon Mrs. Gavin.

"My sweet little Magic!"

The porter bowed and smiled again before he turned away. "I'll have the car up front for you in just a minute, Miz Montague."

"And did he have a good time? Did my sweet Magic have a lovely time after his mommy and daddy *sent him away* from me?"

It was a strange kind of tableau: the parsnip couple motionless and glaring, the stout woman in furs and diamonds on her knees with her arms wrapped about the boy as though she were a suppliant importuning an idol, the sallow, black-haired youth smoking off to one side, the conductor's dark face like basalt.

"Mr. and Mrs. Harlow?" the conductor said.

"My! Hasn't he gotten big since he was sent away! Just look at him!"

The parsnip couple nodded and, after the husband had signed the conductor's receipt, advanced on the boy, who, despite—or maybe because of—the attentions of the stout woman, stood with lowered head, his eyes fixed on the floor five feet in front of him, his left hand in his jacket pocket, his right hand, curiously, balled save for the index finger and thumb, which jutted spastically out at right angles as he made short, choppy jabs into the empty air.

"I have so many things to show my dear little boy now that he's back! His room is all fixed up and waiting for him! Does he know that his parents forgot to tell me that he was coming home today?"

Mr. Harlow said something. Mrs. Gavin ignored him.

"What's that, sweetie? What are you saying?"

The jerks of the boy's right hand became, if anything, even more distinct.

"What?"

And then Mrs. Gavin apparently understood, for, as though startled, she looked up and got to her feet. Her stockings were laddered from the worn, wooden floor.

"Benny!"

The sallow youth's cigarette vanished instantly. Alma could not even tell where it had gone.

"Benny! I want to talk to you!"

Which gave Mr. and Mrs. Harlow time and opportunity enough to grab the boy's arm and pull him toward the side door.

"Benny! I want to talk to you!"

But then Mrs. Gavin appeared to notice that Magic

was no longer with the conductor (who had returned to the train) and no longer near her. With a cry, she turned in time to see Mr. and Mrs. Harlow—and Magic—vanishing through the door.

"My sweetie!"

And the porter was back, smiling, bowing.

"Yo' car is here, Miz Montague."

ABOUT THE AUTHOR

Gael Baudino is the award winning author of *Gossamer Axe*, the highly acclaimed *Water!* trilogy, the popular *Strands* series and *Dragonsword* trilogy. She has also written articles and short fiction for magazines and anthologies. As a professional harper, she has recorded an album and played in concerts throughout the Denver area where she resides. She is currently hard at work on a new fantasy series for Roc.